DIANA PALMER

'Palmer demonstrates, yet again, why she's the
queen of…quests for justice and true love.'
—*Publishers Weekly* on *Dangerous*

'Nobody does it better.'
—*New York Times* bestselling author
Linda Howard

'The popular Palmer has penned another winning
novel, a perfect blend of romance and suspense.'
—*Booklist* on *Lawman*

'Palmer knows how to make the sparks fly…
heartwarming.'
—*Publishers Weekly* on *Renegade*

'Diana Palmer is a mesmerising storyteller who
captures the essence of what a romance should be.'
—*Affaire de Coeur*

'Sensual and suspenseful'
—*Booklist* on *Lawless*

DIANA PALMER

WHITE CHRISTMAS

MILLS & BOON

Published in Great Britain 2014
by Mills & Boon, an imprint of Harlequin (UK) Limited,
Eton House, 18-24 Paradise Road, Richmond, Surrey, TW9 1SR

WHITE CHRISTMAS © 2014 Harlequin Books S.A.

Woman Hater © 1987 Diana Palmer
The Humbug Man © 1987 Diana Palmer

ISBN: 978-0-263-25094-7

011-1114

Harlequin (UK) policy is to use papers that are natural, renewable and recyclable products and made from wood grown in sustainable forests. The logging and manufacturing processes conform to the legal environmental regulations of the country of origin.

Printed and bound in Spain
by Blackprint CPI, Barcelona

CONTENTS

WOMAN HATER
DIANA PALMER

One

When Gerald Christopher first suggested going to his family ranch in Montana to rest his recently diagnosed ulcer for a few weeks, Nicole had instant reservations. He was the boss, of course, and if he wanted to go to Montana, there was no reason he shouldn't. But Nicole liked the pleasant routine of life in Chicago, where she'd spent the last two years working for the Christopher Corporation. At twenty-two, Nicole White had found a nice, pleasant rut for herself and she didn't particularly like change.

The problem was that if Mr. Christopher went to Montana for a month, as he was threatening, and closed down his personal office while he was gone, Nicole would be out of a job until his return. Despite her adequate wages, trying to live for a month without any salary was a frightening thought. That was almost laughable considering her background, because Nicole's family had been one of the old moneyed ones of Kentucky. Her father, in fact, was still one of the jet set, a noted sportsman as well as a horse-racing magnate, and lived the part. Nicole had long since renounced her share of the family fortune and gone to work for a living.

Her mother's death had been the last straw. Her father had been with his latest mistress at the time, not that he'd ever been home a lot. That hadn't mattered at the time, because Nicole had been sure that her new fiancé, Chase James, would set up their marriage and that his job as a real estate agent would make it possible for him to support the two of them. She'd figured wrong. Once Chase found out that Nicole had been foolish enough to give up her family fortune—and when he realized that she couldn't possibly be talked out of it—he asked for his ring back. His immediate defection to one of Nicole's moneyed and eligible girlfriends had shattered her young life.

At the age of twenty, she'd left the elegant brick mansion of her childhood in Lexington, Kentucky, and a racehorse farm worth millions, to live the frugal life as a secretary in Chicago, where she had a friend with whom she could room. She smiled, remembering her lack of skills at the time, and how patient Mr. Christopher had been until she'd crammed in some courses at the local secretarial school. Lucky for her that he'd liked her personality and had decided to take a chance on her secretarial skills improving. They had. She'd graduated from the course at the top of her class.

It all seemed a long time ago now, a part of her life that was like some slowly fading photograph of a reality she no longer belonged to....

"You'll like it there, Nicky," Gerald Christopher said dreamily, staring out the window. "The ranch is in the southern part of the state, nestled in the Rocky Mountains. It's rich with forests, lakes, rivers, peace and quiet. Just the thing to help me get over this ulcer they've diagnosed. We can work in peace and you can have plenty of free time to yourself."

"But your brother and his family—won't they mind having your secretary to house and feed?" she asked, her pale green eyes hesitant in a plain but interesting oval face, surrounded by naturally curling short dark hair. Despite the fact that she'd worked for him for two years, she knew very little about his private life. He'd never made a habit of talking casually about anything personal, as some employers did. She knew he had a brother, and he'd mentioned a woman named Mary, whom she'd assumed was his sister-in-law. But that was really all she knew about him in any personal way.

"Winthrop doesn't have a family," he said, smiling as he turned toward her. He was tall with brown hair and dark brown eyes. Not a bad-looking man and he seemed pleasant enough, but he wasn't a woman chaser or a ladies' man. He was very businesslike and a terrific boss, and Nicky adored him. In a purely businesslike way, of course. Her heart was pretty impregnable these days, hardened by Chase's cruel defection. That had ended her dreams of marriage. The hated wealth that had blinded her to men's greed was gone now, too. And without her designer clothing and her diamonds, men didn't seem to notice her at all. Of course, her manner was stiff and off-putting with most men, but she didn't even realize it.

"Your brother came to the office once, didn't he?" she ventured, recalling vaguely a tall, very cold sort of man she'd barely glimpsed on an unusually hectic day and had learned later that it was Mr. Christopher's mysterious older brother.

"Yes, he did," he said. "Winthrop owns a small share in the corporation, you see, but he's the silent partner. He doesn't care for desks and boardrooms. Dad left him the ranch, which is worth a mint, and I have an equally small share in that. He's primarily a cattleman, and I'm a businessman, so we each have what we like most. He's something of a loner. But as long as we keep out of his way, we won't have any trouble."

That sounded ominous. She looked at the green-lined white steno pad in her lap. "A month is a long time," she said slowly.

"Come on, Nicky, what have you got going

that you can't walk away from?" he chided gently. "No boyfriends, no evening classes. A month in the country would do you good. If that wealth of potted plants you surround your desk with is any indication, you must be a country girl at heart. Or at the very least, a frustrated gardener."

She laughed. "I do love plants. And, yes, I'm a country girl. I was born and bred in Kentucky," she confessed, "and I guess I do miss it sometimes. My people were farmers," she added, tossing off the white lie as easily as she twirled the pen in her slender hand. That was the story she told people, anyway, and it prevented a lot of embarrassing questions about why she'd given up all that money.

"And farming isn't the best profession to be in these days," he agreed with a fond smile. "I can see why you came to the big city. But since you do like the country, I presume, where's the problem?"

She sighed. "It's not quite orthodox."

"No, little puritan, it isn't," he agreed. "But for the next month, you're my private secretary and I'll even increase your salary to make it more acceptable."

"Oh, but that's not nec—" she began.

"Certainly it is," he countered, waving a lean hand at her. "I'm tired of the rat race, Nicky. I need rest or this ulcer is going to put me in the hospital. We'll both benefit from some mountain air."

"It's October," she reminded him. "Late October. Doesn't it snow in Montana in late October?"

"Oh, frequently," he agreed. "And the ranch is way up in the Rockies, near the Todd place—" he paused, glancing at her with an odd expression "—you remember Sadie, don't you?"

"Yes. She was very nice." A nurse, in fact, and Nicole's taciturn young boss had dated her and had been devastated when she left several months ago to take care of her invalid mother. Hmm, Nicole thought, that was about the time his health problems reared their ugly head.

"Anyway, the ranch is near the Todd place," he continued, "and we used to get snowed in a good bit. But we always get a chinook when we need one, and we can dig our way out. Stop worrying."

"What's a chinook?"

"A warm wind that comes unexpectedly to melt the snow," he said, smiling. "You'll love it there, Nicky. I promise."

I hope so, she thought. All at once she wondered if he had more than just health reasons for wanting to work at home. Sadie had managed to drag him out of his shell, and there had been a tangible something between them before her abrupt departure. It might turn out to be an interesting trip. "All right, I'll go," she agreed. "But you're sure your brother won't mind?"

He looked vaguely disturbed for a second. Then he smiled. "Of course I'm sure."

Nicky wondered later about that hesitation. Mr. Christopher had hardly ever mentioned his brother in all the time she'd worked for him. But through the office grapevine there had been some small bit of gossip about the Montana rancher, something someone had whispered just after his brief visit. If only she could remember it.

Becky, a blonde and vivacious woman who worked for one of the vice presidents, breezed into the office after Mr. Christopher had left for the day.

"What's this I hear about some exotic vacation you're taking with the big boss?" she teased.

Nicky laughed. "If you call the backwoods of Montana exotic, then I guess it's true." She sighed as she covered the computer. "I do hope you'll come to my funeral. I have visions of being eaten by a puma or carried off by a moose."

"You might be carried off by Winthrop." Becky grinned. "Or haven't you heard the grizzly tales about him?"

Nicole turned, her eyes wide and curious. "Is he terrible?"

"A wild man, from what we hear. They said some society girl threw him over a few years back, and he actually went to her engagement party with a Hollywood movie star—a girl who turned out to have been a school friend of his and owed him a favor. He called up the friend and paid her expenses all the way from Hollywood, just for the occasion. Ruined the event, of course, since the movie star got all the attention. He used to be a ladies' man and he's always been well-to-do, and he traveled in those very ritzy circles. But since then, he's pretty much given up his playboy status and turned to the great outdoors. They say his experience with the blonde heiress has soured him against rich women in a big way. Can't blame him too much, can you?"

"He sounds…interesting." Nicky chose her words carefully; it wouldn't do to show her fear.

"Looks that way, too, except for the scars and the limp. Although the scars had faded nicely the day he was in here." She grinned at Nicky. "He sure gave you a look, but you were so busy you didn't even notice him."

"I remember him, but I didn't look long enough to see the limp." She frowned. "How did he get it?"

"From the wreck. Deanne Sharp—of the Aspen Sharps, you know, ski-resort wear and accessories, and Winthrop's fiancée at the time—was driving. They crashed. He almost lost his leg, and during his recovery, she walked out on him. I guess she only liked him for his athletic ability. He was an Olympic-quality skier and they met on the ski slopes. He missed the Olympic team by a few points when he was younger."

"That was what I was trying to remember. Someone said he'd been in a wreck, but I forgot what happened."

"The lovely Deanne happened. I hear she's on husband number three now, and has millions. But all that happened three years ago, the year before you came to work," Becky said. "We all heard about it. What he did at that woman's engagement party might have sounded cruel, if you didn't know it all. We were in Winthrop's corner, all of us. He got a bad break. As it is, he gets around pretty good, but he isn't the pinup he used to be. An experience like that could make a man bitter, you know."

Nicky drew in a slow breath. "A real woman hater."

"Now that's the truth," Becky laughed. "No, he doesn't like women. So if you go to the ranch with the big boss, make sure you take lots of warm clothing. That way you won't get frozen—by the weather or Winthrop."

"We may get snowed in," Nicky moaned.

"The snows come big in Montana," she was told. "Six feet deep and more, sometimes. My best friend worked at the hospital here until she had to go back to Montana to take care of her invalid mother a few months ago. You might remember her—Sadie Todd? The boss used to take her out."

"Yes, I remember," Nicky said with a smile, and kept her mouth shut about what Mr. Christopher had told her.

"They grew up together," Becky added. "I visited her once. Montana is lovely country, but brutal. It's frozen a lot of people, but if you want to get away from the world, there's no better place."

"I don't think I want to go."

"Don't be silly," Becky chided. "The big boss is a doll. Winthrop can't be too horrible."

But Nicky still wasn't sure. She went home and got her small apartment in order, still with misgivings. It didn't take long to pack, because there wasn't a lot to pack. She had jeans and sweaters, some blouses and a single jersey dress, because she had the feeling that she would be roughing it. She took a thick winter coat as well, and some leather boots left over from the past. Her lips twisted in a thin smile when she surveyed the contents of her suitcase and she thought about the clothes and lifestyle she'd once taken for granted. She missed that easy luxury once in a great while, and when she had to pinch pennies to meet the rent, her principles didn't help much. But she was a different girl from the arrogant little miss her parents' financial indulgence and emotional indifference had created. And that meant a lot. She'd learned about reality in the past two years, and about real people, who didn't put a dollar sign on their friendship. Even though her friend Dana, with whom she'd roomed, had married a year ago, Nicole still had friends like Becky, and they often went to movies or the theater together.

She pulled on a pair of cotton pajamas, washed her face and went to bed. It wouldn't do any good to worry about the past or the future. It was enough to cope with the present.

A week later, Nicole and Mr. Christopher flew out to Montana in the corporation jet. She wore the gray jersey dress for the flight, along with a minimum of makeup. She looked sweet and young and totally unlike a glamorous socialite. She didn't want to start off on the wrong foot by deliberately antagonizing the elder Mr. Christopher, who had plenty of reason to dislike that type of woman.

"You don't mind if I work?" Gerald Christopher asked with a smile, looking up from the papers in front of him.

"Not at all," she assured him. "I'm not nervous of flying."

The flight seemed to take a long time, but perhaps that was because Nicole wasn't reading. She stared out at passing clouds, a little anxious about the welcome she was going to get when they got off the plane.

"Mr. Christopher, your brother does know I'm coming?" she asked him when they were over Butte and about to land.

His dark eyebrows arched. "Of course. Don't worry, Nicky, everything's going to be fine."

Sure it was. She knew that the instant they got off the plane and she got a good look at the expression on Winthrop Christopher's face.

She recognized him at once. He was a big man. Taller than his brother, broad shouldered and lean hipped. He was wearing work clothing—jeans and dusty boots, with a checked shirt under a massive sheepskin jacket. On his head was a battered black Stetson twisted into an arrogant slant over one dark eye. He looked like a desperado. He hadn't shaved, and the white line of a scar curved from one cheek into the stubble on his square chin with its faint dimple. His face was rather square, too, and his features severe. He had a straight, rather imposing nose, and his black eyes gleamed with a cold light. In one lean, dark-skinned hand he held a burning cigarette. And the look he was giving Nicky would have curdled fresh milk.

"Hello, Winthrop," Gerald said, shaking his brother's hand. He glanced at Nicky with a smile. "In our childhood days, I used to call him Winnie, but I gave it up when he blacked one of my eyes. Despite all that, I know he'd die for me," he added with a grin, which the older brother didn't return. He was too busy glaring at Nicole, his dark eyes cutting into her oval face, looking for imperfections, making an unpleasant inventory of what he saw. "Winthrop," Gerald continued quickly, "this is my private secretary, Nicole White."

"How do you do, Mr. Christopher," Nicky said politely and she actually managed to smile, but her knees felt unsteady. This was no welcome at all. *Dislike* was too mild a word for what she read in those eyes. Wounded man, she thought, even while she wished she could run. She understood the meaning of betrayal, because she knew it intimately. For the first few months of her exile, Chase's handsome face had imposed itself over every letter she typed, every book she read, every television program she watched.

Winthrop's dark eyes narrowed. His thin, chiseled lips pursed thoughtfully, but there was no smile to ease the hardness of that rugged, unshaven face. "Yes, I remember you," he said curtly. His voice was deep and curt. "You're young."

"I'm twenty-two," she said.

"Young." He turned abruptly, with a care that no physically fit man would have had to take. "I've got the pickup. Does your pilot want to come out to the ranch and have something to eat?"

"No, he's due back to fly one of the other executives over to New York," Gerald replied, clapping an affectionate hand on Winthrop's shoulder. Brave man, to touch that walking inferno, Nicky thought as she fell into step behind them.

"I'll get the luggage." Winthrop started toward the plane, favoring one leg, and Nicky hesitated, her eyes speaking her thoughts. He gave her a look that stopped her from moving or speaking. He could have stopped a brawl with that glance. Her half-formed offer to help was frozen solid on her lips. With a violent flush, she turned away and followed Gerald.

"Don't ever offer to help him," her boss cautioned in a soft, quiet tone. "He's a little less sensitive about it these days, but soon after it happened, he threw a punch at one of the cowboys just for offering."

"I'll remember." She felt stung. The older brother was going to be hard going, and her first impulse was to ask if she could go back to Chicago.

Gerald Christopher seemed to sense her feelings, because he put an affectionately careless arm around her shoulder. "Don't panic," he teased. "He doesn't bite."

"Thank God I've had all my inoculations." She sighed, but she smiled back.

Behind them, the older man was watching that exchange of smiles and the arm around Nicky and putting his own connotation on what was going on between his younger brother and his secretary. The look in his eyes was both threatening and disapproving as he picked up the cases and followed them to the cream-colored pickup truck.

It was a long ride to the ranch, down a highway dwarfed by the towering, autumn-hued peaks of the Rockies. Soon Winthrop turned off onto some mountainous dirt roads that didn't actually seem like roads at all. To Nicky, squashed between the two men, it was a cold and unnerving experience. She could feel Winthrop Christopher's long, powerful leg come in contact with hers every time he pressed on the accelerator, and her body was reacting to the feel of his shoulder against hers in ways she hadn't expected. He made her tremble with awakening sensation, made her feel alive as she hadn't felt since her late teens. She didn't like that, or him, and her face took on the hardness of stone as the road wound on and on, through fir trees so tall and thick that Nicky stared in fascination at their girth. The forested areas were becoming thick now that they were off the rolling plain that had led to them, down country roads where houses were miles apart and traffic was practically nonexistent. Nicky, who'd read about Montana, hadn't been prepared for its vastness, or for the glory of orange-tipped aspens with their thin silvery trunks, and cottonwoods fluffy and yellow-hued, and those incredibly big pines. Or for the sheer splendor of the mountains and the crisp, clean coldness of mountain air. She watched, rapt, as the mountains shot up in front of them. Winthrop turned onto a tiny dirt road and they started to go up.

"Not what you expected, Miss White?" Winthrop chided as she stiffened on a sudden hair-raising curve as he gunned the truck up what seemed like a mountainside. "Montana isn't all pretty little photographs in coffee-table books."

"It's very mountainous," she began.

"That it is." He wheeled around another curve, and she got a sickening view of the valley below. It was just like the Great Smoky Mountains, only worse. The Smokies were high and rounded with age, but the Rockies were sharp and young and much higher. Nicky, who had no head at all for heights, began to feel sick.

"Are you all right, Nicky?" Gerald asked with concern. "You've gone white."

"I'm fine." She swallowed. Not for the world would she let Winthrop see what his careless wheeling was accomplishing. She held on to her purse for dear life and stared straight ahead, her jaw set, her green eyes unblinking.

Winthrop, who saw her stubborn resolve, smiled faintly to himself. Nicky might have been surprised to know how much it took to make him smile these days.

Another few miles, and they began to descend. The valley that opened before them took Nicky's breath away. She forgot her nausea in the sheer joy of appreciation. She leaned forward, with her slender hand on the dash, her eyes wide, her breath whispering out softly.

"Heaven," she breathed, smiling at maples gone scarlet and gold, at huge fir trees, delicate aspens and fluffy cottonwoods and the wide swath of a river cutting through it all, leading far into the distance like a silver ribbon. "Oh, it's heaven!"

Winthrop's eyebrows levered up another fraction as he slowed the truck to give her a better view. At the end of the road was a house, a huge sprawling two-story house that seemed part of its environs. It was made of redwood, with decks on all sides and an enormous porch that seemed to go all the way around it. It had to have fireplaces, because smoke was coming from two chimneys. Maples were all around it, too ordered not to have been planted deliberately years before, and with the mountains all around, it had a majesty that a castle would have envied.

"Lovely, isn't it?" Gerald sighed. "Every time I leave it, I get homesick. Winthrop hasn't changed a single thing about it, either. It's been this way for forty years or more, since our mother planted those maples around the house when our father built it."

"I thought they looked as if someone had planted them." Nicky laughed. "They're in a perfect semi-circle around the back of the house."

"Some city people might think that trees grow in perfect order," Winthrop mused, glancing coldly at Nicky. "Amazing, that you were able to pick it out so easily."

"Oh, Nicky grew up on a farm, didn't you, country girl?" Gerald grinned, tweaking her hair. "Way over in Kentucky."

"Good thing they plant trees in perfect order in Kentucky, and teach native sons and daughters to recognize the difference between a planted tree and a naturally seeded tree," Winthrop said without looking at her. "I guess there are people who assume God planted them in rows."

That was a dig, and Nicky wondered what the big man would do if she leaned over and bit him. That amused her and she had to fight to keep from grinning. He was watching her again, his eyes darkly piercing. He disturbed her so much that she dragged her gaze away and felt her cheeks go hot. It was incredible how easily this man got through her defenses. She was going to have to be careful to keep out of his way.

"Did I write you about the Eastern sportsmen I'm expecting week after next?" Winthrop asked Gerald unexpectedly. "I've organized a moose hunt for them, but I'll warn you in plenty of time to keep out of the section I'm planning to hunt."

"I remember." Gerald nodded. "I hope they have some savvy about weapons. Remember the solitary hunter who came one winter and shot your prize bull?"

Winthrop glared at him. "That wasn't funny," he said and glared at his two passengers, who were fighting smiles.

"Damned fool couldn't tell a stud bull from a deer...." Winthrop wheeled the truck up the dirt drive. "These are my Herefords," he added, nodding toward the red-and white-coated herds grazing across the flat plain toward the river. "They're in winter pasture now. I rent some government land for grazing, but I own most of it. It's been a bumper crop of hay this year. There's enough to spare for a change."

Nicole, who knew about farming and winter feed, nodded. "The southern states aren't having such luck," she remarked. "Drought has very nearly ruined a lot of cattlemen and farmers." She didn't question the way he spoke with possession about the family ranch, since Gerald had already told her that Winthrop had complete control of it.

Winthrop frowned as he glanced at her, but he didn't say anything. Her name, her last name, rang a bell, but he couldn't remember why. No matter, he thought; he'd remember eventually where he'd heard it before.

He parked the truck at the door of the huge house and got out, leaving Gerald to help Nicky to the ground.

A big, elderly woman came ambling out onto the front porch to meet them. She had high cheek-bones and a straight nose, and she was very dark.

"That's Mary," Winthrop said, introducing her. "She's been here since I was a boy. She keeps house and cooks. Her husband, Mack, is my horse wran-gler."

"Nice girl," Mary muttered, watching Nicole closely as the three newcomers came up onto the porch. "Long legs, good lines. Plain face but hon-est. Which one of you is going to marry her?" she demanded, looking from Gerald to Winthrop with a mischievous smile.

"I wouldn't have a woman, fried, with catsup," Winthrop replied without blinking, "but Gerald may have hopes."

Before Gerald could say anything, Nicky got herself together enough to reply. She did it with-out looking at Winthrop, because her cheeks were flushed with temper and embarrassment.

"I'm Mr. Christopher's secretary, Nicole White," Nicky said quickly, and forced a smile as she extended her hand. "Sorry to disappoint you, but I'm only here to work."

"And that is a disappointment," the woman sighed. "Two bachelors, all the time. It weighs heavy on my heart. Come. I will settle you."

"Mary is Sioux," Winthrop told Nicole. "And plainspoken. Too plainspoken, at times," he added, glaring at Mary's broad back.

Mary whirled with amazing speed for such a big woman and made some strange gestures with her hand. Winthrop's eyes gleamed. He made some back. Mary huffed and went up the long, smooth staircase.

"What did you do?" Nicole asked, amazed.

Winthrop looked down at her from his great height, his eyes faintly hostile but temporarily indulgent. "The Plains Indians spoke different languages. They had to have some way to communicate, in the old days, so they did it with signs. This," he added, drawing his hand, palm down, across his forehead, "for instance, means white man or paleface. The sign refers to this part of a man's forehead that was usually covered by a hat and so didn't get tanned like the rest of him. It was pale. This," he continued, rubbing two fingers in a long oval on the back of his left hand, "means Indian."

"Winthrop and Mary used to talk about the rest of us at the table—" Gerald chuckled, tugging affectionately at a short curl beside Nicky's ear

"—using sign language. None of us could understand a word."

"It's fascinating," Nicky said, and meant it.

"If you ask Mary, she might teach you a little,"
Winthrop told Nicky, smiling with cool arrogance.
In other words, that look said, don't expect any such
favors from me.

She wondered how she was going to survive a
month around him, but she did come from a long
line of Irishmen, so maybe her spirit was tough
enough to cope. She turned back to Gerald. "Do
you want to work today?"

"No," Gerald said with certainty. "Today we
both rest. Get on some jeans and I'll show you
around."

"Great!" She ran upstairs, careful not to look at
Winthrop Christopher. It was going to be impera-
tive that she keep out of his way while she was here.
He wasn't going to pull his punches, apparently, or
accord her any more courtesy than he would have
given to any other woman. Remembering what
Becky had told her, it was even understandable.
But it was going to make her stay here more uncomfortable than she'd expected. The fact that he
disturbed her only added to her discomfort. Becky
had said that Winthrop had been watching her the
day he came to the office. And it was vaguely unnerving to think of those black eyes watching her
in an unguarded moment. And why had he? Did
she remind him of the woman who'd crippled him?

She wasn't blonde, of course, but perhaps her facial features were similar. She'd have to ask Gerald.

She was only sorry that she couldn't dislike Winthrop as forcefully as he seemed to dislike her. Quite the contrary; he disturbed her as no man ever had, scarred face, limp and all.

Two

✳ ✳ ✤ ✳ ✳

The room Mary led Nicole into was delightful. It had pink accents against a background of creamy white, complete with a canopied bed and ornate mirror and even a small sitting area with pink, satin-covered chairs.

"This was their mother's room," Mary said. "Pretty, yes?"

"Are you sure I was meant to go in here?" Nicole asked hesitantly.

"Oh, yes, very sure. Mr. Winthrop said so." She winked at Nicole without smiling. "With his hands, you see."

Nicole shook her head. "He seems very…" She turned, shrugging as she tried to find words.

"His path has not been an easy one," Mary told her. Those dark eyes were sizing her up while she spoke. "Gerald was the favorite. He was a gentle, easy child. Winthrop was forever in trouble, always fighting, always in turmoil. He was the eldest, but not the most loved. And then came her. She with the blond hair and city ways, who was like a clear morning to me, and I saw through her. But Winthrop could not see through to the greed that motivated her. She crippled him and left him."

Nicole searched the smooth old face quietly. "He hides," she said perceptively.

Mary smiled. "You see deep."

"I know a survival instinct for what it is," came the quiet reply. "We all hide inside ourselves when we've been hurt." She met the dark eyes levelly. "I won't hurt him."

"I see deep, too," Mary mused. "He won't let you close enough to do harm. But watch yourself. He has no love for women. He might take out old wounds on you."

"I'm a survivor," Nicole said, laughing. "I'll manage. But thank you for the warning."

Mary only nodded. "Come down when you are ready. Are you hungry?"

"I could eat a moose," the younger woman sighed.

"Lovely idea. I have moose in the freezer. How would you like it? Baked, fried or in a stew?"

Nicole burst out laughing. "I love stew."

"Me, too." Mary grinned and left her.

Nicole put on a pair of faded jeans with a long-sleeved, gray knit shirt, because the air was chilly, and her pink sneakers and went downstairs without bothering to fix her makeup or comb her hair. She wasn't trying to catch any eyes, after all, so why irritate Winthrop by making it look as if she were making a play for him?

There was no one around, so she went outside and found a comfortable seat on the porch swing. It was peaceful. Birds twittered and somewhere a dog barked. Farther away, cattle were lowing. Nicole closed her eyes as the breeze washed around her. Heaven.

"I see you've found the swing."

She jerked upright as Winthrop came out onto the porch. He was bareheaded, still in the jeans and blue-checked shirt he'd worn to the airport. He'd taken time to shave, because his face was dark and smooth now, with the hairline white scar more visible without the stubble of a beard to hide it.

"I like swings," she said. Her pale green eyes wandered over him. He was terribly attractive without his jacket. Muscles rippled in his long legs when he walked, in his arms when he lifted them to light a cigarette. Despite his size, there wasn't a spare ounce of fat on him. He looked lean and fit and a little dangerous, despite the faint limp when he moved toward her.

"Deer come up into the yard sometimes," he observed. He dropped into a big rocking chair and crossed his long legs. "Moose, elk…it's still pretty wild here in the valley. That's why we attract so many bored Eastern sportsmen. They come here to hunt and pretend to 'rough it' but they've lost something that mountain people have all their lives. They've lost hope." He glanced down at her. "I hate rich people."

She felt as if he knew something, but she was afraid to bring the subject out into the open. "I'm not rich," she said, and it was the truth. "But I thought you were."

It was the wrong thing to say. His dark eyes kindled and his face took on the sheen of stone. "Did you?" he asked deliberately, and the mockery in his face was daunting. "Was that why you came with Gerald, or is it his money you're after?"

"You don't understand—" she began.

"I understand women all too well," he returned coldly. He moved away from her without another word, almost colliding with Gerald, who was coming out of the house as he was entering it.

"Sorry, Winthrop," Gerald murmured, curious about the expression on his brother's face. "I was looking for Nicky."

"I'm out here, Mr. Christopher!" she called.

"Oh, for God's sake, I'm Gerald here," he said shortly, joining her with a resigned glance over his shoulder as the door slammed behind Winthrop. He looked even younger in jeans and a pullover shirt. Nicky moved over to make room for him on the swing, and struggled to regain her lost poise.

Winthrop was going to make her life miserable, she just knew it, and her stupid careless remark had provoked him. "Mr. Christopher was my father," Gerald continued, "and he was *Mister* Christopher, too," he added with a faint smile. "Our mother was on a camping trip up here. She wandered off and he found her. He nursed her back to health and she left, thinking that was the end of it."

"Was it?" Nicole asked.

Gerald laughed. "No. As a matter of fact, Dad followed her all the way to New York, found her at some social gathering, picked her up and carried her to the train station and brought her here. Eventually, to save her reputation, she agreed to marry him."

"I guess he was used to getting his own way," Nicky mused, and in her mind's eye she could see Winthrop doing exactly the same thing. Her fine skin flushed just a little at the unexpected thought.

"They were happy together," Gerald said. "She died one spring of pneumonia. He died six months later. They said it was a heart attack, but I've often wondered if it wasn't loneliness that did it." He paused for a moment, then said suddenly, "I'm sorry Winthrop's so inhospitable." He glanced at Nicole's quiet face. "You aren't afraid of him, are you? If you are, don't ever let him see it. He's a good man, but he's pretty hard on women."

"I'm not afraid of him," she said. And she meant it. She wondered if there was any chance that he found her as disturbing as she found him. That didn't bear thinking about.

"You must miss all this in Chicago," Nicole said, looking up at her boss.

"I miss this, and other things," he replied. He stared at a house far on a hill in the distance, his eyes narrowed and unexpectedly sad. "Sadie Todd lives over there," he said absently, "with her invalid mother. We'll have to go and visit her while we're here."

"She was nursing at the general hospital, wasn't she?"

"Yes. She had to give up her job and come home when her mother had a stroke. Mrs. Todd is completely paralyzed on one side and doesn't seem to want to get any better. Sadie said she couldn't leave her at the mercy of strangers. Her father is dead."

She knew almost to the day when Sadie had left, because Gerald Christopher had withdrawn into a tight little shell afterward and seemed to walk around in a fog. He'd put enough pressure on himself thereafter to give him that ulcer. But it had surprised her that he wanted to come home, because he worked like a Trojan all the time lately. She was almost sure that Sadie was the reason he felt the need of a month's vacation in Montana. She smiled to herself.

"I'd like very much to go and see her," she said.

He smiled down at her. "You're a nice person,

Nicole." He got up. "I'm going to make a few phone calls. Just sit and enjoy the view, if you like."

"Yes, sir," she promised.

He went inside, and she lounged in the swing until Mary called her to have a sandwich. She sat in the spacious kitchen, enjoying a huge ham sandwich and a glass of iced tea while Mary prepared what promised to be the world's largest moose stew. They talked about the ranch and the country and the weather, and then Nicole went out the back door and wandered down to the river, just to look around.

She could imagine this country in the years of the Lewis and Clark expedition. She'd read a copy of their actual journal, enjoying its rather anecdotal style, seeing the country through their eyes in the days before supersonic jets and superhighways. Trappers would have come through here, she mused, kneeling beside the river with her eyes on the distant peaks. They'd have trapped beaver and fox and they'd have hunted.

Kentucky had its own mountain country, and Nicole had been in it a few times in her life. It had been a different setting then. Elegance. Parties. Sophisticated people. Wealth. She sat down on a huge rock beside the river and tore at a twig, listening to the watery bubble of the river working its way downstream. She much preferred this kind of wealth. Trees and cattle and land. Yes.

"Daydreaming?"

She turned to find Winthrop Christopher sitting astride a big black stallion, watching her.

"I like the river," she explained. "We have one in Chicago, of course, but it's not the same. We have concrete and steel instead of trees."

"I know. I've been to Chicago. Even to the office, in fact." His eyes narrowed. "You don't remember me, do you?"

She did. Even that brief glance had stamped him onto her memory, but it wouldn't do to let him know that. She avoided a direct answer. "It's always hectic. I don't pay a lot of attention to visitors, I'm afraid."

"The morning I came, you were sitting at that computer with a stack of steno pads at your elbow and a telephone in your hand. You barely looked up when I went into Gerald's office." He smiled mockingly. "I was wearing a suit. Maybe I looked different."

"I can't quite imagine you in a suit, Mr. Christopher," she said, thinking, top that, cattle king.

"Winthrop," he corrected. "I'm not that much older than you. Eleven years or so. I'm thirty-four."

"How old is your brother?" she asked, curious. He lifted his chin. "Thirty."

"Sometimes he seems older," she mused. "When they call the stockholders' meetings, for instance."

He glanced into the distance. "No doubt. I'm glad I don't have to deal with those damned things. That's Gerald's sole province now. I just run my ranch, and the only stockholder I have to please is myself. Gerald doesn't own enough shares to squabble over the decisions I make."

"You inherited the ranch, didn't you?"

He stared at her for a minute, and she swallowed hard, sure that he was going to give her some sarcastic financial rundown and chide her for asking. But, surprisingly, he didn't. He just nodded. "That was the way my father wanted it. He knew I'd hold it as long as I lived, no matter what. You'll find that Gerald isn't terribly sentimental. He'd just as soon have a photograph as the object itself."

She pursed her full lips and studied him. "I'll bet you saved bobby pins and bits of ribbon when you were a teenager," she said daringly, just to see what he'd say.

He blinked, then laughed, but it wasn't a pleasant sound. "I had my weak moments when I was younger," he agreed. His eyes darkened. "Not anymore, though, Kentucky girl. I'm steel right through."

She wouldn't have touched that line. She turned, glancing at the distant ribbon the river made running into those towering, majestic peaks. "I was thinking about Lewis and Clark," she murmured, glancing toward the horizon, so that she didn't catch the look on his face. "A man died during the expedition. What they described sounded just like food poisoning. They wouldn't have known, of course. How much we've learned in over a hundred years. How far we've come. And yet," she said softly, "how much we've lost in the process."

"The expedition went down the Missouri and Jefferson rivers," he said slowly. "We're on a tributary of the Jefferson, so they may have camped in this valley." He looked away. "They used to call it Buffalo Flats. The buffalo are gone, though. Like the way of life that existed here long ago." He shifted restlessly. "Where's Gerald?"

"Back at the house, I suppose," she said, bothered by the curtness of his tone. "He said he had some important phone calls to make. I would have stayed, but he said we wouldn't work today."

"Want a ride back?" he offered, and then seemed to withdraw, as if he regretted the words even as he was speaking them.

Some devilish imp made her smile at him. "Suppose I say yes?" she asked, driven to taunt him. "You look as if you'd rather sacrifice the horse than let me on him." And she grinned, daring him to mock her.

He felt a burst of light, but he wouldn't give in to it. "Damn you."

She grinned even more. "I won't accept, if you'd rather not let me aboard. Anyway—" she shuddered with deliberate mockery and more sarcasm than he could know, because she'd practically grown up on horses "—I'd probably fall off. It looks very high."

"It is. But I won't let you fall off. Come on." He kicked his foot out of the stirrup and held down a long arm, giving in to an impulse he didn't even understand. He wanted her closer. He wanted to hold her. That should have warned him, but it didn't.

He had enormous feet, she noticed, as she put a foot in the stirrup and let him pull her up in front of him. He was amazingly strong, too.

She hadn't realized how intimate it was going to be. His hard arm went around her middle and pulled her back against a body that was warm and strong and smelled of leather and spice. She felt her heart run away, and that arm under her breast would feel it, she knew.

"Nervous?" he asked at her ear, and laughed softly, without any real humor. "I'm not dangerous. I don't like women, or haven't they filled you in yet?" *She's a woman,* he was reminding himself. *Watch it, watch yourself—she'll sucker you in and kick you down, just like the other one did.*

"Yes, I'm nervous," she said. "Yes, you're dangerous, and you may not like women, but I'll bet they chase you like a walking mink."

His eyebrows arched. "You're plainspoken, aren't you?" he asked, gathering her even closer as he urged the restless stallion into motion, controlling him carefully with lean, powerful hands and legs.

"I try to be," she said, still uneasy about the double life she'd led since leaving Kentucky. To a man who'd been betrayed once, it might seem as if she were misleading him deliberately. But the past was still painful, and she'd forsaken it. She wanted it to stay in the past, like the bad memories of her own betrayal. Besides, there was no danger of Winthrop becoming involved with her. He was too invulnerable.

She held on to the pommel, her eyes on his long fingers. "You have beautiful hands, for a man," she remarked.

"I don't like flattery."

"Suit yourself, you ugly old artifact," she shot right back.

It had been a long time since anything had made him laugh. But this plain-faced, mysterious woman struck a chord in him that had never sounded. She brought color and light into his own private darkness. He felt the sound bubbling up in his chest, like thunder, and then overflowing. He couldn't hold it back this time, and the rush of it was incomprehensible to him.

She felt his chest shaking, heard the deep rumble of sound from inside it. She would have bet that he didn't laugh genuinely very often at anything. But she seemed to have a knack for dragging it out of him, and that pleased her beyond rational thought.

The lean arm contracted, and for an instant she felt him in an embrace that made her go hot all over. What would it be like, she wondered wildly, if he turned her and wrapped her up in his embrace and put that hard, cruel mouth over hers....

She tingled from head to toe, her breath catching in her throat. It shouldn't have been like this, she shouldn't still be vulnerable. She had to stop this, or it was going to be an unendurable month.

"Watch out, Miss White," he said at her ear, his voice deep and soft and dangerous. "Save the heavy flirting for Gerald. You'll be safer that way."

He let her down at the porch, holding her so that she slid down to the ground. For an instant his dark face was very close, so close that she saw his dark eyes at point-blank range and something shot through her like lightning. She pulled back slowly, her eyes still linked to his. What had he said? Something about flirting with Gerald. But why should she want to flirt with her boss?

"See you." He wheeled his stallion and rode off, and she watched him with mingled emotions.

Supper was an unexpectedly quiet affair. Winthrop was out when she and Gerald sat down to eat, along with the ranch foreman, Michael Slade, a burly man of thirty who seemed perfectly capable of handling anything.

"Boss said he wouldn't get back in time for chow," Michael told Gerald with a grin. "Had to go into Butte for some supplies he needed. I offered, but he said he had some other things to do as well."

"Odd that he didn't do it before he met us at the airport." Gerald sighed as he took his medicine and glared at his plate. The doctor had told him that they didn't treat ulcers with bland diets anymore, but Mary hadn't believed him. Amazing, how disgusting green pea soup looked in a bowl, and he did hate applesauce. He glanced at Mary, sighed and then gave in to her, as he had done even as a child. He picked up his spoon and began to sip the soup. "Oh, well, that's Winthrop. Unpredictable. How's it going, Mike?"

The foreman launched into grand detail about seeing to the winter pasture, fixing fences, storing hay, culling cows, doing embryo transplants for the spring calving and organizing other facets of ranch life that he'd expected would go right over Nicole's head.

"One of my family was into embryo transplants when it was barely theory," Nicole interrupted. "They had some great successes. Now there's a new system underway, implanting computer chips just under the skin to keep track of herds...."

"Say, I've read about that," Mike agreed, and Gerald sat and stared while the two of them discussed cattle.

"Mr. Christopher must be feeling pretty proud of himself to have someone like you on the payroll," Nicole told the foreman when they reached a stopping point. "You know your business."

"Forgive me, ma'am, but so do you." Mike grinned, his ruddy face almost handsome with his blue eyes flashing. "I never knew a woman who could talk cattle before."

"I never knew a man who talked it as well." She grinned back.

"I thought you were from Chicago," Gerald sighed, shaking his head, when Mike had gone and they were sipping coffee in the living room. "Until you admitted that you were a Kentuckian, at least," he added. His gaze was warm and faintly questioning. "Amazing, that we worked together for two years and knew nothing about each other."

She smiled at him. "I guess most bosses and secretaries are like that, really," she agreed. "You're very nice to work for, though. You don't yell, like some of your vice presidents do."

He laughed. "I try not to. Winthrop, now," he said, watching her face as he spoke, "never yells. But it's worse that way, somehow. He has a voice like an icy wind when he loses his temper, which isn't often. I've seen him look at men who were about to start fights and back them down. One of our ancestors was a French fur trader up in Canada. Our grandmother used to say Winthrop takes after him."

"He has expressive eyes," she agreed, glancing at Gerald warily. "He doesn't want me here, you know."

His shoulders rose and fell. "He's buried himself up here for three solid years," he said irritably, staring into his coffee. "No company, except these hunting parties that he tolerates because it gives some variety to his life. No women. No dating. He's avoided women like the plague since Deanne left him. He uses that limp like a stick, have you noticed?" he asked, lifting troubled eyes to hers. "It isn't all that bad, and he could walk well enough if he cared to try, but it's as if he needs it to remind him that women are treacherous."

"I'd heard that he was something of a playboy in his younger days," she probed, curious about Winthrop in new and exciting ways.

"He was," Gerald agreed with a faint, musing smile. "He broke hearts right and left. But Deanne liked him because he was a new experience. I don't think she really meant to hurt him. She was young and he spoiled her, and she liked it. But when he got hurt, she had visions of being tied to a cripple for life, and she ran. Winthrop was shattered by the experience. His black pride couldn't deal with the humiliation of being lamed and deserted, all at once."

"Poor man," she said gently, and meant it.

"Don't make that mistake, either," he cautioned quietly. "Don't ever pity him. He's steel clean through, and if you give him half an opening, he'll make a scapegoat of you. Don't let him hurt you, Nicky."

She colored delicately. "You think he might?"

"I think you attract him," he said bluntly. "And I have a feeling that you aren't immune to him, either. He doesn't like being vulnerable, so look out."

Hours later, when she went up to bed, she was still turning that threat over in her mind. She could picture Winthrop behind her closed eyes, and the image made her sigh with mingled emotions. She'd never felt so empty before, so alone. She wanted him in ways that she'd never dreamed she could want a man. She wanted to be with him, to share with him, to ease his hurt and make him whole again. She didn't quite know how to cope with the new and frightening sensations. Nicky had her own scars and she didn't want involvement any more than Winthrop did. But there was something between them. Something that was new and a little frightening, and like an avalanche, she couldn't stop it.

She was almost asleep when she heard slow steps coming past her door. She knew from the sound that it was Winthrop, and her heart beat faster as he passed her room. Odd, how deeply she could be touched just by his step. She wondered if he was as curious about her as she was about him, despite his understandably deep distrust of women. He was like her, in so many ways, hiding from a world that had been cruel to him. They had more in common than he seemed to realize. Or perhaps he did realize it, and was drawing back because he didn't trust her. She closed her eyes as she heard a door close down the hall. In no time at all, she was asleep, secure because the master of the house was back, and she was safe.

Three

Winthrop's horses attracted Nicole immediately, even though he'd given her a terse warning at breakfast about going too close to them. One of the happiest memories of her childhood was watching old Ernie at her home in Kentucky as he worked the thoroughbreds when they were ready to be trained.

Besides his saddle horses, mostly quarter horses, Winthrop had at least two thoroughbreds with unmistakably Arabian ancestry, judging by their small heads. All American thoroughbreds, she remembered, were able to trace their ancestry to one of three Arabian horses imported into England in the late 1600s and early 1700s: Byerley Turk, Godolphin Barb and Queen Anne.

Winthrop's horses had the exquisite conformation and sleek lines that denoted thoroughbreds, too. She'd watched them during her brief stroll around the stables and corral. One was a mare about to foal, the other a full stallion, both with sleek chestnut coats and exquisite conformation. She'd wanted to ask Winthrop about them over scrambled eggs and steak that morning, but he'd been unapproachable. Frozen over, in fact, and she knew why without even being told. He didn't want her too close, so he was freezing her out.

She'd finished her two hours in the study, taking dictation from Gerald, and now cozy and warm in tailored gray slacks and a white pullover sweater, she was lazing around the corral looking for the horses. The stallion was there, but she didn't see the mare anywhere.

A noise from inside the big barn caught her attention. She couldn't see inside, but it sounded like a horse's whinny of pain. It was followed by a particularly virulent curse from a voice she recognized immediately.

She darted into the dim warmth of the big barn, down the neat corridor between the stalls that was covered with pine shavings.

"Winthrop?" she called quickly.

"In here."

She followed his voice to the end stall. The mare was down on her side, making snuffling sounds, and Winthrop was bending over her, his sleeves rolled up, bareheaded, scowling.

"Something's wrong," she said, glancing at him.

"Brilliant observation," he muttered, probing at the mare's distended belly with tender, sure hands. "This is her first foal and it's a breech, damn the luck! Go get Johnny Blake and tell him I said to come here, I can't do this alone. He'll be—"

"The mare will be dead by the time I find him," she said matter-of-factly. She eased into the stall, ignoring Winthrop as she gently approached the mare, talking softly to her with every step. While Winthrop watched, scowling, she slid down to her knees beside the beautiful, intelligent creature, watching the silky brown eyes all the while. She sat down then, reaching out to stroke the mare. And slowly, she eased under the proud head and slowly coaxed it onto her knees. She drew her fingers gently over the velvety muzzle, talking softly to the mare, gentling her.

"She'll let you help her now," she told Winthrop softly, never taking her eyes from the mare's.

"Yes," he said, watching her curiously for a few seconds before he bent to his task. "I believe she might. You'll ruin that fancy sweater," he murmured as he went to work.

"Better it than lose the foal," she said, and smiled at the mare, talking gently to her all along, smoothing the long mane, cuddling the shuddering head, as Winthrop slowly worked to help the colt in its dark cradle. She knew instinctively that the mare would realize that she was trying to help, and not hurt her.

Minutes later, guided by patient, expert lean hands, hind fetlocks appeared suddenly, followed rapidly by the rest of the newborn animal. Winthrop laughed softly, triumphantly, as the tiny new life slid into the hay and he cleared its nostrils.

"A colt," he announced.

Nicole smiled at him over the mare, amazed to find genuine warmth in his dark eyes. "And a very healthy one, too," she agreed. Her eyes searched his softly, and then she felt herself beginning to tremble at the intensity of his level gaze. She drew her gaze away and stroked the mare again before she got slowly to her feet so that the new mother could lick her colt and nuzzle it.

"A thoroughbred, isn't he?" she replied absently, her eyes on the slick colt being lovingly washed by his mother. "The stallion has a superior conformation. So does the mare. He might be a champion."

"The stallion is by Calhammond, out of Dame Savoy," he said, frowning as he moved away to wash his hands and arms in a bucket of water with a bar of soap, drying them on a towel that hung over it. "How did you know?"

"Kentucky is racehorse country," she laughed, sidestepping the question. She didn't want to tell him how much she knew about thoroughbreds, although she'd certainly given herself away just now, and she'd have to soft-pedal over it. "I cut my teeth on thoroughbreds. I used to beg for work around them, and one of the trainers took pity on me. He taught me a lot about them. You see, one of the biggest racing farms in Lexington was near where I lived—Rockhampton Farms." Actually Rockhampton was her grandfather's name; her mother's people had owned the stables there for three generations. But it wouldn't do to admit that to Winthrop, because he'd connect it with Dominic White, who was her father and the current owner. He might even know Dominic, because he entertained sportsmen, and her father was one of the best.

"I've heard of it," Winthrop told her after a minute. He turned, staring hard at her with dark, curious eyes as he rolled down the sleeves of his brown Western shirt and buttoned the cuffs with lazy elegance. White. Her name was White. Wasn't that the name of that jet-setting sportsman from Kentucky who was coming with the Eastern hunting party? Yes, by God it was, and Dominic White owned Rockhampton Farms. He lifted his head. "The owner of Rockhampton is a White," he said in a direct attack, watching closely for reaction. "Any kin of yours?"

She held on to her wits with a steely hand. She even smiled. "White is a pretty common name, I'm afraid," she said. "Do I look like an heiress?"

"You don't dress like one," he commented, with narrowed eyes. "And I guess you wouldn't be working for Gerald if you had that kind of money," he said finally, relaxing a little. He didn't want her, but it was a relief all the same to know that she wasn't

some bored little rich girl looking for a good time.
He couldn't have borne going through that again.
"I've been to Kentucky, but I've never been on the
White place. My stallion and mare came from the
O'Hara place."

"Yes, Meadowbrook Farms," she murmured.
She could have fainted with relief. She didn't want
him to know about her background. Of course,
there was always the danger that he might someday find out that she was one of those Whites, but
with any luck she'd be back in Chicago before he
did, and it wouldn't matter anymore. Right now,
the important thing was to get her boss well and
not upset him with any confrontations between
herself and Winthrop.

Winthrop had every reason to hate rich society
girls, and he might be tempted to make her life
hell if he knew the truth. And probably it would
be worse because she hadn't told him about it in the
beginning. Her character would be even blacker in
his eyes for the subterfuge. For one wild instant, she
considered telling him. But she knew she couldn't.
He disliked her enough already. And it was suddenly important, somehow, to keep him from find-
ing new reasons to dislike her. It did occur to her
that someday he might hate her for not being truth-
ful with him. But she'd discovered a tender streak
in his turbulent nature while he was working with
the mare, and she wanted to learn more about that

shadowy side of him. That might not be possible if he knew the truth about her.

"I couldn't have managed that alone," he said quietly, watching her. "I'm obliged for the help."

"I like horses," she said simply. "And he's a grand colt."

"His father has been a consistent winner, but he was hurt in a race last year. I bought him to stand at stud rather than see him put down. I had a lot of money that was lying spare, so I developed an interest in racehorses. I've spent a good deal of time at racetracks in the past year."

Another chink in the armor, she thought, thinking about his compassion for the stallion as she looked up at him.

He saw that speculative gleam and it irritated him. She wasn't working out the way he'd expected. She had too many interesting qualities, and he didn't like the feelings she aroused in him. He'd buried his emotions, and she was digging down to them with irritating ease.

"You don't like me, do you?" she asked bluntly. "Why? Is it because I'm plain, or because I'm only a secretary…"

"You aren't plain," he said unexpectedly, his dark eyes tracing the soft oval of her face. Big green eyes. Pretty mouth. High cheekbones. Skin like satin, creamy and young. She was young. He sighed wistfully. "And I'm no snob. I just don't want women around."

"That's straightforward," she said softly. "And I hope it won't offend you if I speak as bluntly. I know a little about what happened to you and why. I'm very sorry. But hating me and making my life miserable for the next few weeks isn't going to erase your scars. It will only create new ones for both of us. So can't we be sporting enemies?" she asked, her green eyes twinkling. "And I'll promise not to seduce you in the hay."

His eyebrows shot straight up. *Unexpected* wasn't the word for this little firecracker. He'd have to think up a new one.

"What do you know about seduction, Red Riding Hood?" he asked with blithe humor, and she got a tiny glimpse of the man he'd been before the accident.

"Not much, actually," she said pleasantly, "but that's probably in your favor, because it will save you a lot of embarrassing moments. Just imagine if I were experienced and sophisticated and out to sink my claws into you!"

Her earnestly teasing expression made him feel as if he were sipping potent wine. He had a hard time drawing his eyes away from her soft mouth and back up to her laughing eyes. Incredibly long lashes, on those eyes. Sexy. Like the rest of her. She was tall, but she wasn't overly thin. He liked the way she looked in tailored slacks and that white sweater. Both were thick with horsehair about now, and she'd smell of horse....

"She'll want some water now," she reminded him, unnerved by that slow, bold scrutiny and hoping that it didn't show.

It did. His chin lifted just a little, in a purely male way, and his chiseled mouth twitched. "Nervous of me?"

"If all the gossip I've heard about you is true, I have good reason to be, and that isn't conceit on my part," she added proudly. "Playboys don't usually mind who they charm, because it's all a game to them."

The light in his eyes went out, like a cavern succumbing to darkness. "I don't play games with virgins, honey," he said unexpectedly, catching her chin with a lean, steely hand. "And you'd better remember it. I've forgotten more about lovemaking in my time than you've ever learned, but I'm not low enough to take out my hurt on you."

He was so close that she could feel the strong warmth of him. Her heart ran wild. She'd never had such a powerful, immediate reaction to a man before. Not even to Chase. This was new and wildly exciting, and she wanted more.

"How do you know that…about me?" she whispered, shocked that he could so easily discuss the most intimate subjects.

"I don't know," he replied quietly, searching her soft eyes. His blood warmed in his veins, and he felt his heartbeat slowly increase. Her scent was overpowering, drowning him, seducing his senses. He knew a lot about her, knowledge that only instinct could have supplied.

Her lips parted on a rush of breath. The dimness of the barn was warm and cozy, shutting them away from the world. Winthrop was closer than ever, towering over her, drowning her in a narcotic kind of hunger.

She took an involuntary step toward him. "I... don't understand," she whispered, her voice shaking. One slender hand went hesitantly to his chest and pressed against it, feeling the shock of warm muscle and a spongy wiriness that might have been hair underneath. She felt him tense, even before his hand came up to remove hers with abrupt impatience.

"Don't do that," he ground out, glaring at her. "I don't want your hands on me."

Her own forwardness shocked her more than his irritable statement. She turned away, feeling a rush of tears that she couldn't let him see.

"I'd better get back to the house," she said quickly. "Your brother was going to make a phone call and then finish his dictation. I'm glad the mare's okay." She said it all in a mad rush and threw a vague smile in his direction before she went out of the barn as if her shoes were on fire.

He watched her go with mingled emotions. Anger. Irritation. Hunger. Frustration. He couldn't sort them out, so he didn't bother. He went back to feed and water the mare and see about the colt.

Damn women everywhere, he thought, and limped more than usual as he went about his business.

Nicole made a point of avoiding her boss's unpredictable brother for the rest of the day. But there was no getting away from him at the supper table, and she had to fight not to look at him.

Cleaned up and freshly shaved, wearing a white shirt that suited his darkness, he would have drawn any woman's eyes. It was easy to see how he'd appealed to women when he was younger. He was still a striking man, and it wasn't just his looks. There was an indefinable something about him, a vibrant masculinity that was almost tangible and certainly overpowering at close range. Her hands trembled just sitting next to him at the long table.

Gerald was quoting figures on some real estate he'd acquired, and Winthrop was listening with barely half his mind. He was watching Nicky while he pared his steak and chewed it deliberately, trying not to let her know that he was watching her. She was wearing that gray jersey dress that clung so lovingly to her curves, and the memory of the effect she'd had on him in the barn wasn't doing his appetite any good.

He finally grew impatient with her downbent head and stopped eating and just stared at her intently while Gerald went on talking without realizing that he was talking to himself.

Nicole felt that intent stare and looked up into Winthrop's dark eyes. And her heart stopped beating.

Electricity danced between them. She couldn't drag her eyes from his, any more than his were willing to be tugged away. The look they exchanged was long and piercing and shattering in its intensity. It was as personal as a kiss, so steady and unblinking that she felt her body tremble in intimate response to his blatant interest.

His gaze held hers for a shuddering moment, and then it dropped to her mouth, and she felt her lips part helplessly for him.

"Winthrop, are you listening?" Gerald asked suddenly, breaking the silence when he discovered that his brother was apparently staring into space.

"What?" Winthrop turned back to him. "Something about real estate values?" he asked absently. He didn't like the way his body responded to that look in Nicole's eyes. He was going to have to do something. But what?

Nicole was having as difficult a time with her own body. She shifted restlessly and drank coffee that was, by now, hopelessly oversugared. While Winthrop's dark eyes had been openly making love to hers, she'd put six spoons of sugar in the black liquid. She took a sip and shuddered and left it in favor of the glass of water Mary had provided for each of them. So much for common sense. It was time to retreat.

For the next few days, she and Winthrop avoided each other—ignored each other—to the extent that everybody noticed, and Mary began asking gentle questions that Nicole smiled at and avoided answering. And that might have gone on for another week if she hadn't tripped on the steps coming in from a walk late one afternoon, to be caught by Winthrop in the gathering darkness.

He'd apparently just come in from the corral himself. He smelled of cattle and he needed a shave, but his arms in the sheepskin jacket felt strong and warm, and instead of pulling away like a sensible girl, Nicole had sighed and relaxed against his tall, strong body.

Winthrop muttered something, but he didn't push her away. His hard arms contracted, drawing her against him under the unbuttoned jacket, and he stood holding her in the dusky light, savoring her softness, his cheek against her dark hair.

It seemed so natural, somehow. So right. His eyes closed and all the reasons why he shouldn't allow her this close vanished. He didn't make a sound, and neither did she. The wind sang through the tall lodgepole pines, whispered through the aspen and maples, whipped her hair against her flushed cheek. She pressed closer with a tiny, inarticulate sound, too hungry for the contact to listen to the warning bells going off in her head. He was warm and strong, and it was sheer delight to be held by him. She felt her body tremble with exquisite pleasure.

"We could hurt each other badly," he whispered in her ear, his voice deep and soft and slow. "You don't have the experience to understand the risk, and I can't be sure that I wouldn't take out old hurts on you, even though I wouldn't do it consciously. This is crazy."

"Yes."

He nuzzled his cheek against her hair. "I mean it, Nicky."

She sighed, reluctantly drawing away from him. She looked up, curious, excited. "Afraid of me, cattle baron?" she asked softly.

"In a way," he agreed unexpectedly, but he wasn't smiling. He touched her cheek with the back of his fingers in a soft caress. "I don't like to start things I can't finish."

"Meaning?" she persisted. If it was digging her own emotional grave, she couldn't help it. She had to know.

He stared into her eyes for just a second, and then drew back, physically and emotionally. "You'll figure it out. Don't wander out of the yard when you go walking. One of the men thinks he spotted a wolf today. I don't want anything to happen to you, little Eastern girl. I may never be your lover, but I'll take care of you, all the same, while you're here."

And with that surprising statement, he turned and walked off. Nicole stared after him with eyes that brimmed with unshed tears. He was very protective of her, and she wondered if he realized it. He wasn't saying what he felt, but she knew instinctively that he shared some of the warm feeling that was growing inside her. But whether he'd ever give in to it was anyone's guess. As for Nicole, it had shocked her to realize that she had none of her usual defenses when he was near her. And that realization kept her quiet all through supper and beyond bedtime. What an unexpectedly complicated thing this vacation of her boss's had become. She hoped that she was going to be able to cope with the new and disturbing feelings that Winthrop had unearthed in her.

Life sailed into a pleasant routine after that. She and Gerald settled down to work, and Nicole spent her free time exploring outdoors or watching Mary in the kitchen. Winthrop was pleasant enough, but he kept things cool, although from time to time she found those dark, quiet eyes watching her in a way that excited her beyond bearing.

Two days later, she heard cattle bawling and excited male voices, and she succumbed to the need to see Winthrop. The cattle were massed at a makeshift corral just away from the barn and the stables, and Winthrop was on his horse, helping to drive cattle into a holding pen where they were apparently being vetted and vaccinated and examined and treated for diseases or infestation by grubs.

That weak leg didn't seem to bother the big man one bit on horseback. He could cut and rope with the best of them, and the wilder the horse, the better he seemed to enjoy himself. He laughed deeply and with obvious pleasure the whole time.

She imagined that when he was in the saddle he could forget how ungraceful he was on the ground.

Not that a limp made him any less a man. He bristled with masculine sensuality. She could see quite easily how he'd gained a reputation in his youth as a playboy. He was devastating physically, and he had a voice that even in memory could make her flush with pleasure. Her heart hadn't been the same since that unexpected embrace on the porch. She could close her eyes and hear his voice all over again, as it had been that evening, and she could almost imagine it in a dark room, coaxing, deliberately seductive....

Warmth coursed through her and she forced herself to watch the men and the cattle. Winthrop had climbed off the horse to help catch a calf, apparently one that needed doctoring. He looped his rope and undid it, lazily coiling it while one of the other cowboys threw the calf and began to do something to it. Winthrop was rubbing his leg, and the limp was even more pronounced when he turned, leading his horse by the reins.

He saw Nicole at the fence, and he stood very still for an instant. She could feel his anger even at the distance, and made a discreet and quick withdrawal. He was headed in her direction, so she changed it and walked quickly into the forest that encircled the house.

Why she should have been embarrassed, she

didn't know. But she knew he was angry, even before he caught up with her minutes later.

She stopped, catching her breath. He was right behind her, still leading the horse. As he walked, he favored that right leg.

"Running away?" he taunted. "Why?"

She stared at him. It was silly to be so ill at ease with him, but his expression wasn't at all welcoming. "I don't know," she said quietly. She was wearing jeans and a long-sleeved yellow sweater. He had on a shirt the same shade of yellow and brown as his jeans, and she thought illogically how well they matched.

He lifted his dark head. "Don't you? What are you doing—spying? Did you want to see if the cripple could still throw a calf?"

She went forward without thinking and put her soft hand over his mouth. "Don't," she said softly. "Don't do that to yourself. You're not a cripple. You're a man with a limp."

The feel of her fingers shocked him. The gesture was unexpected and it threw him off balance. He caught her smooth hand, holding it near his cheek as if he couldn't quite decide what to do with it.

He stood over her, breathing roughly, his eyes dark with pain and anger as they searched hers. His fingers contracted absently around hers, bruising a little, but she didn't protest.

"I don't want you here," he said quietly, his eyes narrow, piercing.

"Yes, I know." She moved her fingers experimentally, and he let them go. She touched his cheek, tracing the long scar down his jaw, into the dimple in his chin. It was incredible how secure she felt with him, and not the least bit afraid. She sensed something in him, something vulnerable and tender, and she wanted to reach it. She needed to reach it, although she didn't understand why. "You don't talk about it, do you? Not ever."

His broad chest rose and fell. He was very close. Too close. She could feel the muscles ripple when he moved, feel him breathing, feel the warmth of him in the chill air.

His fingers slid into her hair, hesitantly, feeling the curls as he moved his hands to her nape and turned her head up with firm gentleness.

"It's been one hell of a long time since I kissed a woman," he said half under his breath, looking down at her coldly. "Don't you realize that you've been inviting that for days? I'm not a boy, and I've gone hungry in recent years. I can't play games, I even told you so. You could start something that would ruin both our lives."

She let him pull her head back. She looked up at him unafraid, her eyes soft with understanding and compassion. "I'm not afraid of you," she said softly.

"I could make you afraid, Nicole."

His voice was velvety soft and deep. Her lips parted, because it was as sensuous as she'd imagined it would be. She liked being close to him. She wanted his mouth and her lips parted in subtle invitation. She might have imagined herself in love with Chase James, but never in her life had she felt anything as sweet as this.

He looked down at her soft mouth, seeing it open, and something in him snapped. He bent quickly, covering it with his hard lips. He wanted to hurt her. She was a child, playing at sensuality, and he wanted to make it so rough that she'd stop tormenting him with emotions he never wanted to feel again....

She yielded completely, no thought of fighting him. His mouth was hard, warm and tasted of tobacco and it was only then that she realized how expert he really was. He made no allowances for her youth, and despite her small experience with Chase, this was her first real taste of passion. It was devastating, this helpless feeling he caused in her. She sighed hungrily, letting him draw her completely against the powerful hard length of his body, letting him crush her against it. Her mouth yielded eagerly to his insistent lips, tasting the tobacco tartness of his tongue as it pushed into her mouth, penetrating her in a silence that blazed with kindling sensations.

Her hands grasped his shirtsleeves, holding on, because her knees were getting weak. His arm at her back arched her, the hand at her nape tangled in her curly hair. He made a sound deep in his throat and lifted his head, his eyes black and blazing as they probed her dazed ones.

"Aren't you going to fight me?" he taunted with a faint, mocking smile as his mouth poised over hers.

"No." She reached up, sliding her arms around his neck. Her mouth was soft, parted and waiting, tempting his. "Oh, no, I want it, too!"

"Nicky..."

It was a groan, her name on his lips. He bent, half lifting her up to him. But this time, he didn't try to hurt her. This time, he was achingly gentle. His hard mouth slowed and softened on hers, and he kissed her with a subdued passion that aroused all her protective instincts. Poor, tormented man, she thought. So much love in him, all wasted on the wrong woman. And now he was driven to hurt back, out of fear that it was going to happen again. But it wasn't, she thought, her heart blazing with compassion. It wasn't, because she'd never hurt him.

She closed her arms tight around his neck and opened her mouth for him, drawing it over his as she was learning he liked it. Her tongue teased at his full lower lip and he made a sound that corresponded with the tautening of his body.

"I'm sorry," she whispered against his lips. "I don't...know much about this. I'm sorry if I did it wrong."

He lifted his head again. He was breathing roughly, and his eyes had a haunted look. The hand in her hair caressed gently. "You really are a virgin, aren't you?" he murmured with a tenderness he wasn't aware of.

"I guess it shows," she whispered dryly. She looked down at his shirt, missing the sudden shocked delight in his eyes. "I haven't had a lot to do with men in the past few years."

He brushed the curly hair away from her face, touching her with pure wonder. Yes, this was what he'd been uneasy about, this vulnerable side of her that attracted him. He'd tried so hard to avoid this confrontation. Ridiculous, really, when it was inevitable that he was going to feel her warmth in his arms, savor the soft nectar of her mouth. He'd known she was nearby, back at the corral. He'd sensed her somehow. "Why were you watching me?" he asked.

"I don't know. I needed to." She shifted, burying her face against his broad shoulder. "You disturb me," she whispered shakily. "It frightens me."

"It shouldn't." He held her, rocked her. His mouth touched her forehead in a kiss as gentle as the arms that held her. "I won't hurt you again."

She nuzzled her face against him. "It's very exciting, being kissed like that," she whispered shyly.

He smiled. "Is it?" He tilted her chin up and searched her eyes. "Then let's do it again," he whispered into her open mouth.

It was wilder this time, hotter, more unbearably sweet. She gave him her mouth and melted into the hard contours of his body with a soft moan. It wasn't until she felt the tautening, felt the sudden urgency in the mouth devouring hers, that she realized things were getting out of control.

She put her hands against his wildly thudding chest and pulled her lips away from his. "No," she said shakily.

He bit at her lower lip, his head spinning. "No?"

"You're a man...and experienced," she whispered. "I've never...and I çan't. I'm sorry."

He was breathing roughly, but he didn't seem to be angry. He brushed his mouth over her eyes, closing her eyelids. "Do you want to?" he whispered, smiling.

"What a ridiculous question. I expect you know the answer," she said dazedly.

"I suppose I do, at that." He sighed, wrapping her up against him. "Hold tight. They say it passes, eventually. I can't vouch for it, of course. I'm not in the habit of drawing back at this point."

"Oh, I'm sorry," she moaned.

"I won't die." He nuzzled his cheek against hers, rocking her. His arms had a faint tremor, but his breathing was calmer now and his heartbeat had stopped shaking them both. "What a potent little package you are. I didn't plan this. I meant to... hell, I don't know what I meant to do. Scare you, maybe."

"You did."

He laughed. "Like hell I did, you were with me

every step of the way. I could have laid you down in the grass and—"

"Hush!"

He drew back then and looked down at her, frowning, his eyes wary and searching. She was flushed, and her eyes had an unnatural brightness, as if she were holding back tears.

"What are you so afraid of?" he asked quietly, touching her eyelid gently to release a long, silver tear. "It was passionate, but still just a kiss. I didn't even try to touch you in any way that would have offended you."

"It isn't fear," she whispered. She lowered her eyes. How could she explain to him the intensity of her feelings, the aching tenderness she was beginning to feel for him?

"Are you afraid of intimacy?" he asked very quietly.

She lowered her eyes to his chest and closed them. "I'm afraid of getting involved. Just as afraid as you are," she added. And it was true. She'd given her heart to Chase—she'd almost given her body to him. And he'd betrayed her trust. How could she risk it again?

"Why?"

She looked up at him. "Why are you?" she countered, searching his quiet eyes.

He bent and touched her forehead with lips that were breathlessly gentle. "I loved her," he whispered, "in my way. It was the first time I'd ever felt more than a physical hunger for a woman. When she walked away from me, I wanted to die. I swore I'd get over it, but I don't know that I really have. The scars go deep."

She touched his face gently, running her fingers slowly along his hard cheek. Amazing, how exquisite it was to be near him.

"I got thrown over by my fiancé," she confessed. "He decided he wanted a rich girl, and I wasn't…" She almost added "anymore" but she caught the word in time.

He searched her soft green eyes. "You didn't sleep with him," he said, gazing at her intently.

"That's hard to explain." She stared at his top shirt button. It was undone, and thick dark hair peeked out against his tanned skin. "I wanted the first time to mean something. What hurts the most is that I never felt that way about him. I thought I loved him, but I never thought about sleeping with him."

That was the truth. Seeing how fast living had ruled her parents' lives had soured her on that part of life. Intimacy had become to them as careless as handshakes, and Nicole had determined that it would be treated more reverently in her own life. Perhaps, in retrospect, that was one of the reasons Chase had left her. He'd pushed her toward intimacy more and more after their engagement, but she'd resisted stubbornly. And now, standing close in Winthrop's arms, she was savagely glad she'd resisted.

There was more to it than that, he knew, but she wasn't volunteering any more information. He studied her quietly, thinking how much like him she was. He ran his finger down her cheek. Secretive, too, but he'd get more of an explanation eventually. It was insane to be so pleased that she was still innocent. It excited him, as sophisticated women never had.

"I could eat a moose," he said conversationally. "Why don't we rush back to the house and raid the freezer? Can you cook, in case Mary decides to try out for the Rockettes one day?"

She laughed at him. His humor had surprised her. Was this the real man? Had that cold veneer finally melted away? "Yes, of course I can cook. Why would Mary want to try out for the Rockettes?"

He shrugged. "She threatens it once or twice a winter. She saw them on television once and was sure she was just the right height, even though her legs were a bit large. I haven't taken her seriously in past years, but as I get older, my stomach worries."

"Don't you worry, Mr. Christopher, I'll take care of you," she murmured and turned toward the house. "Are you walking or riding?"

He sighed and grimaced. "I guess I'm riding," he muttered. "Damned leg hurts like hell."

She had a feeling he wouldn't have admitted that to anyone but her. It was the best kind of compliment. She smiled and shook her head when he offered to let her ride with him after he'd painstakingly mounted the horse and was sitting regally on its back.

"It wouldn't do your leg much good," she reminded him. "I'll just walk alongside and look up at you adoringly, if you don't mind."

"That'll be the day," he mused.

She looked up. "What happened to your leg?" she asked softly.

"Bone damage and torn ligaments. I was pinned in the car when she wrecked it," he said simply. "The surgeons repaired it as best they could, but there were complications. I'll always limp. And when I overdo, I'll always hurt." He glanced at her. "I had a choice between limping or giving up the leg. I came in with a matched set and I intend to go out the same way."

She pursed her lips, feeling mischievous, and almost asked an outrageous question. Then she blushed wildly and turned away.

He guessed the question and burst out laughing. "No," he murmured. "It doesn't cramp my style in bed."

She gasped, glaring at him. "I never—"

"You might as well have written it in twelve-inch letters on canvas," he retorted.

Her mouth opened and then closed while she thought up searing retorts, none of which came to mind. Later, she'd think up hundreds, she was sure.

But the thought of him in bed with another woman made her feel jealous and angry. And it showed.

He stopped, fingering the reins in one lean hand and waited for her to look up at him. His dark eyes, shadowy under the wide brim of his hat, watched her. "I'll qualify that," he said after a long exchange of eyes. "I don't think it will cramp my style. I haven't been with a woman since it happened."

Her breath caught, but she didn't look away. It was such an intimate thing to know about him, and she struggled to think of a suitable reply.

"That wasn't fair, was it?" he asked with a slow smile. "And I can't tell you for the life of me why I wanted you to know that. But I did. We'd better get home. It's getting dark."

She lowered her eyes to the trail that led back to the house. His revelation shouldn't have mattered to her, but it did. She smiled softly to herself, unaware that he saw the smile, and understood it.

He lit a cigarette and rode along beside her with a carefully hidden smug expression while he smoked it. "How about dinner tomorrow night? I'll drive you into Butte."

She felt chills to the tips of her toes and a wild excitement that was new, like the sudden tenderness between herself and Winthrop. "If Gerald doesn't need me, I'd love to," she said.

He hesitated. He looked down at her curiously, but he didn't speak. "Okay."

She wondered about the reason for his withdrawn expression and the odd silence the rest of the way to the house. That was good, because it kept her from thinking about the way he'd kissed her. She'd never felt more threatened in her life, and the worst of it was that she wasn't even afraid of what might happen between them.

He glanced at her just once, shocked by the surge of jealousy he felt at her remark about Gerald. It was that, too. Jealousy. He was afraid that there was something between this woman and his brother, and his own sense of honor and family wouldn't allow him to trespass on Gerald's territory. He wanted her to be heart-whole. He wanted that desperately. Could she have kissed him that way and still belong to Gerald? Surely not!

He pulled his emotions up short. It wouldn't do to give in to this unexpected yen for her. He was playing with fire, and God forbid he should get burned a second time.

Nicole, unaware of his thoughts, was having some difficulties of her own trying to figure out his taciturn somberness after the new and delicate camaraderie between them. She guessed, rightly, that he was holding back out of apprehension, and she even understood. But she didn't want him to leave her alone. She was beginning to love him, and it was only when she admitted it that she realized how desperately she wanted him.

Four

Winthrop wasn't at the supper table. Nicole didn't really expect him to be, because it was early November now, and according to Gerald, the boss was getting his management program in gear for winter. That included culling cattle; weaning, pre-conditioning and delivering calves; making the initial selection of replacement cattle and starting them on feed; and all the veterinarian-related chores that that entailed. With the sheer immensity of the cow-calf operation, it was a full-time job for the boss to keep up with what was going on. Mike, the foreman, relieved Winthrop of a lot of headaches, but even with a firm of accountants to do the paperwork, Winthrop still had to make the big decisions. No wonder he was putting in so many late hours, Nicole thought after Gerald had explained his absence.

Later that evening, Gerald had some correspondence for her. They went into the study to work. The room had Winthrop's personality stamped all over it. There was a bear's head on the wall, and burgundy leather furniture. The rugs were Indian, and the huge stone fireplace was made of native rock in comparable colors. The desk was oak, the chairs man-size and comfortable. There was a copper kettle on the hearth, and it reminded Nicole of the huge copper mining operation she'd seen as they came through Butte on the day they'd arrived. On the wall was a portrait of a man in buckskin, and she wondered if that was the French trader who was an ancestor of the Christophers.

"By the way, Sadie's invited us for dinner Friday night," Gerald said as he sorted out his mail, which had been forwarded from Chicago that afternoon. "Is that convenient for you?"

"That's fine," she said. "I look forward to meeting her again." She sat poised with her steno pad on her lap. "Uh, Winthrop asked if I'd go into Butte with him tomorrow night. To a restaurant."

Gerald pursed his lips and smiled mischievously. "I see," he mused. "So Winthrop's out to take my girl away from me, is he? I'm not sure if I like that."

It was an old joke between them, dating from her first six months as his secretary when two of the vice presidents had tried to steal her out from under his nose. She laughed and he was smiling. But the man out in the hall, overhearing him, didn't see that. Winthrop was within reach of the doorknob, but his lean hand faltered.

"He's not likely to try to take me away from you, so you can stop worrying," she said, tongue in cheek. "Anyway, he couldn't do it, you're quite unmatchable. Are you reassured?"

"I am." Gerald sighed theatrically, his brown eyes playful. He wasn't at all bad-looking. He just seemed very young beside his brother. "What a frightening thought!" he added with a mock shudder. "That I could lose you to my own brother. But Winthrop is too much a gentleman to steal from people, so I can relax. Now, suppose we get down to work?"

Winthrop turned and walked out the front door. His footsteps were so soft, and the closing of the door so quiet, that the occupants of the study didn't hear him.

He hadn't expected Nicole to be like that. He'd been sure that her ardor was real, that she'd felt the same tenderness he had. And here she was telling Gerald that there was no chance Winthrop could turn her head. He felt sick to his stomach and furiously angry. He couldn't bear the thought of being near her anymore, not after hearing her conversation with Gerald. What a close call, but at least he'd been spared. His face hardened as he began to work out what he was going to do. Thank God, she'd never know just how close she'd come to getting under his skin.

There was no sign of Winthrop for the rest of the evening, and the next morning, Gerald found a note waiting for him when they sat down to breakfast. He read over it, obviously puzzled.

"Winthrop," he said, waving the slip of paper. "He's gone to Omaha, God knows why. Something about a cattle deal. He said he's sorry about this evening, but he'll have to take a rain check on your dinner date."

"That's all right," she said, hiding her disappointment. "I'm sure he couldn't help it."

Gerald, who knew his older brother a little better than Nicole did, was uneasy. Winthrop hadn't offered to take a woman out to dinner since that blonde barracuda did him in. Nicky had touched something in him, something cold and dormant, and now Winthrop seemed determined to fight it to the last breath. Gerald studied Nicky, wondering if she had any idea how disturbing Winthrop must find her. Probably not. She was a sweet person, a little reserved most of the time. Gerald was fond of her, in a brotherly way, and he felt responsible for Winthrop's unexpected coolness toward her. Knowing how his brother felt, Gerald should have been more wary of bringing a woman to the ranch. But it had been Winthrop who'd mentioned bringing Nicky. Come to think of it, Winthrop had asked a lot of questions about her after he'd seen her that day at the Chicago office. He pursed his lips. Well, well. Big brother had an Achilles' heel, it seemed. He smiled as the thought warmed his mind. And now that Winthrop had the quarry near the hook, he was going to play her for a while, was that it? Or had he gotten cold feet and was now running?

"You're very quiet," Nicole said hesitantly.

"I'm just thinking. By the way, with Winthrop gone, would you rather spend tonight at Sadie's?" he asked with old-world politeness.

She smiled. "You're a nice man. Would you mind?"

"Heavens, no," he murmured. Besides, it would give him an excuse to see Sadie again the next day, when he went to fetch Nicky. And it would kill any potential gossip stone dead. Winthrop might appreciate that one day.

They went that night to have dinner with Sadie. She was a tall woman with blond hair and soft brown eyes. Nicky had always liked her, and the two of them found plenty to talk about when Sadie had come by the office to wait for Gerald.

"I'll be delighted to have you stay the night," Sadie told her enthusiastically. "It gets lonely with just me for company. Mother likes people."

"How is she?" Gerald asked gently.

Sadie sighed and shook her head. "No better. No worse. She just lies and looks at the wall and begs to die." She bit back tears. "Here, Nicky, help me get the food on the table, will you? Gerald, would you like to go in and ask Mother if she needs anything?"

"Certainly," he agreed, and paused to exchange a look with Sadie that was long and bittersweet.

Sadie watched him leave the room, her eyes wandering over his tall figure in the becoming tan suit.

"I'm hopeless," Sadie sighed, smiling shyly. "I love him to death, but there's not a thing I can do about it. I love Mother, too. I can't leave her."

Nicky studied the wan face. "He hasn't been well, either," she said.

Sadie glanced up. "Oh, dear."

"An ulcer," Nicole said. "Just an ulcer. But he pushes so hard."

"He always has. Competing, you know," she added with a loving smile. "He feels he has to come up to par with Winthrop."

"That would be a tall order," Nicky said without thinking as she laid the table.

Sadie glanced at her as she filled cups with steaming black coffee. "He's a cold man."

"Not really," Nicole replied softly. "He's just hurt, that's all."

The older woman pursed her lips. "How did you wind up on the ranch?"

"Mr. Christopher wanted to come home for a month to rest and work. I have car payments, furniture payments, payment payments..." She grinned. "I couldn't afford to lose a month's pay, so I came, too."

"And now Winthrop's done a vanishing act. Why?"

"I don't know," Nicky said honestly. "He asked me out to dinner tonight, and then this morning he left." She shrugged. "He's very difficult to understand."

"He always was. I've known the two brothers for years. I went to school with Gerald." She filled the coffee cups and then placed them in their lovely china saucers on the linen tablecloth. "Winthrop was always a loner, although he was something of a rounder in his younger days. He broke hearts…"

"I'll bet he did," Nicky murmured. She looked up. "Did you know about the blonde?"

"Everybody around here knew about the blonde," Sadie replied. "It was a nine-day wonder. The gossip went on forever, as it does in small communities. Winthrop got back on his feet and lived it down, but I imagine he hasn't really gotten over it. She was a first-class barracuda. She'd have cut him up like fish bait if they hadn't been in that wreck. She'd have taken him for everything he had, and left him bleeding without a backward glance. She married an oil millionaire, you know. They say she's got a closet full of mink coats."

"How sad," Nicky said genuinely, her green eyes full of bitterness. "So many people marry for money. Or try to."

"I'll bet you never would," Sadie said unexpectedly. "Gerald always did like you. I'm a bit jealous of you."

"Me?" Nicky grinned. "Thanks, but he's too nice a man to make a play for his secretary. I'd do anything for him, but only in the line of duty. I'm shy that way. Most men don't appeal to me physically."

"Does Winthrop?"

Nicole flushed and flapped around while Sadie burst out laughing.

"I'm sorry, but your guilty secret is safe with me," Sadie said with a laugh. "Oh, Nicky, what a man to get hot and bothered by. The iceman!"

"It could be worse. I could develop a case for some married man with twenty kids."

"True, true." She put the finishing touches on the table arrangement. "Come and meet Mother, and then I'll show you where to put your overnight case."

"You're nice to let me stay," Nicky said. "You and I know that nothing would go on, but people talk. I don't want any gossip about my nice boss."

"Neither do I, and I'm glad you're old-fashioned." The nurse narrowed her eyes. "You really are old-fashioned, aren't you?" she asked with startling perception.

Nicky cleared her throat. "I always thought... well, marriage is nice. They say white only means it's your first marriage, but it means a lot more than that to me. I had old-fashioned grandparents."

She didn't add that she had wildly liberated parents and a succession of stepparents, or that her grandparents had gone to court to save her from the glitter.

"Good for them," Sadie said. "Her room's through here."

Sadie's mother was small and withered and very quiet. She looked like a little doll lying there, white hair and pale blue eyes and a beaten look about her. She could only move one side of her body—even one eye and part of her mouth were affected. It must have been a massive stroke.

"Mama, this is Nicky," Sadie introduced her.

Gerald moved. He'd been sitting on the bed beside the little old woman, holding her hand. He got up so that Nicky could sit and take the wrinkled little fingers in hers.

"Hello, Mama." Nicky grinned. "Or should I call you Mrs. Todd?" She raised her eyebrows.

"You may call me Mama if you like," Sadie's mother said, with the first hint of a twinkle in her eyes.

"That would be nice," Nicky said, smiling. "Mine died a long time ago. I don't have one. So if Sadie doesn't mind, I can share you. It's a pretty big deal," she added with mock solemnity. "I live on a tight budget, so working another person into my Christmas shopping list is a great honor. I give Godiva chocolates as presents," she whispered.

The old lady actually laughed. Her thin fingers tightened on Nicky's. "Do you?" she whispered.

"Do you like chocolates?"

Mama managed to smile. "I love them!"

"Lucky you, to have just adopted me," Nicky said. She searched the tired old eyes. "I'll bet you were as beautiful as Sadie, at her age," she mused.

"Yes, I was," the old woman said emphatically. "Sadie...show her."

"This was Mother at my age." Sadie held up a small portrait study. The woman in the photograph was standing beside a tall, dark man, and she was the image of Sadie.

"Weren't you a dish?" Nicole sighed, studying it. "You're still a dish," she added, glancing down at the smiling woman. "What can we bring you to eat? I saw roast beef and mashed potatoes and a salad...."

"Mashed potatoes and gravy," the woman replied eagerly. "And is there pudding?"

"Yes," Sadie said quickly, although there wasn't and she'd have to rush back and make one.

"I'll have pudding, too," came the pleased reply. "Now go and eat," her mother said. "Then Nicole can visit with me while you and Gerald put everything away."

"Nicky's staying the night. Winthrop's away," Sadie explained.

"If it's all right," Nicky asked.

"It's all right," the old woman said fiercely. "Go and eat, child. If I adopt you, you must be fattened up. I don't want any thin children."

Nicky laughed, her green eyes sparkling in her elfin face as she got to her feet. "I'll double up on portions. And I'll bring your pudding myself."

Sadie just shook her head when they were back in the dining room. "Never," she whispered, smiling. "I've never seen her so animated. She just lies there and hates it. Tonight, for the first time, she came alive. Nicky, what did you do?"

"I stirred her up," Nicky said with twinkling eyes. "That's all. People need stirring up now and again, especially when they're bitter."

"You should see what Nicole did to Winthrop," Gerald mused. "He left home."

"That wasn't my fault."

"Tell me about it," Gerald invited, a mischievous twinkle in his dark eyes.

"It wasn't. All I did was…" She hesitated, her face turning red as she thought about what she'd done and the way she and Winthrop had kissed so hungrily in the woods.

Gerald raised an eyebrow and exchanged a glance with Sadie.

"Is everything on the table?" Nicky asked quickly, sitting down.

With the subject safely changed, they took their places and began to eat. Watching Gerald and Sadie, she could easily see that they felt something for each other. Nicole's gentle heart went out to them, because it was obvious that they couldn't have any kind of future together in this situation. Putting Mrs. Todd in a nursing home would be condemning her to death. And Nicole had a feeling that she was very possessive about her daughter, perhaps without realizing it. Sadie was shy and so was Gerald, to a large extent. It was a difficult situation.

Sadie made a vanilla pudding and when it was dished up, Nicole took a tray to Mrs. Todd's room.

"I haven't enjoyed anything so much for a long time," Mrs. Todd sighed when she finished. "It's so hard to bear, being like this. I was always active, able to do as I pleased. And now..."

"Won't you get better?" Nicole asked quietly.

"I don't know. The doctors said I might. But that was a year ago; I think they've given up now."

Nicole put the tray to one side. "That's a nice bird feeder outside the window," she remarked, glancing at the elaborate chrome and glass affair.

"I love birds," the old lady explained. "I can watch them."

Nicole pursed her lips. "Do you have any binoculars?"

Her eyes gleamed. "No."

"I'll get you some. How about a book on birds, so you can identify them?"

The old eyes got brighter. "I'd love it!"

"Done. Just give me a few days. Now, how about

a good murder mystery? There's one on television, one of those Agatha Christie ones, and I won't even tell you who done it."

Mrs. Todd actually laughed. "You should be with the young people, Nicole."

"The young people are—what did you flappers call it—spooning," she whispered conspiratorially. "At least, I hope they are. Gerald's very shy, and I think your daughter is, too."

"Yes, she is, poor child. She's such a good girl, and she's been so sweet to come and look after me. A lot of children would have turned their backs, or put me in a nursing home," Mrs. Todd said worriedly. "She hasn't said anything about it, but I know she's lonely here."

Nicole patted the old hand. "She loves you."

Mrs. Todd looked up. "And that young man... is he yours?"

She shook her head. "But I think he might be Sadie's. Would you mind?"

Mrs. Todd thought about it for a minute. "Well, no. He's a good boy. Not a patch on Winthrop, mind you, but the Christophers are fine people. I knew their mother. She was a dream girl."

"I hear their father was a nightmare man," Nicole said, fishing for information.

"Oh, no. He was a dynamo. We were all so jealous when he went to New York after Margaret. She didn't want to come, they'd had some terrible falling out. But he made her, kept her down at that house a virtual prisoner, until she agreed to marry him. Just between you and me, I think he took unfair advantage, too, but she loved him like a tigress. They were very happy."

"Did he look like Winthrop?" Nicole asked softly.

The old eyes seemed suddenly young. "Yes."

"A big man?"

"Body and heart. How is Winthrop? Is he getting over that woman?"

"I don't know him that well."

"Of course you don't, but you light up when I mention him, all the same. Turn on the television, child, and save your blushes. And then why don't you say good-night to the young lovers for us both and we'll hope something nice develops."

Nicole laughed delightedly as she followed the smug instructions. She tiptoed down the hall. It was unusually quiet, and when she reached the hall door, she saw why. Gerald, who seemed such a quiet and shy man, had Sadie in an embrace that spoke volumes and the way they were kissing said everything. Nicole tiptoed back and shut Mrs. Todd's door.

"Did you say good-night?" she asked Nicky.

Nicky said no with a straight face. "They're having a lively discussion. I expect it will be some time before we hear from them."

Mrs. Todd settled back against her pillows.

"Lovely. I think it would do Sadie good to have company more often."

Nicole just smiled and settled down to watch the movie.

It was late the next morning before Nicole heard the sound of a vehicle coming up the driveway. That would be Gerald, she thought and she smiled at Sadie.

"I've had a lovely time," she told the other woman. "Thanks for letting me stay."

"I'm glad you did," Sadie mused. "Mother hasn't enjoyed herself that much since the stroke. You were just what she needed to shake her out of her lethargy. And now that I know you aren't making eyes at my Gerald, I'll be your best friend."

Nicole's eyebrows arched in surprise. "You didn't think that?"

"Of course I did," Sadie replied, amused. "So did everybody else. Gerald isn't the kind of man who brings women home, even secretaries, unless they mean something to him. Or at least, that's what we all figured."

Nicole wondered then about Winthrop's strange behavior, and if he could have thought the same thing. She went back over her easy friendship with her boss and began to see what an outsider might have seen.

"He's a very nice man," Nicole began quietly, "but…"

"That 'but' saved your life," Sadie whispered conspiratorially. She looked up as a knock sounded on the door and she went to open it with wide, bright eyes. But it wasn't Gerald standing outside. It was Winthrop.

Five

Sadie's face fell, although she tried not to let her disappointment show. "Oh, hello," she faltered. Winthrop's expression didn't encourage any pleasurable outbursts. He looked out of humor and unapproachable. Nicole, watching him, thought that he'd had time to build walls again, and he'd done it with enthusiasm. So much for her optimistic outlook on the future; the iceman had frozen over.

"Where's Gerald?" Nicole asked hesitantly. Her question made the situation even worse.

He positively glared at her. "He's at home on the phone, coping with some office disaster that one of his vice presidents is in the middle of. He's drinking buttermilk by the gallon, eating antacid tablets by the handful and generally getting sicker by the minute."

"Winthrop, you should have disconnected the phone," Sadie sighed.

He smiled at Sadie. "How's your mother?"

"Doing better, thanks, and all because of Nicky. She built a fire under Mama." Sadie grinned.

Winthrop stared at Nicole speculatively. "She's good at starting fires, all right," he said, but it wasn't a compliment. He was spoiling for a fight.

Nicole glared back. He was wearing jeans with a chambray shirt and the familiar sheepskin jacket, and a wide-brimmed hat shadowed his cold face. He looked very Western and deliciously sexy. Nicole wondered why he always seemed to button his shirts up almost to the throat, and found herself unexpectedly curious about what was underneath. Hair peeked out at his throat, and she remembered the springy feel of his chest under her hands that evening he'd caught her on the steps....

Winthrop was telling Sadie something about a party.

Nicole snapped back to the present. "A party?"

"Gerald thinks you're getting bored without some fun, buried out here in the sticks," Winthrop told her. "He wants to give a party. There'll be a band and all the neighbors will come. You too, Sadie. I'll drive Mary up to sit with your mother."

"I haven't been to a party in a long time," Sadie confessed wistfully.

"Neither have I, but I guess we'll have to make the best of it," Winthrop said with unflattering resignation. "It'll be Friday night, around six. I'll drive Mary up and fetch you."

"Couldn't Gerald?" Nicole suggested.

Winthrop openly gaped at her. "What?"

"He'll have to welcome his guests and so will you," Sadie reminded Nicole.

Nicky sighed. "I guess so." She picked up her case, which Winthrop promptly took away from her, and followed him out to the truck with a rueful wave at Sadie.

He got in under the wheel, threw up a hand at Sadie and reversed the pickup with deft, controlled movements. He didn't speak until he had it headed down the long, winding road toward the ranch.

"I didn't expect to find you here," he said curtly, lighting a cigarette as he drove. The wind was fierce and the truck lurched. It was getting dark against the horizon, heavy blue clouds building over the peaks.

"It wouldn't have looked right, to have Gerald and me under the same roof alone," she faltered.

He glanced at her. "Then, my God, how does it look to have the three of us under one roof?" he shot back.

She hadn't thought about that. She flushed scarlet and moved her gaze out the window. "How was your trip?"

"Fine."

"When did you get back?"

"About an hour ago."

She stared at her hands in her lap. She'd felt her heart soar when he walked into Sadie's living room, but now all she felt was miserable. He'd left town because he didn't want to take her out, and now he was as remote as the clouds. She felt abandoned.

"Don't look like that," he said abruptly.

"Like what?" she muttered.

"Lost. Wounded."

She studied her hands in her lap, twisting the small emerald ring she wore on her right ring finger. "You've been spoiling for a fight ever since you came in the door."

"And you don't know why?" he taunted, and his eyes cut at her. "Or hasn't it occurred to you yet that I want you?"

It had, but only in a vague way. She felt her face flush at hearing it put into words, and so bluntly. She couldn't even look at him. She was feeling a tenderness she'd never experienced, and he'd reduced it to something casual and physical and faintly irritating.

"That's plain enough," she said in a soft tone, forcing herself not to react violently when what she wanted most to do was push him out the door and down a sharp ravine.

He wouldn't back down, he told himself, no matter how miserable she looked. His jaw tautened as he wheeled the truck around a sharp curve, scattering dirt and gravel on the unsurfaced road.

"You get under my skin," he said abruptly. "I don't like it."

Her heart shifted uncomfortably. She stared out at the tall trees in the graying horizon. "You have the same effect on me," she said curtly, "and I don't like it, either."

"Then suppose we keep out of each other's way," he suggested. "You won't be here that much longer."

"That might be wise."

He drew on his cigarette, and then he turned and looked at her just as she lifted her eyes to his. The truck almost went off the road. He braked easily enough to stop the truck, but his gaze didn't waver. Her eyes were greener than new leaves on spring trees, he thought absently, his own narrowing with kindling hunger. She was young and soft and sweet and she made him ache as he had in his youth, made him feel invulnerable and all male.

Her lips parted, but she couldn't look away. It was like holding a live wire in bare hands. Her breath shuddered out of her throat and she felt throbbing fire in her blood.

"If I touched you now, there wouldn't be any stopping for either of us," he said in a deep, slow tone. His broad chest rose and fell heavily, and his eyes were narrow, dark. "You knock me off balance."

"You said yourself," she whispered, trying to be

rational, "that you'd been away from women for a long time."

"And you think it's proximity that's causing my reaction to you?" he asked with a mocking smile. He reached out a lean hand and idly linked her fingers into his with a caressing pressure that was as arousing as a kiss. Her heart began to race, and her breath came in smothered whispers that she tried not to let him see.

"That," he whispered, "is chemistry. It doesn't have anything to do with proximity, or age, or sanity. I touch you, and my body aches. And if the way you're breathing is any indication, Kentucky girl, you're on fire for me."

She bit her lip, hard. But the tremors wouldn't stop. She tugged her hand away from his and he released it with careless indifference and went back to smoking his cigarette.

"Don't worry," he said with cool mockery, "I won't tell your boss. I love my brother. His happiness comes first."

She frowned slightly. "I don't understand."

"Don't you?" He turned back to the steering wheel and put the truck into gear without another word.

She rode beside him in an uncomfortable silence. She wanted to tell him that he'd gotten it all wrong, that she and Gerald were only boss and secretary. But he looked too unapproachable and she wasn't sure of him. Her feelings for Winthrop were new and a little frightening. She didn't want to have to face them.

When they got back to the house, he got out to carry her bag up to the front porch, all bristling masculine humor. He limped more than he usually did, too, and she wondered if it was due to his bad temper or if he was in pain from the walking he must have had to do on his trip.

"I don't understand why you're so angry at me," she murmured as she joined him on the porch. "I haven't done anything…."

"This is why," he said quietly. He looked down at her from his formidable height and, aware of Mary standing just inside the door, he did something with his hands, in sign language—first a movement like someone drinking out of a cup, and then an odd movement with his elbows and closed fists. "See if you can get Mary to translate that," he chided, turning. "And you'll know it all."

She stared after him wistfully, loving the lines of his elegant body, the muscular fitness that emanated from him despite that limp. He was the most attractive man she'd ever known. And if he'd looked back, and seen her standing there watching him, it might have erased some of the ill humor from his dark face. But he went away without a backward glance and Mary seemed to vanish into thin air as Nicole went inside with her overnight case.

"There you are," Gerald moaned, rubbing his stomach as he appeared in the doorway of Winthrop's study. "My ulcer is killing me. Have Mary pour me some buttermilk, will you? Then we've got to get some paperwork done and see if we can sort out this mix-up in taxes. Hurry, Nicky!"

"Yes, sir!"

She got the milk from the kitchen, curious about Mary's oddly smug look.

"There's something I want to ask you." Nicole hesitated. "Those signs Winthrop made on the front porch—you saw them. What did they mean?"

Mary grinned, showing even white teeth. "Interesting things."

"What did he say?"

Mary folded her arms over her ample bosom. "Much."

"Well?"

"Hard to translate into English," Mary continued. "Many Indian signs have no equivalent in English."

"Yes, but you must have some idea what he said," Nicole persisted.

"Good idea, all right, but I must give thought to the proper manner of expressing it to you." Mary turned back to making a thick-crusted apple pie. "Some time soon, I will translate it for you." Then she grinned again over her shoulder and giggled.

Nicole, no wiser than before, sighed and carried the milk to Gerald.

The tangle took time to straighten out, especially over the phone, and by the time it was done,

Nicole was too tired to do anything except eat a light supper and go to bed. Winthrop, as usual, was out working, so she didn't have to worry about keeping peace with him.

During the next few days, as she helped Gerald plan the party in her honor, Nicole puzzled over Winthrop's cool behavior and Gerald's continued stomach pain. Gerald and Sadie had gotten off to such a great start, and now he seemed morose and moody and worried.

Nicole had planned a menu of hors d'oeuvres and finger foods for a buffet, and arranged for a local band to play. Gerald had called the neighbors to invite them.

"This will be fun," he said as he finished. "There hasn't been any music in this house since Winthrop announced his engagement." He seemed far away for a minute and wistful. "There was music that night, and the neighbors came over, and we danced until after midnight. Mrs. Todd was fit as a fiddle back then, and she danced, too." He glanced at Nicole from his comfortable armchair. "Winthrop hasn't allowed music in the house since, although I can't blame him. He won't go near a party, either. He says he can't dance because of his leg, but I think the memories are stopping him more than any physical pain."

"I guess he really loved her," she said, remembering what little Winthrop had told her about his feelings at the time.

"It's been three years. He should be healing, mentally at least."

She didn't like to think about Winthrop's broken heart, or the cause of it. Her feelings were too turbulent, and jealousy was still topmost.

"Will he even come to the party?" she asked.

"He'll have to," he chuckled. "Or the neighbors will talk about him. He hates gossip more than he hates music. At least, he does since the accident. It never used to matter in the old days."

"We haven't heard from Sadie lately," she said with deliberate casualness.

He looked uncomfortable. "Her mother hasn't been well."

She studied his wan face. "Hasn't she?"

He shifted restlessly, crossing his legs. "She doesn't want to lose Sadie," he said curtly. "She's afraid of being alone, or at the mercy of strangers in some nursing home. I can't blame her, Nicole. It's just that Sadie's so young to be buried alive like that."

"Couldn't Mrs. Todd get better if she had more interest in life, in living?"

"Perhaps," he agreed. "But it's very hard to keep that interest going. You made a good start with her. Unfortunately, she's only enthusiastic when people are around. The minute they leave, she goes back to brooding."

"Doesn't she have relatives besides Sadie?"

"She has a sister in Florida," he murmured. "Ten years her junior and a live wire. She wants Mrs. Todd to come and visit, but Mrs. Todd is terrified to leave here. She has some idea that she'll die if she does. Meanwhile—" he sighed "—Sadie is trapped. She loves her mother, you know."

"And you love Sadie," she said quietly.

He started to deny it, and then he saw the gentle compassion in Nicole's green eyes. "Yes."

"Give it time," she said. "And we needn't rush back to Chicago," she added with a faint grin.

"Even if that means watching Winthrop do a job on your nerves?" he probed. "Because he's wearing them down, isn't he?"

"I bother him," she said, then looked up at Gerald. "He bothers me, too."

"Good. You both need a little shaking up," he said with a smile. He got to his feet, grimacing. "I need some more buttermilk."

"And your tablets," she added.

"And my tablets. But you're good medicine, Nicky."

She smiled. "Thank you. And thanks for the party, too. It was a nice thought."

"I hope you enjoy it."

"Oh, I think I will," she said. She was already thinking about breezing down the staircase in a billowy white gown, dragging a black mink coat behind her, dripping diamonds so that Winthrop would fall at her feet. Of course, she didn't have a white gown or a black mink or any diamonds. It would be the gray jersey dress and he'd be too out of humor about the whole thing to notice if she waltzed down the staircase stark naked. She sighed and went back to the typewriter.

The night of the party, Nicole dressed carefully in the hated gray jersey and did her face with a minimum of makeup. The band, a very good country and western one, was already in full swing when she went to answer the door with Gerald.

Winthrop came in behind Sadie, glaring at Nicole and Gerald with coal dark eyes. He was wearing white shirt with dark slacks and a leather jacket, a creamy dress Stetson atop his neatly combed straight hair. He and Nicky had barely spoken in recent days. He'd commented that a party was just what he needed the night before his group of Eastern hunters arrived—which they were scheduled to do that Saturday. But Gerald had made soothing noises to the big man and he'd calmed down.

But only temporarily. His eyes were already promising retribution on Nicky's poor head.

"Good evening, Winthrop," she drawled softly as Gerald led Sadie off to the punch bowl, since she was the last to arrive and there were no more guests to receive.

"Good evening, Miss White," he replied. His

dark eyes ran down her body like exploring hands, slow and very thorough. "I gather that you only brought one dress with you?"

"I didn't think I'd need more than one," she explained quietly. Her pale green eyes swept over his dark face and she felt tingles of pleasure from just looking at him. "It isn't too drab, is it?"

"You know you look lovely in anything you wear," he said suavely. He took off his Stetson, settled it on the hat rack, then hung up his jacket.

Watching the muscles ripple under the white shirt he wore with a blue patterned tie, Nicole wanted to stand in his arms and feel him holding her. It was a hunger that bordered on obsession. She moved closer to him as the band swung into a slow dance tune.

"I want to dance," she said quietly, aware of the guests watching them. Nobody was dancing yet; everybody seemed to be waiting for someone else to get things started.

He stared her down. "I don't dance anymore," he said coolly. "I can't. My leg won't hold me up under sudden turns and dips."

"It would if you danced slowly," she said. She moved even closer, her perfume floating up into his nostrils, her warmth teasing, seductive. "Hold me, Winthrop," she whispered, laying both palms slowly, hesitantly, flat down over the hard muscles of his chest.

He shuddered a little, and his chiseled lips parted. "I won't, damn it," he bit off.

She laid her head against his shoulder. "You want to," she whispered, "and I want to. Everybody's watching." Her own forwardness was beginning to embarrass her, but the need to be held by him was so strong that she fought down the urge to give in.

"No!" he bit off.

He started to turn, but she blocked his path. Everyone stopped talking, and she held her breath while he decided.

With a glance behind them and a muffled curse, he pulled her into his hard embrace and began to move very carefully to the slow rhythm of the music.

Gerald and Sadie watched the tall man's slow, hesitant movements with quiet smiles, amazed that Nicole had been able to manage such a small miracle. Winthrop was giving in, at least for the moment. His dark face was threatening, but he was holding her with such tenderness that it was almost tangible despite his temper.

Nicky savored her small victory, closing her eyes in wonder. Dancing with him was as sweet as she'd imagined it would be. He might hate her for it, but right now it seemed worth every expected bit of pain. He was tall and strong and warm, and he smelled of spice and soap. The lean, sure hand that held her made her feel safe and protected. She sighed with pure delight.

He felt that soft yielding and was furious at her for making a spectacle of him, for drawing everyone's eyes to his disability. Damn her, what was she trying to do to him?

He gave in with ill-concealed irritation and drew her slowly against him, one lean hand possessing hers. He began to move to the rhythm, a little clumsily at first, but quickly with more and more confidence. She melted into him, then, careful not to knock him off balance, she smiled against his shoulder.

"There," she mumbled happily, "I knew you could."

"I could wring your neck," he said, forcing himself to smile at her while all around them other people were finally joining them on the dance floor.

"It's your house," she reminded him. "The host is supposed to open the dancing. There are rules about that kind of thing."

"I can't dance with this leg," he said through his teeth.

"You're doing it, aren't you?" She drew back a little and looked up into his darkly glittering eyes. "But if you're sure you can't do it, then why don't you fall on the floor or something?"

"Lady," he breathed through his teeth, "you're brave in company."

"If we were alone, what would you do to me?" she asked with open curiosity, her green eyes wide and twinkling.

The look in them softened him, just a little. She was a handful, but her heart was in the right place. She wouldn't let him feel sorry for himself, or slide into thinking he had to give up living because he had a bum leg. And until now, he hadn't even realized how much he'd used that leg to keep him away from people. It had become his excuse for being a recluse, his excuse for avoiding involvement.

His fingers edged between hers and caressed them as he turned her with amazing flexibility. He smiled then, the cold anger in his eyes melting into reluctant pleasure.

"You danced before the accident, didn't you?" she asked, smiling. "You loved it, too. You're very good, despite that leg. You move with such grace for a big man."

"And what would you have done, Pollyanna, if I'd gone down on the floor with the first turn?" he asked.

"Oh, I'd have made sure I went down with you," she said matter-of-factly, "so that everyone would have thought I tripped you."

He felt his heart start pounding. Something stirred in him that he hadn't felt since his youth, something young and daring and utterly reckless. He pulled her against him and stood there for one long minute, fighting the urge to kiss her in front of everyone. He liked the way her body melted into his when he drew her close, he liked the faint trembling of her legs against his. She was his the minute he touched her, and he especially liked that. His eyes narrowed as he remembered the feel of her soft mouth, the exquisite pleasure it gave him to kiss her. She'd been engaged once, she'd told him. He felt a sudden heat of unreasonable jealousy. What had the man been like? Why had he jilted her? Was there some secret in her past that she was afraid to share with him?

"Are we doing statue imitations?" she asked breathlessly.

His lips pursed. "I'm trying to decide whether to kiss you."

"Not in front of all these people, for heaven's sake," she burst out.

"These people—or Gerald?" he asked softly.

Her eyebrows went straight up with surprise. "Well, come to think of it, I'm not sure how he'd react to it," she had to admit. Gerald hadn't said anything about her interest in Winthrop, and she didn't think he'd fire her over it. But, then again, she wasn't sure....

Winthrop sighed, and drew her back against him. "Never mind, daffodil. Just dance."

"Why did you call me that?"

He smiled against her temple. "There's nothing more full of hope than a daffodil. It comes before the last snow is gone, fluffing up yellow and pretty and optimistic in the middle of all that freezing white. It takes a lot to kill a daffodil. They're glorious."

Tears stung her eyes. He could call her daffodil forever, if he liked. She snuggled closer. "What a nice compliment," she said.

"I meant it."

"I know. You're not the kind of man who spouts insincere flattery."

"Perceptive of you, Miss White."

"You bet, Mr. Christopher."

He was quiet then, circling the floor lazily with her soft weight against him, feeling his head whirl with delicious sensations. His leg was beginning to throb from the unfamiliar strain, but he'd have fallen on the floor before he'd have given in to it now. He didn't want to let go of her. He wanted to pull her closer, and bend his head and take her soft mouth fully under his....

All too soon the music stopped, and Gerald was there, waiting.

"My turn." He grinned. "Sorry, big brother."

Winthrop stared at his brother for a long minute, searching the younger man's eyes curiously. And for just a minute, he thought about refusing. Then he came to his senses. She was just a woman, for God's sake, and women were treacherous. He wasn't going to fight with his brother. If Gerald wanted her, he could have her, Winthrop thought angrily. He smiled, but there was no humor in it. He nodded with a mocking smile at Nicole and then walked slowly away to the punch bowl, pausing to talk to some of the other men on the way.

"You angel," Gerald said, hugging her. "At first I thought he was going to breathe fire at you."

"So did I, but I bluffed him out. Doesn't he dance beautifully?" she murmured dreamily, staring past Gerald at Winthrop.

"Indeed he does, with the right partner." He whirled her around. "You've brought him back to life. I'd given up hope that he was ever going to put things into perspective. You're very good for him."

"Where's Sadie?" she asked.

"Phoning Mary to make sure Mrs. Todd is all right." He slowed down a little. "I wish I could decide what to do about it."

"Why don't you do what you want to and solve all your problems when the time comes? You can't cross a bridge until it's in front of you."

"Where did you learn so much?" he asked curiously. "You're not at all what you seem."

"I've had plenty of practice," was all she'd admit. And then that dance, too, was over, and she went from partner to partner for the rest of the evening.

Winthrop didn't dance with her again, but she felt his gaze on her wherever she went. Her eyes were on him just as much, when she thought he wasn't looking. He was so good to look at. Dressing up suited him. Even in a simple white cotton shirt and dressy tie, he looked elegant. It made him seem darker than ever, more sensuous. She wasn't even surprised to discover that she loved him. That seemed as natural as breathing.

All too soon, the guests were leaving. Nicole had the crazy idea of being alone with Winthrop while Gerald took Sadie home. But he looked in her direction with an expression on his face that chilled her to the bone. It was as if he hated her, and perhaps he did for what she'd done to him. Dragging him onto the dance floor in front of all the neighbors might not have been the way to his heart, she realized. And because she was confused and a little hurt by his coldness, she asked if she could ride with Gerald and Sadie. They took one look at her face and agreed without protest.

When they got to Sadie's house, Mrs. Todd was asleep, and Mary was watching a gory horror film on television. It was just ending and Mary sat with a big bowl of popcorn on her ample lap, refusing to budge until the last drop of blood was spilled.

"Good movie," she enthused, walking out with Nicole while Sadie and Gerald said a lingering good-night indoors. "You like horror films?" she asked.

"I like vampire movies," Nicole said. "But I like science fiction better."

"You and Winthrop." She shook her head. "Those films are noisy. Too noisy. I like quiet movies."

"With screaming and lots of victims," Nicole chided.

Mary stared at her, stone-faced. "Beats all those noisy machines."

Nicole laughed delightfully. "I guess so. How did Mrs. Todd do tonight?"

"Done fine. We had pudding. I like pudding."

"So do I," Nicole said, smiling. "It was a good party. Winthrop and I started the dancing."

Mary's eyes widened. "Winthrop was dancing?"

"Yes. He does it very well."

"He used to," Mary agreed. "But I have not seen him dance since the accident. How did you manage it?"

Nicole chewed her lip a little and peeked at Mary. "I stood in front of him on the dance floor and wouldn't move."

Mary laughed. She did it seldom, but when she did, it was wholeheartedly. "Good medicine," she told the younger woman. "We should bottle you."

"I'd most likely ferment and become illegal. There's Gerald."

He joined them, looking a bit hot under the collar and flustered. He grinned. "Ready to go?"

"Been ready quite some time," Mary said. "Long past my bedtime."

"There, there, too much sleep can kill a good woman," Gerald said soothingly. "Think of how I'm saving you from certain death."

"Saving me from much needed rest," Mary countered, climbing into the pickup between him and Nicole. "Winthrop danced, she tell you?"

"She didn't have to. I saw it with my own eyes," he volunteered, grinning past her at Nicole. "I wish I could have taken a picture. Nobody will believe it."

"Isn't it cloudy tonight?" Nicole was trying to change the subject, but it really did look cloudy, and it was getting colder.

"Snow clouds," Mary said. "We get buried in snow pretty soon."

"Not in November," Nicole said.

"This is Montana. Snow comes early and late—you can't predict mountain weather. And snow in November is pretty routine," her boss informed her. "Lord, I hope we don't get shut up with that horsey set from back East. They'll be here tomorrow." He glanced at Nicole. "By the way, one of Winthrop's guests is from Kentucky, an expert on thoroughbreds. Winthrop wants him to take a look at the colt and give him an opinion. He wouldn't be able to race it for a couple of years, of course, but he's thinking along those lines."

Nicole knew a number of people in the horsey set. She was afraid of meeting someone from her old life, someone who knew her father, who might tell him where she was and what she was doing now. She didn't want him to know anything about her new life. There were deep scars from those young years. She wanted nothing to do with the man who'd driven her mother into a succession of lovers, followed by a fatal accident. Nothing at all.

"Did he tell you the man's name?" Nicole asked quietly.

Gerald glanced at her. "As a matter of fact he did," he replied. He grinned ruefully. "But I was on the phone at the time and I didn't catch it. There's a Murdock woman, and a couple of brothers named Harris. But I don't think the Harrises know much about horses."

Nicole consoled herself with the thought that there must be hundreds of horsey sportsmen in the world besides her father. She only nodded, closing her eyes as they went back to the Christopher ranch.

The house was quiet when they got there. If Nicole had hoped to see Winthrop again, she was disappointed. He was nowhere in sight. She said good-night to Mary and Gerald and went reluctantly to her room.

She didn't sleep. She lay awake staring at the ceiling for what seemed hours. Finally she got up and decided to make herself a cup of hot chocolate. Perhaps that would do the trick; she really couldn't stay awake all night.

Since the household was asleep, she didn't stop to fumble through the closet for a robe. Besides, her long flannel pajamas were more than decent, with their pale-pink rose pattern. She looked very young without her makeup and barefoot, as she went down the long, dark staircase. She hoped the house didn't have ghosts, she didn't fancy meeting one.

The kitchen light was on. She opened the door and paused, stopping dead at the sight of Winthrop bending over the stove. He was wearing pajama bottoms, nice brown striped ones, but no top. His chest was…incredible. Broad and bronzed and thick with a wedge of hair that covered his rippling muscles.

He turned, his dark hair tousled, and stared at her. "Looking for someone?" he asked.

"For some hot chocolate," she confessed. "I can't sleep."

"I'm making some," he said. "Come in and find some mugs."

She stared at herself. "I should get a robe…"

"Why?" he asked, glancing at her. "You're covered up in all the right places, and I'm hurting like hell. I'm not in any condition to lay you down on the kitchen table with evil intent."

She smothered a giggle, went in and closed the door behind her. "How savage sounding," she mused as she searched the cupboard for cups. "Think of the splinters!"

"A nice girl like you. Shame on you." He took the hot chocolate off the stove and poured it into the mugs before he put the pan in the sink to soak. He was limping rather badly, and she grimaced as he sat down with a hard wince.

"That's my fault, isn't it?" she asked gently. "I made you dance when you didn't want to, and you hurt it because of me. I'm sorry."

"Nobody makes me do a damned thing," he said curtly. He had two pills. He took them, swallowing them down with a sip of the hot chocolate. "I could have walked away from you if I'd wanted to."

"But you didn't."

He turned, his dark eyes holding hers. "I didn't want to. I like holding you. The excuse isn't particularly relevant."

Her face colored, and he smiled slowly.

She lowered her eyes to her cup and lifted it quickly to her mouth. She sipped at it for a long time, her mind hungry with sweet longings, her eyes darting to his broad, bare chest and back to her cup. He was through with his chocolate, but he sat back, quiet and faintly threatening, and just looked at her until her body began to tremble.

"Did you wonder what I looked like under my shirt, Nicky?" he asked with blatant seduction in his voice.

Her lips parted on a husky sigh. She couldn't quite meet that searching gaze. She clung to her empty mug as if it were a life jacket. The silence was suddenly too sweeping, the loneliness of the deserted room staggering in its implications. They were alone. And he wanted her.

She felt him move before she saw him. He took the mug out of her hands and drew her up in front of him, holding her gently by her upper arms.

"There's nothing to be afraid of," he whispered. "Nothing at all."

He bent his head and she saw the shadow of his face, felt his chocolaty breath as his mouth brushed against hers. She relaxed then, because he was very slow and sure of himself. He wasn't in any hurry, and the leisure of his movements stopped the panic inside her. She began to unwind, feeling the softness of his mouth along with its hardness, liking the delicate probing of his tongue just under her upper lip. Amazing, she thought, how sensitive her mouth was to that light touch.

She lifted toward him a little, and heard his breath catch. She couldn't know that he was on fire with need, that he was in agony trying to hold back enough to keep from frightening her.

"Sweet," he whispered against her lips. "You're so sweet."

He had a lover's voice, she thought, very deep and seductive. She loved to hear him talk anytime, but particularly like this, in hushed whispers. She put her hands against him and felt them tingle where they touched the thick hair that covered him. It was wiry against her palms, deliciously abrasive when she began to draw them over his broad chest, disturbing the muscles so that they rippled under her fingers.

His breath caught. He stopped and suddenly moved back. His eyes held hers, searching them. "I want more than this," he said tautly.

She couldn't look away. "How...how much more?"

His eyes went to her pajama jacket. "Nothing terribly indiscreet," he said quietly. His hands followed his gaze. He hooked his index finger into the V neckline of her pajamas and tugged her toward him. "Don't panic, okay? I promise I won't let it go too far."

She wanted to protest. But her eyes went down to his lean fingers working the buttons with such deftness, and she couldn't look away. He undid them slowly, and then drew the fabric back from her high, pink breasts with a leisurely expertise that hypnotized her.

Then his gaze was on her, looking at her with blatant possession. Winthrop was a man with an eye for beauty, and the expression in his dark eyes told her that he found her beautiful. Her nipples went hard under his scrutiny, and she was embarrassed and tried to cover them. But he stopped her, shaking his head gently.

"It isn't sordid or shameful to let me see you," he said quietly, his voice very slow and deep. "God never made anything more beautiful than a woman's breasts."

Her breath stopped in her throat at his words. She looked up at him, her gaze sharing secrets with him. Then he smiled, and it was like the sun coming out.

He touched her cheek, gently tracing it. "Come here and let me hold you, Nicole," he breathed, drawing her. "Feel my body and let me feel yours. Let me teach you how beautiful it can be to touch skin against skin."

She let him draw her close, feeling the sting of tears as she went into his arms. Her eyes closed at the first contact with his warm, hard body, and she cried out as her nipples stabbed into his skin, burying themselves in the damp, abrasive mat of hair that covered the hard muscles. "Winthrop," she murmured.

"Yes." His hands spread against her silken back, under the pajama top. He drew her very close, closing his own eyes as her soft body melted into him. He was aroused, and she knew it. He felt her stiffen as her legs came into contact with his.

"Don't flinch away from me," he murmured at her temple, coaxing her back against him. "This is natural, too, and good and sweet and right between a man and a woman. Don't be afraid of it."

"It's so intimate," she whispered shakily against his warm, broad chest. His skin tasted of cologne and soap. Masculine smells. Good smells.

"Intimate," he agreed at her ear. "Yes, it's that. It's exquisitely sweet, having you close to me this way." His arms tightened and trembled a little. So did his tall, fit body. "Nicky," he breathed on a groan, bending his head over her. He began to rock her, fostering a new kind of intimacy between them, one that should have shocked her but was strangely familiar now. She clung to him, letting him hold her, yielding to his strength.

"Your leg..." she said a long minute later.

"What leg?" he murmured.

She drew in a long breath, and he shuddered as he felt her breasts swell against his skin.

"It's scary, isn't it?" she whispered. "Holding each other like this."

"Scary enough," he agreed on a bitter laugh. "You can't possibly imagine the thoughts going through my mind."

"I'll bet I can, too," she said. She nuzzled her cheek against him, loving the rough feeling of the hair over his chest. "Do you like that?"

"Can't you feel how much I like it?" he asked with blatant mockery. "Give me your mouth."

She lifted her lips to meet his, her hands sliding around him to his back, loving the feel of him, the vibrant masculinity of him. He kissed her slowly, warmly, and even that was intimate, his tongue probing softly in her mouth.

He shifted her a little so that his hand could find the soft curve of her breast and tease it into arching toward those tormenting fingers.

"Do you want me to keep going?" he whispered at her lips.

"Yes," she whispered back, her voice breaking. She wasn't old enough or sophisticated enough to hide her hunger.

"Like this?" he murmured, with a teasing touch around the nipple, his fingers faintly callused and deliciously abrasive on her soft skin. "Or like this?"

His thumb rubbed suddenly at the tiny hardness and she cried out, a whimper of sound that worked on him like a narcotic. His hand covered her breast and he lifted his head to look into her misty eyes while he caressed her.

"I'm on fire," he whispered. "Burning."

"So am I," she moaned. "Winthrop…"

His head bent to her body, and as she watched, fascinated, he arched her and opened his mouth and put it completely over her breast.

She thought that as long as she lived, she'd never get over the sensation. It went on and on, tearing at her, shaking her, making her too weak to move, to breathe, to think. She was an instrument, and he was playing her with an expert touch, teaching her things about her own body that she'd never known.

She arched farther, her hands in his dark, cool hair, inciting him, begging him. His mouth slid from one breast to the other, and she moaned like a wounded thing, feeding on the sweet ardor of his mouth, living only through him.

Dazed, shuddering with sensation, she barely felt him move. And then she was on his lap in the chair, and he was holding her, cradling her while she cried. She hadn't even been aware of the intensity of her emotions until she felt the tears like rain on her face.

"Shh," he whispered gently, his mouth soothing her now, touching her hot cheeks, her wet eyelids and eyelashes, her nose and mouth and chin. "It's all right. Hush, darling, it's all right now."

"Winthrop," she whispered tearfully.

"Nicole," he breathed, wrapping her up in his arms. He rocked her against him hungrily, laughing a little at her headlong response even now. "Wildcat! Never in my life, not ever... You damned near pushed me over the edge with those little cries you made."

"I couldn't help it," she said, hot-faced. "It was what you were doing to me..."

"I couldn't help that, either," he murmured dryly. He kissed her gently. "You have exquisite breasts, Miss White," he breathed huskily. "As soft as satin, as warm as velvet. I'd rather cut off my arm than cover them, but if I don't, you and I are very likely to become lovers within the next few seconds, right here on the floor."

And while she was getting over the shock from that statement, he sat her up on his lap like a big doll and proceeded to do up the buttons on her pajamas. When she was covered again, he drew her back down, holding her lazily while he pressed tender, undemanding kisses on her damp face.

"You're very quiet," he remarked finally. "Why? Are you shocked? Outraged? Embarrassed?"

"I don't know," she confessed, snuggling closer. "Not outraged or ashamed, although I suppose I should be embarrassed. I'm not in the habit of... behaving this way with men."

"I know that." He brushed the damp hair away from her cheeks. His dark eyes held hers. "Is this all new to you?"

It wouldn't do to lie to him, she supposed. She searched his dark eyes. "Yes," she said quietly. "My fiancé…" she said quietly. "He wanted me, but I could never give in to him. I…didn't like it when he tried to touch me." She lowered her eyes to his broad chest. "And when I found out what he really wanted, I felt used and cheap and ashamed. I don't feel any of those things with you." She lifted her eyes again, because it was important to make him understand. "It isn't like a physical thing with you, however silly that sounds. It's…" She searched for the right words. "It's…"

"Beautiful," he said for her. "Poignant. Profound."

"Yes." Her pale eyes lit up, making her beautiful.

He kissed her very tenderly. "Any other woman I'd have in bed by now," he murmured. "But you aren't the kind of woman who can play around with sex. Not even in the throes of an urgent need."

"Nevertheless," she said slowly, choosing her words, "I wouldn't refuse you."

"I know. That makes it worse. I can't take the responsibility alone." He touched her mouth with a gentle finger.

"Responsibility?" she whispered.

"I could make you pregnant," he said gently.

Her body felt wildly hungry. Her lips parted and the look in her eyes made him want to throw back his head and scream.

His fingers trembled as they touched her face. "Nicky," he whispered.

"Do you want a son?" she asked in a husky, loving tone.

"Yes," he bit off. "I want one with you...."

Her body shuddered. She looked into his eyes and knew that she was lost, that she couldn't stop, that he couldn't. In his eyes, she saw the coolness of white sheets and the outline of two bodies in the darkness....

And all at once, she was standing and he was five feet away from her with a burning cigarette in his hand.

She was so numb she could hardly feel. Her eyes traced him, saw the faint shudder of his long legs.

"Go to bed, sweetheart," he said without looking at her.

"You aren't angry?"

"No," he said, his voice deep and slightly choked. "I'm not angry."

She turned toward the door, only half understanding. She paused with her hand on the knob and glanced back. "Winthrop, are you all right?" she asked, her tone exquisitely gentle.

"Team sports and cold showers will save me," he said on a husky laugh. "Go to bed."

She flushed because that explained it all. "I'm sorry," she said. "Really sorry."

"For what?" He glanced at her finally, and she was shocked at how pale and drawn his face was.

"Nicky, you were in as deep as I was. I'm a little shell-shocked, that's all. But we can't stay here. Things are getting out of hand. I don't want anything to happen that we might regret."

She smiled at him. "I wouldn't regret anything."

"I can't be sure of that. It's easy to lose sight of things in the darkness. I want you very badly. I know you want me just as much. But let's stop and think before we commit ourselves that completely. I can't take you to bed one night and walk away from you the next morning. At my age, sex is a commitment, not a toy."

Her face colored. "I guess it is, when you start talking about making people pregnant," she murmured dryly.

"That, Miss White, I would enjoy," he said lazily, and his dark eyes glittered playfully. "And so would you; I'd make sure of it. So suppose you go up to bed and give it some thought. And tomorrow we'll discuss terms."

"What kind of terms?"

He smiled slowly. "That would be telling."

She turned back to the door. "If it means I get to live with you, I'll agree to most anything," she said and ran for it. Behind her, she heard rich, thunderous laughter, and by the time she got to the top of the staircase, she was laughing, too. Life was sweet and Winthrop had to feel the same way she did, because he was hinting at a lot more than a brief affair.

If he trusted her that much, it must mean that he

loved her. And God knew, she loved him with all her heart. She was so preoccupied dreaming about Winthrop's arms holding her in the darkness, and little boys and never leaving this exquisite valley as long as she lived that it was hard to fall asleep.

For an instant, she had a twinge of guilt about not sharing her past with him. But there was still time, she told herself as she snuggled under the covers. Plenty of time, to explain why she'd kept it a secret, to show him that she loved him, that she'd never betray him. Yes, there was time.

Six

When Nicole woke up the next morning, it was to an odd kind of silence. Although she was used to that particular stillness in winter, it was unfamiliar in autumn. But usually it meant snow.

She threw off the covers and ran to the window. Sure enough, the lacy white flakes were coming down like cotton out of the clouds, gently blanketing the trees and the grass. She sighed, vividly remembering last night and the newness of what she'd shared with Winthrop. Like a daydreaming child, she propped her elbows on the windowsill, put her face in her hands and mused about how it would be if she and Winthrop had been snowed in together, just the two of them.

Her daydreams were rudely shattered by the loud

noise of an approaching vehicle—a four-wheel-drive vehicle, at that.

A huge Cherokee wagon came into view with Winthrop at the wheel, and several passengers. They must be the hunting party, she guessed. The group didn't look too bad. There was a willowy redhead dressed from head to toe in white fur, followed by two older men, one in a wool plaid coat, the other in leather. And there was one more passenger, a big, white-headed man with an imposing nose, wearing tweeds....

Nicky came away from the window feeling sick. She'd go back to Chicago alone, right now. She'd pack her things and get out while she could. The memories came back hauntingly. The loud arguments, the fights that never seemed to end. Her father apologizing halfheartedly for his latest infidelity, her mother's mocking laughter. She put her hands against her eyes, feeling all over again like the little girl who used to run into the kitchen and hide her face against Lalla's ample bosom and cry her eyes out until the argument ended.

"Nicky!" came Gerald's voice outside the door. "Nicky, come down! Guess who one of our visitors is? It's your father!"

Along with that horror came a new one. She hadn't told Winthrop who her father was, or that she'd renounced her inheritance. What was he going to think?

"I'll be right down," Nicky called back.

She got dressed in a daze, pulling on her gray slacks and white sweater, the ones Mary had miraculously cleaned. She'd been wearing them the day she'd helped Winthrop deliver the colt. Perhaps that memory, if her clothing triggered it, would make the next hours easier.

She ran a brush through her hair and smoothed on some lipstick. She looked pale and haunted, but that couldn't be helped. Why did it have to be her father? she wondered miserably. Of all the sportsmen in the world, why him? She'd suspected it, of course, when Winthrop had mentioned that he'd been to Kentucky and knew Rockhampton Farms. Since her father was a well-known sportsman, it wasn't farfetched to imagine that he might enjoy hunting in Montana.

There were voices in the living room when she went downstairs, but the only face she saw immediately was Winthrop's. The tender lover of last night might have been a dream. His expression was hard, ice-cold. He barely looked at her before he turned back to his guests, a cup of coffee in one lean hand.

"Here she is," Gerald said with a grin, coming to meet her. His hand on her arm gave her the strength to walk into the room. "Look who's here," he added, pulling her toward the big white-haired man in tweed.

"Hello, Nicky," her father said coldly. "Long time, no see."

"Not long enough," she replied, and the bitterness of the past was in her eyes.

Winthrop frowned. It wasn't the reunion he'd expected to see at all.

Dominic White stood up, but he didn't approach her. His careless green eyes swept over her wan face and dismissed it. "This is Carol Murdock," he said, introducing the willowy, very young redhead in ski pants and a mohair sweater under all the fur. "She's visiting with me for a while."

"Hi," Carol said breathily. She beamed up at Dominic, who was at least fifteen years her senior, probably more like twenty. "Your dad sure is a lot of fun. He's going to show me how to shoot a moose."

"Oh, you'll enjoy that, I'm sure," Nicky told her. "It's easy. You just load the gun and point it and pull the trigger."

"I taught Nicky to shoot when she was twelve," Dominic told the group. "She could match any man on the place with a rifle. Even won trophies at it."

Winthrop, quietly smoking a cigarette, studied her curiously. "A girl of unusual talents."

"An unusual girl altogether," her father replied. He laughed shortly. "We haven't spoken in two years, have we, Nicky? I'm in disgrace, you see. I made the unforgivable error of falling out of love with her mother. Nicky holds me responsible for Brianna's death. And for cutting her off without a dime after the funeral," he added with killing precision. "She's been living by her wits ever since, haven't you, darling? Which one of these rich Christophers have you set your cap for?"

Just like old times, Nicky thought, feeling panicky. Her father was turning everything around, taking the blame off himself and throwing it at others. Winthrop's expression told her that he believed her father, and it grew even harder.

"I'm Gerald's secretary," she said with what little pride she had left. "And I'm not chasing anyone."

"You mean you've learned to love being without those Dior gowns you fancied and having to make do with the same fur several years running?" her father persisted. He looked like some middle-aged playboy even in his hunting clothes, and Nicky wanted to scream at him. All her life he'd made her feel inferior, and now he was destroying her one chance at happiness. He was convincing a once-betrayed man that he was being betrayed all over again. How would she ever make Winthrop listen to her?

Nicky's fists clenched by her sides. Her father had always enjoyed creating scenes. He should have been an actor, she thought bitterly.

"Let me introduce you to the other guests," Winthrop interrupted, wondering even as he did it why in hell he should bother to save her any discomfort after the way she'd deceived him. She'd pay for that, he promised himself. "Ben Harris—" he nodded toward the man in leather "—and Jack, his brother." He indicated the other, thinner man, in the plaid. "They come up every year looking for a good rack to go on their walls back in Kentucky. This year Dominic decided to come with them."

"I don't suppose you knew I was here, of course," Nicky asked her father with some of his own flair of stealing the advantage.

"I haven't known where you were in two years," he replied shortly. His eyes, so like her own, searched her face. "I haven't cared," he added with a mocking smile. "There's been a noticeable financial difference since you moved out, honey. I can balance the checkbook these days."

"Stop it," she whispered, near tears of enraged helplessness. "You know that's not true."

He simply turned away from her, refusing to take any notice of her embarrassment.

It wasn't the way he'd insinuated. She hadn't wanted his money—not even the trust her mother had left her. She'd refused all of it, but he was making sure both Christophers thought he'd done it himself, and that she was out for what she could get in the way of financial security. And it wasn't true.

"I hope you find someone to support you, honey, but it won't ever be me again," Dominic laughed, bending to brush a kiss across Carol's hair. "Your mother was enough."

"Don't you talk about my mother," Nicky said huskily. Her green eyes spit fire at him. "Don't you dare!"

Dominic laughed. "You always were dramatic."

As if he'd have noticed, with his eternal philandering. She almost said so, but Gerald was looking worried, and Winthrop's eyes were promising a confrontation.

"Do you have TV?" Carol asked, searching around. "It's so boring, just sitting around."

The woman was bored already? Nicky thought with surprise. Boy, was Carol in for a shock. Neither Gerald nor Winthrop watched much television. But Nicky was taken aback herself when Winthrop abruptly got up, and led Carol off to show her the TV and VCR in the living room.

"Fast worker, isn't he?" Dominic asked Gerald with a smile that wasn't quite friendly. "He'd better remember that she's my property."

"Your good manners are exceeded only by your arrogance," Nicky remarked coolly. "And if you try it on Winthrop, you'd better be wearing body armor. He doesn't like jet-setters."

Dominic glared at her. He stuck a diamond-ringed hand in his pocket and pulled out a cigarette case. "Something you've already discovered?" he asked with a pointed smile.

"Why did you do that to me?" she asked, searching the face that was so like her own. "Why did you make me out to be a cheap gold digger?"

"Tit for tat, darling," he drawled, and his own eyes kindled angrily. "You didn't think about the effect your defection would have on things at home, did you? I was blamed for everything. I don't like being humiliated. I don't think you will, either. And just for the record," he added coldly, "I didn't kill your mother, although I felt like it a time or two. She was no saint, Nicky, for all that you're trying to canonize her posthumously."

"So you've always said," she returned. "And who are you to judge anyone, you with your bought-and-paid-for playmates?"

"I'm not a plaster saint," he shot at her. "Your mother turned me out on the town as soon as she knew you were on the way, in revenge for what I'd done to her. Making her pregnant was a cardinal sin, in case you didn't know. She paid me back twenty times over. Are you shocked, Nicky? Didn't you realize that people are human?"

Nicky listened, only half hearing him. Why should her mother have hated him for that? She was suddenly aware of Gerald, an unwilling eaves-dropper to the argument. The Harris brothers were sitting in the corner, talking hunting, and hadn't heard much. She shifted away from her father, and tried to smile.

"Do you have anything for me to do?" Nicky asked Gerald, her tone conciliatory and faintly hopeful. He caught on quickly.

"As a matter of fact, we've got about ten letters to get out this morning," Gerald replied. He smiled vaguely at the three men. "If you'll excuse us..."

"Is he your partner?" Dominic asked Nicky, frowning.

"He's my boss," she replied coolly. "I'm his secretary."

Her father stiffened. "You're joking, of course," he said curtly. "No White has worked for a living for three generations—"

"Until now," Nicky interrupted with a mocking smile. "Some of us like the real world better than the artificial life of upper-crust luxury. You ought to try it. It has a humbling effect on a haughty spirit."

"You should know," Dominic countered coldly. "You were a haughty enough child."

"Living in a combat zone does have that effect on children." She turned and left the room.

"So he's your father," Gerald murmured when they were in the study with the door closed. "He wasn't originally supposed to be included in this group. He invited himself along with the Harris brothers at the last minute. Odd that Winthrop didn't connect you with Dominic White, since you were from Kentucky, too."

"He did," she said reluctantly, averting her eyes. "But I lied to him. I told him that White is a common name. I imagine I'm about the most unpopular person in Winthrop's acquaintance right now, especially after what my father just said about me. And it's not true."

"You don't have to defend yourself to me," he

replied gently. "Your father strikes me as a vindic-
tive man."

"You don't know the half of it," she replied.
"He's used to cutting people's throats. That's how
he got so rich."

"Well, he can't be all bad," he said after a minute.

"He's not," she said pleasantly. "He likes his
horses, and once I saw him feed a hungry dog. He
just doesn't like me. He never wanted children."
That was true enough, but she'd always thought
that her mother wanted her. She was still puzzling
over what her father had said.

Gerald didn't press further. Instead he chose a
different tack. He pursed his lips, stared at her and
asked, "Why didn't you tell Winthrop the truth?"

"Because I was sure he'd get the wrong idea,"
she sighed. "He'd think I was a bored heiress out
for a good time. Ironically, that's probably exactly
what he thinks now, thanks to my father and his
big mouth. I must sound like the world's most experienced spendthrift and a gold digger as well."

"You don't like him, do you?"

"My father, you mean?" Her green eyes gleamed.
"I do not. I'm sure he has some good points somewhere, but I've never found them."

He searched her face quietly. But he didn't say
another word. He pulled up a chair and sat down
behind the desk. After a minute, he began to dic-
tate.

Nicky spent the rest of the day trying to avoid

the other guests, and the snow continued to fall. Mary never said a word about the extra people to look after. She just kept cooking, imperturbable even when Carol dashed into the kitchen and asked in all innocence if there was a boutique anywhere close by because she wanted to shop for a new fur.

Nicky had to bite her tongue to keep from asking if the girl knew that in these parts, a mink set consisted of a trap and a skinning knife.

But to Nicky's irritation and her father's frank anger, Winthrop seemed to enjoy Carol's company.

"Maybe she forgot who she came with," Nicky muttered to Mary late that day as she helped the older woman set the long dining table.

"Not likely," Mary said. She glanced at Nicky. "Winthrop looks through you today. Why?"

Nicky hesitated before she put down the last plate. "He thinks I lied to him because I didn't tell him about my background. I let him think I came from a poor family. But it's true in a way," she added, her face open and sad. "I was poor in love, at least."

"And your father?"

Nicole pursed her lips. "You tell me. What kind of man is he?" she asked, because she'd learned how perceptive the Sioux woman really was.

"He is a sad man," Mary said surprisingly. "He draws attention to himself out of loneliness and pain. He has not learned to admit fault, only to find it in others. I pity him. As you should. In your youth, you have twice his wisdom."

Mary left and went into the kitchen, leaving the younger woman thoughtful and quiet.

If Nicole thought the day had been bad, she soon found that the evening meal was an even worse ordeal. Winthrop sat at the head of the table with the hateful Carol on one side and Gerald on the other and completely ignored Nicky and her glum father. The Harris brothers ate and sipped their coffee merrily, exchanging pleasantries and hunting experiences with Nicky, but she hardly heard them. She was watching Winthrop's dark eyes light up as he spoke to the nubile redhead, and hating the other woman for arousing the tender side of the man she could no longer reach.

"You wear your heart on your sleeve," Dominic said coolly. He stared over his coffee cup at his daughter. "Never let it show."

"Never cry. Never show emotion." She laughed shortly. "A page right out of your book. You're frozen clean through. I suppose I'll be just like you when I'm your age. What a lovely future to look forward to."

"It beats having your emotions lacerated twice a day," he said nonchalantly. He stared hard at the redhead. "She's barely your age," he mused. "And your host is a hell of a man, limp and bad temper and all. I won't like losing her to him. I'm not a good loser."

"Winthrop doesn't want a society girl," she replied. "He's had enough misfortune because of one."

"I remember reading about the wreck," her father said surprisingly. "Deanne something-or-other, that ski heiress. I had a fling with her myself. She was a real honey. The kind who'd stroke your fevered brow while stealing your wallet."

It hurt, knowing that her own father was that kind of man. An aging playboy with no real emotion underneath his elegant facade. "You ought to compare notes with Winthrop. I'm sure he'd be interested," she said sweetly.

"Stop sniping at me, Nicky," he said coolly, and his green eyes met hers. "All your regrets and all mine won't change the past. Neither will giving up your rightful legacy. Brianna wouldn't have wanted that. She had high hopes for you."

"Did she? I don't remember her being sober enough to discuss them in the past."

"I thought you'd become wiser with time, but you still see the past with blinders on," he remarked. "Grow up, honey. Life isn't all black and white. Your mother was neurotic. She couldn't handle responsibility. In fact, neither could I. We were two kids playing at life, and when you came along, the dream fell apart. Neither of us could cope and you got caught in the middle. I'm sorry, but I can't remake the past."

"If neither of you wanted me, why did you

bother to have me?" she asked, wounded by the confession. "Or was I just an accident?"

She read the answer in his face before he could even try to disguise it. And suddenly, her whole childhood made more sense. The endless fights, the indifference of her parents to each other's lifestyles, the drinking and womanizing...

"So," she let out the word as a sigh. "So that's why." She smiled ruefully. "Thank you. At least now I know why you both hated me so much."

"Oh, Nicky," he said, "that's not so. We never hated you."

"You never had time for me, either of you."

"That's true," he admitted. His green eyes searched hers and he smiled wearily. "We were just kids when you came along, Nicky. Both of us. Kids playing house. And then there we were with a real live baby, but we couldn't put you back on the shelf. We had to be responsible for you. That wasn't an easy task for two people who'd never known what it was to be responsible."

She stared at him as if she'd been slammed in the head with a pole. She'd never thought of her parents as people, only as parents. This new perspective was enlightening, but disturbing.

"You don't understand, do you?" her father asked quietly. "You thought because we were your parents, we had to be perfect. But it doesn't work that way. Parents make mistakes. They aren't perfect."

She shifted restlessly. "Mother drank herself to

death because of your womanizing," she said accusingly.

"Your mother drank herself to death because she was unhappy," he replied, without heat. He leaned back, and despite the trendy shirt and the gold chains he wore, he looked old and tired. "So was I. I ran after women looking for my rainbow, and she climbed into a bottle looking for hers. Neither of us ever found it." He pursed his lips and studied her. "Have you found yours, Nicky? Does anybody ever really get the brass ring in life?"

"There are better ways to try for it," she began.

"Sure there are," he agreed. "But when you've got all the money in the world, why look past your wallet?"

"I can think of some very good answers to that question," she told him. "I've watched you buy people all your life. I hate the ugliness that money can bring out in people."

"You can't bribe an honest man, honey," he said sagely. "Can you?"

"But everyone has a price. Some prices are less materialistic than others—a promotion, a holiday for a hard-working parent, a hospital bill for a sick child. Those are less obvious prices, but they still mean people can be bought."

He nodded. "So you begin to see."

"What you and mother had wasn't a marriage," she accused him, all the hurt of the past coming back.

"We didn't love each other enough," he said simply. "In the beginning, maybe we did. But we had families that lived in each other's pockets and constant interference. We were never let alone, not even when you came along. You were the last straw, Nicky. You were the knot that we couldn't untie. Divorce, in our day, was scandalous. Our families had never had a divorce."

"Better a divorce than unending war," Nicky shot back.

"My sentiments, exactly. And your mother's. If we'd divorced, she'd have married one of her old beaux and I'd have married—probably several more times," he acknowledged with a wicked grin. "And we'd both have been very happy. As it was, we sought our separate remedies and your mother's was fatal. Nobody's fault," he tacked on, watching her. "Nobody's fault at all. But you can't accept that, can you?"

"Somebody has to be at fault," she said doggedly, glaring at him.

"Why?"

The question threw her off balance. She stared at him. "What?"

"Why does somebody have to be at fault?" He fingered his chains. "Your mother and I were nice people, separately. We just weren't compatible. Who do you blame for that?"

She felt herself losing ground. He always had been like a trial lawyer, able to twist things around to suit himself. If only he didn't make so much sense. She'd blamed him for two years for her mother's untimely death, just as she'd blamed herself. But what if neither of them were responsible?

She shifted a little and finally got to her feet, looking down at him. He always seemed laid back, very relaxed. Nothing seemed to bother him.

"I'm a black sheep, Nicky," he said. "I always have been. I like women and I'm rich enough to indulge that habit, and I try to come out ahead in business. But I never hated you, honey. I never could."

She tried to smile. "No? It seemed like it when you got here."

"That was dirty pool, all right." He glanced down and then up again. "I missed you," he said curtly, as if he hated even saying the words. "I missed Brianna. Everybody left me at one time. Damn it, how do you think I felt?"

He got up and stormed out of the room without even a backward glance. Nicky stared after him with confused emotions. He'd sounded, and looked, hurt. Perhaps he had cared about her mother in his fashion. Maybe even about Nicky, too. But the wounds were still raw and she couldn't cope with this new facet of her father just yet.

She turned, oblivious to the others in the room, and went upstairs. Her father was only forty-one, she realized with a start; he wasn't even old. And there was no reason he shouldn't have women friends. It was just…she'd wanted him to love her mother. She'd wanted her mother to love him. She'd wanted a warm family life…and she'd never had it.

She changed back into her jeans and the yellow sweater, hating the gray dress. She wished she had something as slinky and svelte as Miss Kansas City downstairs, so that she could tempt the antagonism out of Winthrop's dark face. But she'd probably lost her chance with him. He hadn't come near her since her father's arrival; he hadn't spoken to her or acknowledged her. He'd even avoided looking at her.

It was amazing how deeply his turning on her had hurt. She sat down at her vanity and ran a comb through her hair, dreading the return trip downstairs. She'd never felt quite so lost and alone, not even as a child. She missed her mother suddenly and wished that they could have talked. There had been a few precious times when her mother had been sober, when she'd actually listened to her daughter's rambling.

The door opened, cutting into her thoughts, and the comb paused in midair over her short, dark hair as Winthrop walked into the room and slammed the door behind him.

He'd unbuttoned his long-sleeved chambray shirt at the throat. His dark hair caught the light and gleamed, like his unblinking dark eyes under that jutting brow. He stared down his straight nose

at her and bad temper mingled with pure male arrogance in the way he watched her.

"Go ahead," she sighed, putting down the comb
to sit with her hands folded in her lap. "Get it out
of your system. Shall I start it for you? I betrayed
you, lied to you——"

"You could have told me," he replied. His eyes
narrowed on her face. "I even asked you point-
blank if you were related to Dominic White and
you sidestepped the question."

"Guilty as charged," she confessed. "I should
have told you the truth. And if I had," she continued, turning to face him, "you'd have shot me off
the ranch like a bullet."

"Trust comes hard to me," he said unexpectedly. "I won't be able to forget that you didn't level
with me."

Even though she had expected it, the words hurt.
She tilted her chin up and looked at him, drinking in the sight of his face, adoring it with her soft
green eyes. "I'm not a bored heiress. I've lived in
Chicago for two years——"

"Patiently," he agreed with a smile that would
have been pleasant any other time. "Waiting for
your chance. Gerald was first choice, I realize that,
but I was the second-string, wasn't I?"

She blinked. "I don't follow you."

"You set your sights on Gerald, honey," he replied. "He was going to be your meal ticket. You
played him for two years——"

"I what?" She got to her feet.

"I'm no fool," he ground out. "You've been hanging on him ever since you got here! I overheard what you said to him, about no other man ever being able to take you away from him. I heard it all. And you even held back last night, because you were afraid of what he might say if he saw us together."

"I did? Amazing, how much restraint I showed in the kitchen, wasn't it?" she taunted.

His jaw tautened angrily. "I'm no innocent boy. I've had my share of adventures with women. And this morning, I got a good look at the real Nicole White. No, honey, you won't pull the wool over my eyes again. I'm onto you now. And there's no way I'm going to be your meal ticket. Neither is Gerald. I'll see to that."

She couldn't believe what she was hearing. All the growing tenderness between them, everything he'd said last night… After all of that, he could believe her father's lies, could he? How could he believe that she was just a gold digger?

"Gerald's in love with Sadie," she said, almost in a daze.

"Is he? Too bad. I guess you're brokenhearted. So that's why you turned to me, was it?" he laughed coldly. "And if your father hadn't arrived, I might still be deluding myself. What a lucky break. One cheap adventuress in a lifetime is damned enough."

"Oh, Winthrop," she sighed achingly. "Are you

so afraid to believe what you feel, instead of what you hear? Can't you take my word for it?"

"I did," he reminded her, his tone icy. "And look where it landed me."

"My father was getting even," she said, moving closer. "He was paying me back for walking out on him after Mama's funeral. It was just revenge. He's over it now, he'll tell you the truth if you ask him!"

"I know the truth." He lifted his chin as she came closer, and the expression on his hard face was not welcoming. "You've been stalking me. I knew it was no accident that you wound up at the corral that day and you deliberately came on to me at the dance last night."

"That's right," she said sarcastically as she looked up at him. Her heart was breaking and he didn't even care. "That's right, all I wanted was to get my hands on your wallet. I never cared a fig for you!"

She pressed against him and his steely hands caught her, holding her away.

"Do I make you nervous, big, bad rancher?" she teased, moving as close as his hands would allow. Her eyelashes fluttered at him, her fingers went to his chest and her nails drew lazily across the cotton fabric, making sensuous little scratchy sounds there. His heartbeat increased sharply.

"No," he denied. But he was looking down at where her hands were touching him, and something flickered in his dark eyes.

"Well, you make me nervous," she whispered.

"You make me shake all over when you touch me, and that doesn't have a thing to do with how much money you've got in the bank. And I didn't lie to you about being innocent, I am."

"You and Madame Bovary..." he chided, but his touch had become caressing on her arms.

"And when we made love in the kitchen, I would have died for you," she breathed ardently, her lips parted, welcoming, pleading as she looked up into his eyes.

His hands tightened while he tried to fight what she made him feel. His body suddenly went taut but he couldn't help it, he wanted that soft mouth under his until it was madness.

"Damn you, Nicky."

"Winthrop." It was a moan, and he covered it with his lips.

He muttered something under his breath, but Nicky didn't hear it. She was lost in the strength of his arms, the ardent hunger of his hard mouth as it moved breathlessly on hers.

It seemed to take a long time for him to realize what was happening. Her warm body in his arms drugged him. The soft warmth of her mouth, trembling gently as he explored it, made him vulnerable. But minute by aching minute, the past came back. Deanne had once melted like this against his hard body. She'd murmured words of love, promised heaven. And then...

He eased his mouth away from Nicky's, steeling

himself not to care about the soft accusation in her drowsy eyes as she watched him pull away.

"Please..." she whispered, and made a move to go to him.

"No, thanks," he said quietly. And the very tone of his voice halted her in her tracks. He was as politely indifferent as if he were refusing a drink of water when he wasn't thirsty.

She looked up at him with slow comprehension. He didn't even seem to be affected by that sweet interlude. He was just indifferent. She felt a sudden, sharp emptiness. Was this how it was going to be from now on? Was he so uninvolved that it didn't require any effort for him to draw away from her? She'd banked everything on his desire for her; she'd seen it as her one way to reach him. But it hadn't. She'd lost. He didn't trust her. And now he was showing her that he didn't even want her anymore.

"I'm not a gold digger," she said with what pride she had left. She was trembling, and he had to know it. She wrapped her arms around herself and watched him, like a hurt child. "Money doesn't matter to me. Surely you can see that?"

"I don't know you," he answered. His dark eyes narrowed as he studied her face. "And maybe it's better this way. I remember telling you once that we could hurt each other badly. I let you get to me last night, honey, but I won't make that mistake again. The last thing I want is involvement."

"But you said...I mean, I thought..." She faltered, trying to put into words what she'd felt the night before, what she'd thought he meant.

"I've been alone a long time, daffodil," he said with a mocking smile. "And I'm no saint. A man gets lonely from time to time."

In other words, she'd been a nice little interlude with no strings attached, but now it was broad daylight and he'd come to his senses. He'd just proved his indifference by showing her that he could pull away from her anytime he wanted to without regret.

"That's plain enough," she said quietly, studying his dark, impassive face. It was a long way up, despite her own height, and she felt at a disadvantage. "I guess I misread the whole situation."

"Just as long as you realize you'll never get to first base around here, except in business. Get my drift?"

She should have pasted him one, but she was disillusioned and sick at heart. Her dreams were shattered. "I can't really blame you for the way you feel," she said dully. "I should have told you the truth in the beginning. I guess it was a hard knock."

"Nothing I couldn't handle," he replied coolly. "Don't flatter yourself too much. A few kisses doesn't make a relationship."

"Oh, I know that," she laughed coldly. "And just for the record, I was lonely, too. You see, men haven't noticed me for a long time; not since I had money, in fact," she said with a cynicism that suddenly matched his. She felt old and world-weary and battered. "Too bad I can't go home to Daddy and accept that trust my mother left me. That would up my bank balance by about three million."

She went to the door and opened it, watching him scowl as her remark registered.

"Dream on, honey," he said, but without a lot of conviction.

"You don't believe that, either, of course." She nodded. "Why don't you ask my father why my fiancé threw me over? The answer might open your eyes."

He stared at her for a long moment. "If you've got that kind of money, why work for my brother?"

"Because I got sick of a warped lifestyle where promiscuity and alcohol and pills seemed to replace love in my parents' relationship! Because I got lost somewhere and went hungry for just a little love!" Tears welled up in her eyes and she set her lips together to try to stop the trembling. "The man I thought I loved walked out on me the day he found out I'd given up all that nice money. And here I am, two years later, being accused of the very thing he was guilty of. You think I'm mercenary," she said in a husky whisper. She laughed tearfully. "How's that for irony?"

He stopped in the doorway to look down at her. His conscience and his pride were at war. "You lied to me once, damn it!"

"So you can't ever trust me again," she returned.

"Okay, you've judged me and found me guilty. I don't want your pity. I don't want you at all. My father was right all along—everybody's got a price. I should go home with him and let him teach me how to buy people!"

"You're talking nonsense," he said curtly.

"I'm talking sense," she said on a laugh, although her chin was trembling. "I've been chasing rainbows. Thanks for putting me back on the right track."

"You're crying," he said half under his breath and lifted a hand to catch a stray tear.

But she jerked away from his hand like a wounded thing, raw from his rejection, sick at heart. "Go away," she whispered furiously. "I hate you! I hate you, Winthrop! I wish I could leave here tomorrow and never have to see you again as long as I live!"

He tried to speak, but he couldn't seem to find words. In the end he turned and stormed off down the hall, smoldering. He was the wronged party, so why in hell did he feel guilty? He didn't even want to think about how he might have messed up things if she was telling the truth. Surely she wasn't. She'd lied to him once, hadn't she? He closed his mind tight. He just wouldn't think about it. She was another Deanne. He was well rid of her.

She watched him go with a sore heart. Well, if he wouldn't believe the truth when it was staring him in the face, who cared? She closed the door and gave up any idea of going downstairs again. She took off her clothes and cried herself to sleep.

Seven

Somehow, Nicky got through the night. Winthrop had excused himself and gone out to help his men keep a check on the cattle. The snow had made the mountain roads impassable except with a four-wheel drive. The hunters didn't seem to mind. In fact, they were apparently used to mountain weather and since they were planning a weeklong outing on the ranch, they settled in with easy acceptance.

Carol, however, became a pill. Nothing pleased her. Her room was too cold, the bed was lumpy, there were no shopping centers and she couldn't even get a manicure. Furthermore, she missed her parents, whom she visited every few days. She wanted to go home.

Nicky's father spent the better part of the second

day, in between cleaning his hunting rifle and getting himself kitted out with the proper attire, calming down his playmate. It seemed he had a knack for communicating with Carol, because he finally got through to her that it would be impossible to get out until a chinook blew in. That could be any day, he'd added with careful insight.

Mary had already told Nicky that the snow could go on for days or even weeks, but Nicky wasn't sharing that tidbit with the excitable redhead. After Dominic's comforting statement, anyway, Carol went off into the living room and watched a popular science-fiction thriller until even Winthrop started to grow tired of the film.

At dawn on the third day, the hunters piled into Winthrop's Jeep and headed down the valley. Gerald and Nicky worked alone in the study, leaving Carol to her science-fiction habit.

"I can't tell you how sick I am of light sabers," Nicky remarked after the sound became louder in the next room.

"Sure you can," Gerald invited, leaning back in his chair. "Go ahead. Then I'll tell you how sick I am of laser cannons. And then we'll make silly faces in the mirror and see about renting straitjackets in a matched set."

She giggled. "Let's pray for a chinook."

"I'm for that. The Sioux used to have a prayer for it, come to think of it. We'll ask Mary."

She looked at her steno pad. "Winthrop said

something to her at breakfast with sign language. Mary's been teaching me a little bit of signing, so I tried to watch carefully."

"I watched for years and never learned a thing," he confessed. "What did he say, do you know?"

She smiled ruefully. "Either he wanted bicarbonate of soda or he was melancholy."

He frowned. "What?"

"When you want to express melancholy or gloom, you make the sign for *heart* and then the sign for *sick*. It's really a fascinating insight into another language," she added. "For instance, if you want to say that you're disgusted, you sign *heart* and then *tired*. The sign for enemy is *friend* and *not*. Drunk—" she grinned "—is expressed by making the signs for *whiskey*, *to drink*, *much* and *mad*. See?"

He shook his head. "Fascinating. Smart girl."

"Intelligence is this," she said, touching her right index and middle fingers to her forehead.

"How about smart aleck?" he taunted.

"I'm not that good, yet," she sighed. But she was learning. Already, Mary had taught her enough that she could translate what Winthrop had "said" to her on the porch the morning he'd brought her home from the Todds'. He'd said that he was jealous of Gerald, and that he wanted her very much. How different things might have been if she'd known that at the time. But Winthrop had become a coolly considerate host and nothing more. All the lovely

soft feeling that had been growing so gently between them was gone forever.

"I'm worried about Sadie and Mrs. Todd," Gerald said abruptly, tapping a pencil on the blotter. "I
tried to phone them an hour or so ago, and the lines
are down. Sadie had to put their Jeep in the shop a
couple of days ago, so I know they don't have any
transportation. I drove by there before the snow
started, just to say hello."

"Could you get Winthrop to run up and check
on them?" she asked.

"Winthrop is in a snit lately, haven't you noticed?" he asked miserably, his gaze apologetic as
he added, "Your father did a job on your character.
Although, to give the man credit, he tried to tell
Winthrop it was mostly just bad temper and ven-
geance. But Winthrop didn't listen. He walks off
every time your name is mentioned."

"We had an argument and didn't exactly part
friends," she told him, without going into details.
She didn't add that Winthrop's attitude had broken
her heart. "You wouldn't want to go back to Chicago anytime soon?" she added hopefully.

"Poor Nicky," he said, smiling at her knowingly.
"I'm sorry it turned out like this. In the beginning,
Winthrop was so different when you were around.
He smiled and laughed and seemed to enjoy life
for the first time since the accident. I'm sorry it
fell apart."

"So am I," she confessed, feeling her eyes sting

with unshed tears. "I guess he's soured on me because I didn't tell him who my father was. He thinks I lied to him. And perhaps, in a sense, I did. But I didn't mean to be devious. I was only trying to forget the past. My childhood was pretty rough, and my mother's death shook me up. There are so many scars. I guess that's why I understand Winthrop so well. I have scars, too, and time isn't all that healing when your emotions have been ravaged."

"I guess so." He got up and went to the window. "I wondered why Winthrop was flirting with Carol. I supposed he was trying to make you jealous."

"On the contrary," she laughed, "he was showing me that I don't matter. And believe me, he's succeeded. I wouldn't go near him now with a whip and a chair."

"I can understand how you feel," he said, turning. "But you have to understand how it's been for my brother, Nicky. It was several months after the accident before he was even able to walk without a cane, and they'd threatened at first to take off the leg entirely. Winthrop said they'd take it off after he was dead, and he meant it, but he doesn't realize even now how close it came to that. It took one of the best orthopedic surgeons in the country to save it—and he performed an operation that used techniques he invented as he went along. One of the bones in his lower leg was shattered; the surgeon completely rebuilt it, like putting a jigsaw puzzle together."

"He said there were complications," she probed.

"His impatience," he said, confirming her suspicions. "They told him exactly what he could and couldn't do, and he ignored them and tried to ride a horse the day after he came out of the hospital. He tore the cartilage and had to go back into surgery to have it resewn. Consequently it hasn't healed as well as it could have. But the doctors said he could get rid of that limp if he'd work half as hard at his exercises as he's worked at fighting them tooth and nail over the manner of his recovery. Winthrop," he added dryly, "is impatient."

As if she hadn't already noticed that, she mused sadly. "I suppose at the time he didn't much care what happened to him."

"It was the closest I've ever seen him come to the edge," Gerald agreed. "He took chances and pushed himself even harder than he used to in his wild days. Finally I asked him if the stupid woman was worth his life. And that seemed to snap him out of it. But he's not the same man he was."

"What was he like then?" she asked, because she wanted to know everything there was to know about him.

"Full of fun," he said. "Reckless, with a devil-may-care attitude, but in a suave kind of way. He liked music and parties and skiing—in the water or in the snow. He was forever on the go. The ranch was important to him, but not in the way that it is now. He left Mike in charge and went out to beat the world. Now," he said softly, "he just sits up here in the mountains and broods. Less since you've been here, I have to admit, but he still has that streak of melancholy."

"Maybe he found out that money and glitter don't wear well," she said. "I learned it young."

"Perhaps he did." He studied her quietly for a long moment. "It hurts you that he believes your father, doesn't it?"

"More than I can tell you."

"Give him time, Nicky. Trust comes hard to a man who's been betrayed. But if the feeling is there, inevitably it's going to break through the ice."

"Think so?" She smiled. "I wonder."

They went back to work, but she brooded about what Gerald had said. Would Winthrop eventually come to his senses? Or had it been just a mild physical attraction and he wanted nothing more to do with her? She didn't know.

Later that afternoon, Gerald began to pace, and rubbed his stomach as if it were troubling him.

"Need an antacid?" Nicky asked.

"What?" He glanced at his stomach. "Oh. It's just acting up. I forgot my medicine. I guess I'd better take it. No, it isn't that," he said suddenly, turning. "I'm worried about Sadie."

"Then let's go see her. Isn't there a four-wheel drive around here somewhere that we can use?"

He grinned. "Sure. Are you game? It could be dangerous."

"I'd like some fresh air myself." She glanced toward the living room door, where the sound of laser blasts was echoing loudly. "And I need a reprieve from that movie that I loved until we got snowed in with her."

"My sentiments, exactly. I'll tell Mary where we're going. Dress warmly."

Warmly meant putting on her jeans, two pair of socks, boots, a long-sleeved shirt, a sweater, and her heavy coat, gloves and a stocking cap. Even that was hardly enough against the thick snow and biting wind. The mountains were cold in November, she learned quickly. And the snow was flying at them in an unending sheet of white, provoked by a wild wind. Nicky had misgivings about this trip, but she had more about being cooped up inside with Carol.

Gerald had the old Jeep idling when Nicky climbed in beside him. She glanced around her with a curious smile. "Will it get us there?" she asked hesitantly.

"I hope so," he confided. "It hasn't been used for a while, but Mike has one and Winthrop has the other new one, so we're stuck with this. I think it will be all right."

The vehicle sputtered and lurched as he put it in gear, and the chains on the heavy tires made a nice clanking sound as he shot down the mountain road.

Thank God it was a wide one, but by the time they turned off onto the dirt road that led up to the Todd place, Nicky was regretting her decision to go with him. Gerald wasn't the driver Winthrop was, and as the heavy snow continued to fly at them, Gerald swung too wide around a curve and the Jeep suddenly left the road.

Gerald moaned something. The Jeep lurched crazily sideways and slid down onto a lodgepole pine and hung there, shuddering. Nicky pitched against his shoulder, and got a sudden and terrifying view of a sheer drop out his window.

"Oh, for heaven's sake!" she squeaked.

He caught his breath, staring beside him. "Damn," he breathed. "I couldn't see the roadbed and I ran right off. Nicky, we'll have to get out of here. This is a dead pine, and if it gives way…" He glanced at her with pure terror in his dark eyes.

"Then we'll get out," she said, more calmly than she felt. "How?" she added.

"Well…" He studied the Jeep's position for a minute. "I think it might be easier if we tried to get out on your side. The tree will balance us. You go first. I'll help."

Climbing out of the Jeep looked impossible, but there was no choice; plunging down that deep ravine would be as sure as death. She thought of Winthrop and wondered if he'd miss her if she pitched down there. Morbid thoughts, and she shook them off. No, sir, she wasn't about to give him the satisfaction of dying.

With Gerald's help, she managed to lever herself up to the passenger door and gingerly open it. The Jeep pitched a little, and she caught her breath and shuddered, certain that the end was near, but the vehicle remained fairly secure against the pine. She prayed as she caught hold of the opening and began to drag herself up and over. She got grease from the dirty undercarriage all over herself, but in the end, she managed to tumble out. Then she reached up to help Gerald, who managed the task with more deftness than she had.

They cleared the Jeep and collapsed onto the thick, soft snow, almost buried in it while they caught their breath. Behind them, the Jeep lay on its side against the tall pine, unmoving, despite the fierce wind.

"At least it hasn't gone over," Gerald sighed. He held his stomach and groaned. "Damn. I wish I'd stopped long enough to take that medicine."

She stared at him, snow sticking to her face. She felt bitterly cold. "Can you make it?" she asked, frightened.

"I think so," he sighed. "My ulcer isn't sure, but I am," he said with a wan smile.

"So am I." She smiled back. "Well, shall we start out?"

"We're closer to the ranch than the Todds' place," he said when they were standing in the road.

But the snow was coming harder and thicker, and it was blinding, stinging their eyes. "We can follow the road back…"

We hope, she added silently, because the blizzard wasn't letting up. If anything, it was getting worse. The brilliance of the snow was as blinding as the flakes whipped up by the biting cold wind.

She leaned into that wind, pulled the cap down and her collar up to cover as much of her face as possible, and started walking. Beside her, Gerald kept up the pace. But when they'd gone a few hundred yards, the going got harder and harder. Incredibly, she started to feel hot in all the freezing cold and snow. She wanted to throw off her coat and walk in her sweater, but Gerald shook his head sharply when she started to do it. He mouthed something that looked like "frostbite," but she wasn't sure.

She concentrated on putting one foot in front of the other, watching her boot sink into the deep snow. It came over the boot top and down into her warm socks, wetting them, chilling them. She'd left her gloves in the Jeep, like an idiot, so she had to keep her hands in her pockets, but they were freezing cold, too.

They rounded a bend, and found the road suddenly buried under a huge drift of snow. Nicole stopped, her eyes on the blanket of white around them, but there was no alternative route. They had to get through that drift or die.

Gerald moved close to her, panting. "Oh, God,"

he muttered, clenching his hand over his stomach. "It's hurting, Nicky. How in hell are we going to dig through that?"

She looked at it dubiously. She didn't have gloves and Gerald was in no condition to do it alone. There were no tools. A ranch hat like Winthrop's Stetson would have helped or even a shoe, but if she took off her boot, her foot would freeze. She stared at the huge mound of snow with helpless frustration.

"Oh, damn," she wailed, hating the hot sting of tears in her eyes. She wasn't beaten. Oh, God, she couldn't be beaten! She had to do something, but what?

"I'm so tired," Gerald sighed. He sank down with his back to the snowdrift. "So tired…stomach hurts…"

"You can't go to sleep," she burst out. "It's fatal! Gerald, we have to go on."

"How? The snow's too deep. We can't get through, Nicky." He closed his eyes, leaning back against the bank that angled against the snowdrift. "Nice…"

Nicky shook him, but he was too weary to try anymore. She looked around at the white forest, its tall trees rising over them like shrouds while the wind blew and the snow fell and the world was as hushed as a cathedral.

She sank down beside Gerald and sat there, looking around at the deadly white beauty of it.

A hundred years before, men must have seen such sights and been killed by them, she thought. The Lewis and Clark expedition probably had its share of snowstorms, and they'd survived. But they were strong, well-equipped woodsmen. Nicky was a city woman with no woodcraft skills. She didn't even know how to build a fire, if she could have made her hands do the work.

Her green eyes went up to the sky. Well, it wasn't such a very bad place to die, she mused as drowsiness swept over her. She was near Winthrop, even though he didn't care anymore. Maybe he'd bury her here, and she'd be near him forever...

She closed her eyes. Somewhere she heard an organ. It was making beautiful music in the distance, and there was singing. It was an old hymn of some kind, exquisite in the stillness...

"Amazing Grace."

Her grandfather used to sing it when he worked with the horses. "Amazing Grace, how sweet the sound..." she began to hum.

Voices...coming close. The organ stopped, but a cat was purring. Something touched her. Shook her. That voice—it was deep and urgent and somehow familiar—but she didn't understand what it was asking. She was warm and safe and she protested when someone tried to move her. She fought, but she was subdued. Then she was rising, floating. White clouds. Snow. Cold. The organ drifted in and out. She tried to open her eyes, but it was just too much work. She slept.

Her head ached. She sneezed and the sound echoed around her. Was she dead?

She opened her eyes slowly. A ceiling. Very white. A canopy, pink, overhead. She turned her head and there was Winthrop. He was unshaven, his hair needed combing. He was sprawled beside the bed in a chair half his size, his booted feet splayed, his mouth open. He was snoring.

She stared at him for a long moment, memorizing him. He looked good, even without a shave. His shirt was open, and his hair-roughened chest looked like leather. She wanted to touch it, smooth her hands over its masculine contours, feel his heart beating under that rough skin. His hands were clasped over his lean waist, darkly beautiful masculine hands, their strength evident even in rest. She remembered their delicate touch on her soft flesh, and trembled a little with pleasure.

"Winthrop." His name sounded rusty. She frowned, because it had hurt her throat to call him. Her hand went to it. Her fingers were cold, but they didn't hurt. Had she escaped frostbite? She held out her hands, palms down, and looked at them.

"You were damned lucky," Winthrop said, opening his eyelids without moving a muscle. He glared at her out of eyes as black as night. "You didn't even get frostbite, although you'll have a hell of a cold."

"Gerald?" she rasped.

"He's fine, thank God. What possessed you two greenhorns to scale the Rockies in a blizzard?"

"He was worried about Sadie," she defended.

"Sadie had the good sense to stay inside," he said coldly. "I sent Mike up to take supplies to her and her mother. They're fine. More than I can say for you and Sir Galahad."

"We can't all be brilliant mountain men," she said sweetly.

"Do you want something to drink?" he asked.

"Not until I can have it analyzed for poison," she threw back at him.

"I'll send Mary with it," he replied. "I might not be able to resist the temptation, at that."

She watched him get up and tears gathered behind her eyes. Such an ordeal, only to find him still unforgiving and hateful at the end of it. He might have said he was glad she was alive or smile at her, or something.

"Sorry to put you to the bother," she muttered.

He bent over her, his eyes dangerous. "Don't bait me," he threatened softly. "I've had a hell of a night watching you fade in and out. You little fool, people have died in snowdrifts out here!"

"Sorry, but I do seem to be alive. I hope you aren't too disappointed...oh!"

The exclamation was in response to the sudden, unexpected descent of his mouth, square over hers.

"Disappointed—" he bit off, and kissed harder.

His hand at her throat tilted her face at a more inviting angle and he caught his breath as his lips became gentle and began to play with hers. His breath was as ragged as her own now, but he didn't even care. She could have died. Knowing it made him wild.

Her hands went to his hard cheeks, trembling and cold as they pressed there, holding him to her mouth. Her brows knitted in exquisite anguish. Dreams came true like this, she thought achingly. Dreams. She'd lived on them for so long.

"Oh," she whispered softly, a tiny whimper of sound that echoed in his mind.

His mouth opened against hers, lifting, teasing, his breath mingling wildly with hers while his hands caught hers and pulled them down to the bed beside her head, his fingers interlocking with hers.

"I could ravish you," he ground out huskily, and the eyes that glanced at her were blazing.

"I thought...you hated me," she breathed unsteadily.

"I did. I do. I hate what I feel when I touch you." He bent again, tormenting her mouth with his lips, brushing, lifting, teasing until she began to writhe on the sheets. "Yes, that's exciting, isn't it?" he whispered roughly, watching her face. "I'm going to make you wild, Nicky, and then I'm going to walk off and leave you with it...."

She arched softly, her eyes wide and quiet, her

body trembling. "No, you won't," she whispered. "Because you'll be just as wild as I will."

His jaw tautened as he looked down at her, his pride aching, his body aching. She was killing him. His eyes went to her bodice, where her breasts were outlined under the gossamer-thin white cotton of her gown. The arousal she couldn't help was blatant.

His fingers, linked with hers, contrasted roughly. His eyes adored her breasts, caressed them. "That," he whispered slowly, "is beautiful."

"Everything is beautiful with you," she said, her heart in her eyes as she looked up at him, too much in love with him to even be embarrassed at his bold stare.

"Nicky!" He groaned her name as he bent, his mouth so tender, so exquisitely gentle with hers that tears ran hotly down her cheeks. He was the world, and everything in it. She loved him so.

Even as she thought the words, she whispered them under his warm mouth, breathed the truth against him, echoed her feelings like a prayer.

"No." He drew back suddenly, sharply. His fingers pressed hard against her lips while he sat over her, trying to breathe, with eyes as black as the night outside the window. "No. Don't say it."

"But I do love you," she said, her face like a child's, full of pleading and hope.

His thumb rubbed against her lips roughly in a

reluctant caress. "I don't want that," he said quietly. "I'm sorry. But I…can't, Nicky."

"I can't help it," she whispered softly. "I'm sorry, too, but I do. I do, I do!"

His thumb pressed harder and he caught his breath. "Listen, I've been alone a long time. I've gotten used to my own company. I don't want anyone with me. I don't want ties, commitment. For God's sake, Nicky, I'm not a marrying man!"

Her face flamed when she realized where the conversation was leading. She stared at him, horror-struck. She hadn't meant that, but he'd assumed she was begging him to marry her.

"I…I didn't mean…" She faltered.

"I can't saddle myself with a wife," he said flatly. "And you're too frail for this country, even if I went crazy and invited you to live with me. You're too used to the city. This is a man's country, Nicky, not a woman's. You'd never survive it."

She bit her lower lip. "Are you sure?"

"Yes." He took her hand in his and smoothed over its softness, wondering at the delicious sensation that washed over him as he savored it. "Just as I'm sure that I don't want a woman here," he added deliberately, holding her gaze.

She searched his dark eyes quietly. "All right. I'm sorry if I've embarrassed you."

"I think you're more embarrassed than I am," he mused, smiling gently at her red cheeks. He frowned a little as he studied her. "Are you sure this isn't reaction? You've had a rough time of it lately."

She took the out he was offering her, grateful for a little salvaged pride. "Probably it is. Being rescued, and all," she explained. "You don't hate me anymore, do you?" she added weakly, the expression in her eyes so eloquent that he felt himself choking to death on pride.

"No, I don't hate you," he said shortly. "I never did. I hated being lied to, that's all." And she had lied, he recalled. Numbly, he laid her hand down on the covers, wondering why he felt so empty. It had warmed him when she'd whispered that she loved him, God knew why. Love wasn't something he coveted these days. His eyes drifted up to hers, but she was concealing them under her lids. Could she love him?

He bent toward her, watching her face lift for him, her mouth part. Yes, she wanted his mouth, that was sweetly evident. He looked into her eyes while he kissed her, seeing the pupils dilate, the lids close drowsily. That excited him more, and he drew back before he got in over his head. He scowled down at her curiously. She disturbed him all too much. He didn't need this. She'd already betrayed him once, he wasn't giving her a second shot at him. It might be an act, even this talk of loving. Just an act. He couldn't trust her.

"I'll see about some orange juice," he said with a faint smile. "Want some soup?"

"I guess I could eat something, if it won't put Mary to too much trouble," she added quietly.

"I can't remember the last time any woman guest considered Mary," he mused, his gaze quietly possessive. "Get some rest. I'll be back after a while."

She watched him get up, trying to hide her feelings. But he limped suddenly and she sat up, her breath catching. "Winthrop, you're hurt!" she burst out.

The caring note in her voice cut him to the quick. He didn't want it, or what he was feeling for her. He glared at her. "I don't need a nurse," he bit off. "Get yourself well. I can take care of myself. I've had years of practice."

He went out and slammed the door, leaving her stunned and hurt. She wished she knew what she'd done to make him so angry. She felt like she'd made an utter fool of herself by telling him she loved him. Tears stung her eyes as she lay back. Well, maybe he'd believe she'd lied, or, as he'd said, that it was reaction. He'd made it all too obvious that her love was the last thing on earth he wanted. So she'd just have to learn to hide it from him.

Eight

✳✳✻✳✳

Soon after Winthrop left the room, Nicky had an unexpected visitor. Her father, neatly dressed in a gray suit, came in and took the chair Winthrop had vacated.

"Feeling any better?" he asked, and seemed to be genuinely concerned. Nicky could remember being sick as a child and having neither of her parents come near her.

"I'll be all right," she said. "I just feel a little tired."

"I guess so," he said with a smile. "Your nose is red."

"It feels red, too." She returned the smile. "Did anybody shoot anything?"

"I got a deer," he said. "Six-point buck. Nobody else had any luck." He pursed his lips. "I offered

Carol a jacket made from the skin and she stormed off in a snit. I shot Bambi, you see."

Nicole laughed in spite of herself. "You cold-blooded killer, you."

"I love venison," he sighed. "Mary's fixing us a big stew out of the hindquarter, but you won't get any until lunch tomorrow. She says it has to simmer a long time to get done right."

"She's a good cook."

He leaned back in the chair to study her. "What possessed you and your dim-witted boss to go driving in a snowstorm?" he asked pleasantly.

"He was worried about Sadie Todd," she explained. "And I just wanted to get some fresh air."

"In a snowstorm?" he asked.

"Well, we were kind of getting tired of watching science-fiction movies…"

"That's no reason to commit suicide. Snow is deadly, as you damned near found out. If Winthrop hadn't decided to call it quits early, the two of you would have frozen to death."

"I guess Winthrop was pretty angry."

"Angry." He pursed his lips. "That's an interesting choice of words. Mild, considering his reaction when he found you. I thought I had a good command of four-letter words, but he taught me some new ones. He carried you over that drift all by himself, weak leg and all. I guess he's hurting like hell, from the way he limps, but he was determined."

She felt her heart leap with the pleasure that

knowledge gave her. She toyed with the sheet. "He's quite a man."

"I think so," he agreed. "I told him the truth, by the way. I think you've paid enough for the past."

"Thanks. But it won't do much good. Winthrop isn't a marrying man," she added when he didn't seem to understand. "And I'm not a liberated woman."

Dominic sighed heavily. "Well, different people, different attitudes." His green eyes twinkled. "I'm very liberated, myself. But I'm kind of glad you aren't. And do you think I'm ever going to get any grandkids?" he added thoughtfully.

She flushed, averting her eyes. "Not anytime soon. I'm barely twenty-two."

"Kids are nice. I wish I'd enjoyed you more, while I had the chance." He frowned. "Say, would you like to go to a carnival or something? I could buy you cotton candy and ride the rides with you. Or we could go fishing...."

"This sounds serious," she said with mock fear. "Are you suffering from an attack of fatheritis?"

"Feels like it." He grinned. "We could at least speak. Maybe we could exchange Christmas cards. Then, as time goes by, you might come to Kentucky to see me."

"Or you might come to Chicago to see me." She sighed. "You and Carol," she amended.

"Carol won't last." He shrugged. "She's temporary. They all are. You see...in some crazy way, I loved your mother, even if we couldn't quite get our act together. She's pretty irreplaceable." His eyes fell. "God, it hurt when she died. I couldn't even tell you how it hurt."

"I don't think I would have listened if you'd told me then." She sat up straighter. "I think I understand a little better now. And maybe we could exchange Christmas cards."

He grinned at that dry remark. "Maybe we could." He got up. "Well, I'd better go rescue Mary. Carol is trying to teach her how to walk like a model."

"Carol models?"

"Doesn't it show? She's got style, all right. And Mary was just eating it up." He scowled. "She mentioned something about the Rockettes...."

"That's kind of a family joke," Nicole said, enlightening him. "Thanks for coming up to see me."

"You look a little peaked to me," he said. "Mary was fixing chicken soup in between parading around with a book on her head. I guess she's going to bring you some."

"No, she isn't," Winthrop said from the doorway, limping heavily toward them with a tray on which were perched a soup bowl and a teacup and saucer. "She's too busy trying to do a pivot without falling into the venison stew."

"Sorry about that," Dominic murmured sheepishly. "I did tell Carol to stay out of the kitchen."

"No harm done. Mary seems to be having the

time of her life." With a hard glare, Winthrop bypassed Dominic and put the tray down on the bedside table. "Well, don't just lie there, prop yourself up. You can't eat flat on your back."

"I was just trying to do that," she shot back, "and you don't have to snap at me!"

"I'll check on you again, Nicky," Dominic said as he started toward the door.

"Okay."

He closed the door and Nicky tried to take the soup from Winthrop's steely hands without letting him see how much hers were trembling. But the bowl seemed pretty unsteady even before she touched it.

He looked down into her eyes and they exchanged a glance that set her heart running away.

"Here, this won't do," he said under his breath.

He sat down beside her on the bed and began to ladle the soup gently into her mouth. She watched him, fascinated at his unexpected tenderness. The way he pampered her, the way he looked at her—even the gentle smile that touched his hard mouth as she accepted the soup like a child—tugged at her heart.

"Feeling better?" he asked.

"Much, thank you." She swallowed some soup. "Winthrop, my throat hurts," she whispered.

"Yes, I imagine so. I've got something for that, and for your cold. Nonprescription, but they're

what our doctor always prescribes for head colds.
I'll take care of you, daffodil."

"Somebody needs to take care of you," she said
softly, studying his hard face. "Your leg must hurt
terribly."

"It usually does after a day as hard as this one,"
he said carelessly. "I've got something to take for it."

"Well, thank you for rescuing us, anyway."

"Gerald sounds worse than you do," he told her.
"You're both greenhorns."

"You were out in it, too," she reminded him.

"That's so," he said agreeably. "But I'm a woodsman, honey. I know how to survive a snowstorm.
You and my citified brother are lucky to be alive."

"Yes, I realize that." She took the last bit of
soup and sat quietly while he mopped her up with
a napkin. She knew she must look terrible. Her
hair hadn't been combed, her face was pale and
her throat felt scratchy. But Winthrop was looking
down at her with pure pleasure...almost possession.

"You need sleep," he said.

"I've been asleep on and off since you brought
me home," she said. "I don't want to sleep."

"It will help you heal." He got up, put down the
bowl and offered her a cup of steaming tea to swal-
low down the capsules he'd put in her hand. She
hesitated but he looked determined, so she swallowed them, finished the tea and lay back against
the pillows.

"I hope you don't catch my cold," she said.

"I don't usually get them," he replied. He smiled slowly. "Even from kissing sick little girls."

Her face colored and she lowered her eyes to his chest. That was even worse. He had a sexy chest, and she wanted very much to draw her hands over it.

"You have expressive eyes, Nicole," he murmured, watching her intently. "You want me, don't you?"

The color in her cheeks deepened. She glared at him. "Well, I do realize that it isn't mutual. You don't have to throw it in my face. It isn't something I can help."

His eyebrow arched. "Was I doing that? I didn't mean to. I'm pretty used to speaking my mind."

"Well so am I." She stared at the coverlet. "What I said…earlier." She faltered, glancing at him and then away. "I was overwrought and tired, and I guess I kind of got carried away."

"You mistook a chill for true love?"

She glared at him. Damn that mocking smile. "I got carried away."

"You're one of a kind, Nicky," he mused. "As for getting carried away, if you weren't so frail, I'd throw you back against those pillows and lie down against you. And in a very few minutes, we'd both know what you feel for me."

He was doing it again. She felt completely out of her element when his voice dropped into that sensuous drawl and his eyes began to make love to her body. She felt her breasts tautening and drew the sheet slowly over her bodice so that he wouldn't see what he was doing to her.

But he did see her response. His eyes seemed to darken at the proof of how easily he could arouse her. She couldn't know that it made him feel ten feet tall.

"Don't worry," he said as he picked up the tray, still watching her. "I've got sound survival instincts. I meant what I said about commitment."

"You'll grow old all alone," she said quietly, her eyes steady on his hard, dark face. "You won't have anyone to look after you or care about you. Eventually, you'll grow a thicker shell than you have now, and no one will be able to touch you. Is that really what you want?"

For just an instant, his expression was open. "No," he replied. "But I don't want my heart torn out of my body a second time, either. I like my life as it is."

"Unhampered," she said.

"Exactly." He left her with that parting shot. He was still limping badly, and he was scowling when he left the room.

Nicky must have slept then. She wasn't aware of the quiet, watchful man sitting beside the bed. He looked at her as if he couldn't help himself, staring at the steady rise and fall of her firm young breasts under the sheet. She looked innocent in sleep. Everybody did, he reminded himself.

But there was something different about this woman. She was special. Much too special. He was going to have to get a grip on himself before he pitched headfirst into that sweetly baited trap. He'd fought it too long to give in now.

He closed his eyes finally, with a long sigh, and tried to get comfortable in the chair. His knee was giving him hell. Probably he'd torn a muscle. But he hadn't wanted anyone else to touch Nicky. She belonged to him. She was his responsibility.

The sound of the windup alarm clock was unnaturally loud. It woke Nicky in the early hours just before dawn. She opened her eyes and glanced at the tall man sprawled again in the chair, grimacing as he breathed. His leg was probably hurting, and here he sat, when he could have been comfortable in bed.

Nicky got up, just staring at him. Even unshaven and unkempt, he was a sexy man. His shirttail had been pulled from his jeans, and his shirt was half unbuttoned down a chest thick with hair and dark from exposure to the sun. He might not love her, but he was oddly protective of her these days. That was some small comfort.

She touched his hard, warm cheek with her fingertips, tracing its high cheekbones.

"Winthrop?" she whispered.

He made a sound and his head turned, but his eyes didn't open.

"Winthrop, come to bed," she whispered.

He never did wake up completely. He let her tug him out of the chair and he sprawled onto the bed with a mumbled protest. Nicky was glad that he'd already taken his boots off, as she wouldn't have relished trying to remove them. She eased his legs onto the bed, careful not to jar the bad one. Then, with a mischievous grin, she crawled back under the covers and snuggled close.

His arm came around her instinctively, drawing her cheek to the soft cotton of his shirt. His fingers caressed her hair gently, and she thought that she'd never been quite so close to heaven. She lay quietly beside him in the dim light of the lamp and tried to imagine how it would be if they were married, if she had the right to lie in his arms every night like this, while the wind howled angrily outside the darkened window and snow fell.

It was so sweet that she lost all fear of the future and simply went to sleep, Winthrop's chest rising and falling steadily against her.

A drum was beating somewhere. She heard it in the back of her mind, its steady rhythm comforting. It was nearby. Growing louder. Louder. It stopped suddenly and then increased. Something moved against her. Her head fell back onto a pillow and she mumbled when she felt the mattress lower then return to its normal position.

The sound of footsteps grew dim. A door opened and closed. What a crazy dream, she thought, and drifted back to sleep again.

The light streaming in the window woke her. This time she opened her eyes, and found Mary standing at the curtains.

"How you feel?" the Sioux woman asked.

"Fi..." Her voice sounded hoarse. She tried again. "Fine. I think."

"You look pale. I bring oatmeal. Best thing for scratchy throat and cold. Also buttered toast and coffee with lots of cream. Sound good?"

"Oh, yes," Nicky sighed. "I'm so hungry!"

Mary paused beside the bed and bent down to touch Nicky's forehead. "No fever. Good. You live yet." She pursed her lips at the clear indentation of a head in the pillow beside Nicky's. "You have pajama party last night?"

Nicky grinned. "He was sprawled in the chair and groaning in his sleep. I figured his leg was giving him the devil. So I got up and led him over here and tucked him in. He never knew."

Mary's normally placid face came alive. "He never knew?"

"That's right," Nicky told her, smiling broadly. "He was gone when I woke up, but I'll bet he doesn't remember how he got in the bed."

"Well, well. New weapon, hmm." Mary grinned, too, showing even white teeth. "Poor man. Shame on you. You should not take advantage of the helpless."

"He wasn't very helpless yesterday, was he?"

Nicky asked with pride. "He carried me through a snowbank."

"That leg is not as bad as he thinks it is," Mary returned. "If he exercised it more and favored it less, it would heal properly. It is his hiding place, Nicky. He cannot accept being a whole man again because that would make him vulnerable to his emotions."

"Not so anyone would notice," Nicky sighed ruefully. "He can be pretty formidable."

"He is still only a man." Mary tucked Nicole back into bed. "Need medicine for your throat?"

"A lozenge would be wonderful. It's scratchy." She paused to sneeze and grab for a tissue. "And I think I have a cold."

"It would seem so. I will bring your breakfast. And I will bring you venison stew for lunch. That should help clear your head."

"It may take more than venison stew to do that," Nicky replied.

"I make it with Tabasco sauce." Mary leaned over her. "Trust me." And she grinned again before she went out.

To Nicky's dismay, Winthrop didn't come back all day. She expected him every time the door opened. Mary brought breakfast and then Gerald came, red-nosed and sniffling, followed by her father and even Carol, who gave her a pretty scarf to cheer her up. But no Winthrop, not even when the venison stew was served.

When Mary came back after lunch to pick up

the dishes, she cocked her head at Nicky's forlorn expression.

"Something troubles you?" she asked.

"Of course not." Nicky finished her cup of hot black coffee and set the cup on the tray Mary was holding. "I don't care if he ignores me. I'll just lie here and die."

"He cannot get up just yet," Mary said after a minute.

Nicky was immediately contrite and worried. "It's his leg, isn't it?"

Mary nodded. "The strain, you see. I think he may have pulled a tendon. I have made a poultice for it, which will take away the pain and make it heal. But in the meantime, he is an invalid. Mr. Mike has taken the hunting party out for him, and Miss Carol is watching...would you care to guess?"

"I thought I heard laser cannons," Nicole replied grimly. "Does he have something for pain?" she persisted, her green eyes troubled.

"He will not take it," Mary grumbled. "Even now, he is trying to work with a board across his lap on which to write."

"It sounds as though he might need a little nursing," Nicky suggested.

"You need it more. Lie down."

"I could talk to him. It's only a cold and a reaction," she said and then added when the other woman looked doubtful, "Oh, please, Mary. How can I lie here knowing that he's in pain?"

Mary shrugged. "Good point. All right. But put on your robe and leave door open." Her dark eyes held Nicky's with subtle warning. "He is still a man."

"I love him," Nicky said simply.

"Yes, I know. That will make it harder for you. He is a man who does not trust love." The expression on her face was serious. "He will fight being vulnerable. Now more than ever."

"I wouldn't hurt him," she said.

"You will have to prove that to him. And it will not be easy. But I would think less of you if you did not try," Mary added. And she smiled as she went out.

Nicky put on her long white chenille robe and went along to Winthrop's room, a little nervous about how she'd be received.

Her nervousness was justified as it turned out, because he was moody and restless and more irritable than she'd ever seen him.

He glared at her from his bed, where he lay taut-faced with only a sheet drawn haphazardly over his lean hips for cover. His dark hair was disheveled, his face unshaven. His long, powerfully muscled legs were bare, like his tanned chest, and all of him was covered with a very masculine feathering of black hair. He looked like an outlaw in his sprawled dishabille, and Nicky wondered if any woman could see him like that and not be affected.

Her heart began to run away from her the minute she knocked on the door and was invited to open it.

"What do you want?" he asked curtly, and she noticed the scattered paperwork that had apparently been cast to one side with irritation.

"I thought you might need something," she said, hesitating.

"If I did, Mary could get it."

"Mary's got her hands full with your hunting party."

"They've gone out again. Carol's watching movies. Gerald's on the phone. So all Mary has to do is look after me. In any event," he said with a mocking smile, "that's what she gets paid to do."

"And here I am about to cause a labor dispute by offering to do it for free," she sighed. Her throat still felt a little raw, but at least her nose had stopped running. She moved closer to the bed, eyeing him warily. "How about some fruit juice?"

His dark eyes narrowed. "How about telling me how in hell I wound up in bed with you last night?"

Her eyebrows arched. "You were in bed with me?" she asked with pretended horror. "How scandalous!"

His lips made a thin line. "Don't be cute," he ground out. "And it wasn't scandalous. Nothing happened!"

She lifted her chin. "A likely story," she said.

He sat up, disrupting the sheet, but her eyes stayed on his face so that she didn't see what it revealed. "Nothing happened," he enunciated. "I don't ravish women in their sleep."

"Ah, but you don't know what I might have done to you," she said, lifting her eyebrows mockingly.

The glare got worse. "Cute. Real cute."

"Anyway, you rejected me," she reminded him. "You cut and ran before I woke up. But not," she added with a slow smile, "in time to fool Mary, who saw the imprint of your head on the other pillow and asked how it got there."

His eyes widened. "What did you tell her?"

"Oh, nothing at all," she assured him. "I told her I didn't have the slightest idea how you'd gotten in my bed."

"Oh, my God." He put his face in his hands.

"It's all right, she understands perfectly that these things happen. She didn't say a word; she just grinned."

"Oh, my God," he repeated.

"And she promised she wouldn't tell anyone except family and close friends and any acquaintances that happen past the mailbox."

"Oh, my God!"

"Now, now, you don't have to get upset, this is the twentieth century, after all—"

"This is rural Montana," he said, half shouting. His eyes blazed at her. "You little fool! Your reputation will be in shreds!"

"People in Chicago don't notice things like

that," she reminded him. "And Gerald and I are going back next week, you know. Your reputation will have hardly a blemish. In fact, it might even make you more desirable to some of the local belles if it gets around that you're the same devil-may-care rake you used to be."

He narrowed one eye. "How do you know what I used to be like?"

"I asked Gerald, of course. He said you used to score with every woman you dated—"

"Nicky!"

"Well, not in exactly those words, of course," she amended at his shocked expression.

"Have you lost your sweet mind?" he demanded. "What were you trying to do?"

"Get you comfortable and warm," she said with a smile. "You were groaning and I knew your leg was hurting you. Since you seemed determined to sit up with me, I thought you should be comfortable. So I led you into bed, and you went with me just like a lamb."

"Which wasn't what I felt like when I woke up," he replied curtly. "Your gown was up around your hips and half off your shoulder, and men have it rough early in the morning anyway. Oh, honey, you had a close call you didn't even know about!"

"I did?" Her eyes were wide, trusting and innocent. He sighed impatiently.

"Never mind. What did you really tell Mary?"

"The truth. She grinned and mumbled something about a new weapon."

"It will backfire." He bit his lip suddenly and grimaced. His hand went to his knee, where she noticed a poultice tied with white gauze.

"Will that help?" she asked.

"Mary says so. She usually knows. Even the local doctors have a measure of respect for her way with herbs. In the old days, the Indians had to have a healthy knowledge of it, since they didn't have a neighborhood clinic."

"Mary's told me a lot about Montana and the way it used to be," she said. "It's a fascinating country. Big and sprawling and special."

"That's why I stay here," he said. He leaned back against the pillows, studying her face. "I have no desire to go back to the life I used to lead."

"Well, that's one thing we can both agree on," she said quietly. "Neither do I."

His chiseled lips pursed thoughtfully. "Are you really worth three million?"

She nodded. "If I sign the necessary papers. But I don't want three million dollars. If I refuse that trust, do you know what the money will be used for?"

"No."

He seemed honestly curious, so she told him. "It will fund a research program to find new ways of treating cancer in children."

"Three million would go a long way," he said.

"Yes, wouldn't it?" She smiled. "And since I've gotten used to working for the Christopher Corporation, and nobody's fired me yet, I expect I can support myself without that trust."

He stretched lazily, watching her eyes drop to his chest with the movement and follow the sensuous tautening of muscle under thick hair. He liked the way it felt to let her look at him like this.

"You're a surprising girl, Nicole," he said, his voice dropping an octave, deep and sexy.

"Am I? I thought I was a gold digging adventuress."

"That sounds bitter," he mused.

She shifted from one foot to the other and stared down at the thick beige carpet. "It felt bitter, too. You never believed a word my father said, really, but it gave you the excuse you needed to draw back before things got complicated." She looked up, catching the surprise in his dark eyes even as it registered that she'd hit on the truth.

"I told you at the beginning that I didn't want commitment," he reminded her sulkily.

"I don't remember asking for any," she replied.

"You said you loved me." His dark eyes slid down her body. "Several times."

"You'd just saved my life." She steeled herself not to let him see how vulnerable she was. She'd thrown herself at him for the last time. He didn't want to make a life with her, and there was only one other thing he might offer. She couldn't accept that kind of relationship, so what was left?

His face didn't reveal a single emotion. "And it was only gratitude?"

"Gratitude, and a natural response to a very experienced man. Which you are," she said, watching his eyes narrow. "I must have been a real pushover."

"You're twisting it." His voice was deep, but a little more curt now. "What I saw in your eyes wasn't completely physical."

"I'm young, as you keep reminding me," she shot back.

"Yes." His gaze swept over her face, memorizing lines and curves and expressions. "Eleven years my junior. Almost another generation, especially in sensual ways."

"You don't have to remind me about how experienced you are."

"In my day, I was," he agreed. He propped himself against the pillows, righting the sheet with a careless hand. "But in recent years, I've given up jet-setting around the world. I've changed my values, Nicole."

"Through choice?" she asked gently. "Or just because you were unsure of being accepted with your battle scars?"

"Honey, you believe in cutting to the bone, don't you?" he asked with a half-angry laugh.

"You aren't the kind of man to be spoon-fed things, are you?" she returned gently.

"No." He drew up his left leg and studied her quietly. "Why did you think I'd order you off the place if I knew your real name?"

"You'd already said you hated rich people, and Gerald said you had no use whatsoever for jet-setters. I guessed that if you knew I was in that class, it would make you hate me," she said simply.

"You might have given me the benefit of the doubt."

She managed a smile. "I didn't have enough self-confidence for that. As it was, you were only tolerating me."

"I thought you and Gerald had something going," he said. He studied the coverlet. "I love Gerald. I couldn't take away something he wanted as badly as he seemed to want you."

"And all along, he was in love with Sadie. I've never had ulterior motives," she added, wanting to make him understand. "I don't want a rich man, Winthrop. I have a job I enjoy, I can make my own way in life. I was never looking for a...a meal ticket."

"I didn't know that. All I had left were my instincts, and they'd already let me down once. I haven't trusted a woman since this happened." He touched his knee.

"Were you ever in love before her?" she asked hesitantly, because it was suddenly important that she know that.

He met her searching gaze. "Love is an illusion.

I don't believe in it. I never did. I wanted Deanne until she was an obsession with me. I got drunk on her. When she walked out, I thought I was going to bleed to death, and for two years I felt like a zombie. Is that love? I don't know. It's the most intense thing I'd ever felt, so maybe it was. But I'm over her now and I have no inclination whatsoever to go through it again."

He'd probably never spoken so candidly about his feelings before, and she was flattered that he'd trusted her even that far. She sat down slowly on the bed beside him, her soft weight moving the mattress.

"Love shouldn't be all physical," she told him, her voice as gentle as the fingertips that went hesitantly to his firm mouth and touched it. "It should be a sharing between two people. A bonding of thoughts and hopes and dreams. A linking of intangible things. Companionship. Friendship. Openness and honesty."

"You lied to me," he said curtly. His fingers caught her wrist.

"What do you care?" she asked. "You don't believe in love, and you don't really want it anyway. You're safe from ever being hurt again. Nobody can reach you. If you stay up here another ten years, you'll be a walking dead man!"

"At your age, what do you know about love?" he demanded. "You said you loved me, but we both know all you feel is pity. I've been hurt and I'm scarred, so you see me as a charity case!"

Her eyebrows went up. "You?"

The one word was more expressive than any argument she could have made. He glared at her and let go of her wrist. "You feel sorry for me," he continued doggedly.

"I feel sorry for anybody who gets close to you all right," she mumbled. "You aren't my idea of the perfect lover."

"How would you know, when you've never had one?"

"You said my innocence was all an act—"

"Oh, for God's sake, I was mad as hell, I'd have said anything! I didn't mean it. I know lack of experience when it stares me in the face. You blushed that night in the kitchen when I looked at you."

"I wish you'd stop bringing that up. I was…overwrought," she concluded helplessly.

"You got too damned close," he said suddenly, every last bit of caution gone. His eyes glittered dangerously. "You got under my skin. What did you expect me to do—lie back and enjoy it? I won't be owned by some little city girl with a rich daddy!"

"Now just hold on one minute," she said slowly. "What do you mean 'with a rich daddy'?"

"Your father mentioned that if I wanted to marry you, he'd give us a racehorse for a wedding present, and an interest in the farm to boot."

She was horrified. Absolutely horrified. In his

usual bulldozing way, her father was trying to help. This scheme sounded like his idea of building a fire under the man he thought Nicky wanted.

Somehow she got to her feet, her heart slamming in her throat. "How nice of him," she said huskily.

"He needs looking after," he replied. "He shouldn't be let out alone. And you're not much better. Neither of you do things the right way."

"Which is?" she taunted.

"Straightforward. Don't you know how to get what you want in life?"

"Your way would probably be to reach out and grab it," she muttered.

"You're catching on, sugarplum."

Before she could react, he had her by the wrist again. He levered her down onto the bed, on her back, and loomed over her with a purely arrogant look in his dark eyes.

"I don't want to be another one of your conquests," she told him, struggling.

"Sure you do. If you keep thrashing around like that, you're going to dislodge my sheet and the mystery of life will be over!"

She stopped immediately, glaring at him with wide green eyes as she tried to catch her breath. Smiling down at her, all unshaven and with his hair down over his forehead, he looked sensuous and a little dangerous.

"You don't want commitment, remember?" she reminded him bitterly.

"I don't have to propose marriage to kiss you," he returned, bending.

"I have a cold—I'm contagious!" she squeaked.

"I have a sore leg, and that's not catching. But desire is," he whispered against her lips. "Shall I show you how easy it is to catch?"

"It isn't fair," she wailed.

"Probably not. But it's sweet, all the same." He nuzzled her face with his, in soft, gentle caresses that wore her down all too easily. "You smell of gardenias, Nicky. You smell sweet all over. Here," he breathed, taking her hand in his to press it against his hard, warm chest. "Touch me."

Her hand faltered shyly, but he guided it over the hard muscles, letting her feel the silky hair that covered him, the ripple of muscle under rough skin. "You feel furry," she whispered.

"And you feel like satin." He traced her cheek with his fingers as he kissed her very lightly, and his hand slowly lowered to the buttons of her bodice under the robe.

"No," she protested.

"Go ahead, fight for your honor," he chided. "And I'll wear you down anyway. It's only going to be a token resistance. You want to be touched as much as I want to touch you. So just give in, Nicky, and enjoy it."

"You conceited ape!"

"Enjoy it," he whispered. His fingers moved to the edge of her breast, tracing around it with maddening expertise, making her moan and stiffen suddenly in an explosion of unexpected pleasure.

"Winthrop!" she gasped.

"It isn't new," he whispered, drawing his mouth slowly over hers. "We did this in the kitchen that night...you let me touch you then, too. You let me kiss you."

"You shouldn't," she whispered shakily.

"You belong to me," he said simply as he began to unfasten buttons. "I have every right in the world."

"You don't," she tried to protest, but his hand was inside the gown now, his lean, cool fingers against virgin flesh, teasing, tracing, until she arched up and trembled.

"Mine," he breathed against her mouth. Her movements were exciting him, her little cries caught in his lips, making him hungry. "All of you. Here and here...sweet young body, ripe for my hands. I could make a meal of you, Nicky."

He had her gown around her waist, and she couldn't even protest. Her eyes closed, tears falling down her cheeks while he looked, touched, delicately tasted her pretty, firm breasts. She let him, and his whirling mind registered her complete abandonment to his ardor. She wasn't resisting him anymore—verbally or physically. He could do anything now and she'd let him.

And that realization was what slowed him down. He lifted his head quietly, looking at the helpless reaction of her body to his lovemaking. She was beautiful, he thought, and he stared at her with something akin to reverence in his dark, tender gaze.

His fingers traced around an erect nipple, gently loving. "I've never seen anything so perfect, Nicky," he whispered. "It's like touching satin."

Her eyes opened. She was embarrassed, and her face felt hot as she met his gaze. "I'm afraid," she whispered.

"There's no reason to be frightened. I'm not going to ravish you." He drew the backs of his fingers against her, loving the way she tensed with pleasure. "But I could, couldn't I? You want me pretty badly right now."

"Obsessively," she confessed. Her voice shook a little. "Do you enjoy humiliating me?"

"Is that what you think I'm doing? Think again." He lifted his hand, and she saw its faint tremble. "That isn't faked, Nicky," he added solemnly. "I go just as high as you do when we make love. It's mutual, this chemistry. It has been from the very beginning."

"I won't have an affair with you," she said quietly.

"I wouldn't let you," he returned. He nuzzled her nose with his. "On the other hand, I don't want marriage."

"I'll have to leave," she whispered, feeling her heart break.

"Inevitably," he agreed. He looked down at her as his fingers drew tenderly over her bare breasts and she trembled. "It knocks the very breath out of me to touch you this way," he breathed.

"You aren't the only one," she said shakily.

He bent and put his mouth gently on the soft curve, and then he drew back, while it was still just a whisper of sensation. "You'd better sit up and pull up your gown, honey. Someone's coming up the steps very loudly."

His words registered, but she felt as if she was caught in a dream. In the end, he helped her up, buttoned her gown and belted her robe with exaggerated indulgence. He'd only just finished when Mary ambled into the room with two mugs of steaming black coffee.

"Still here?" She clicked her tongue at Nicky. "You should be in bed. You will never mend this way."

"We were talking," Winthrop said. "Don't run her off just yet. I'm not through."

"Yes, you are," Mary said with unexpected stubbornness. "Must get her well, first, and you back on that leg. Then you can talk. Up!"

Nicky managed a rueful smile at Winthrop, feeling disappointed and a little shy. His expression, on the other hand, gave nothing away. He didn't protest, so she went with Mary, too subdued to even notice the twinkle in the older woman's eyes.

But Nicky didn't go back to Winthrop's room

again, and he didn't ask for her. It was a kind of world-weary truce, but without any fraternizing. She didn't even see him, but Mary said that he was almost on his feet again. That was good news.

Meanwhile, Mike brought Sadie and Mrs. Todd down the mountain for the duration, so at least Nicky had someone to talk to. That was, she had Mrs. Todd to visit with, not Sadie, who was taking a delicious pleasure in nursing her Gerald back to health.

The little group got along very well. That was unexpected and enlightening, because Nicky had thought they wouldn't fare that well. Even Carol found things to talk to Mrs. Todd about. And Dominic White discovered that his lady love had a compassionate side to counterbalance her mercenary tendencies. He didn't seem to want to cut at Nicky anymore, although he did keep mentioning fairs and cotton candy....

Nicky was back taking dictation when Gerald felt up to it, in between wondering why Winthrop hadn't come near her and how she was going to bear to leave him when she and Gerald had to go home to Chicago. Even living in the same house separated from Winthrop was agony. How was it going to feel when she was hundreds of miles away, separated for life?

Nine

❋❋❋❋❋

It was Saturday, and the hunters were packing to go home. A chinook had blown in Friday to take away the snow, unlocking the grip the storm had on the ranch, leaving the roads passable if slushy.

"Well, it's just been great," Carol sighed as she left. "I can't think when I've enjoyed anything as much. Especially your movies," she added, smiling demurely at Winthrop in the hall.

"You'll have to get Dominic to bring you again," he returned with a smile.

"I might be persuaded," Dominic said. He put an arm around Carol. "This one might be worth keeping."

"Well, she's certainly pretty enough," Nicky volunteered. "And I like her, if that carries any weight."

Carol's eyes brightened. Impulsively, she hugged Nicky. "We won't tell anyone that I'm only five years older than you are. We'll just let people gape when you call me Mom, okay?" she laughed.

"Okay," Nicky said gently. She winked at the redhead.

"By the way—" Dominic hesitated, luggage in hand "—I, uh, put my foot in it again, Nicky."

She knew what he was going to say, about trying to buy Winthrop. He was a rascal, but he was still her father. She liked him sometimes, warts and all.

She hugged him briefly. "I've fouled things up all by myself, thanks. You just added your two cents' worth. I like you anyway."

Dominic looked uncomfortably emotional for a minute before he pulled himself together. "Come see an old man once in a while," he managed finally.

"I don't know any old men, but I guess I could come see you. If I get to help Eddie with the horses," she added. "It's been a while since I've ridden."

"We can remedy that. Don't wait too long. See you, Nicky."

"See you, Dad."

They went out, followed by the Harris brothers who were mumbling their own thanks and goodbyes. Nicky found herself alone with Winthrop, who towered over her in jeans and that huge sheepskin jacket he liked to wear with his creamy Stetson.

"You seem to have arrived at a truce with your father," he mused.

"I misunderstood a lot of things. Grief plays havoc with the brain," she said quietly. "I loved my mother very much."

"So did he, unless I miss my guess." He touched her short hair, the simple gesture sending thrills down her spine. "Was she like you, to look at?"

"Oh, no. She was beautiful," she recalled gently. "Long black hair and pale blue eyes—Irish. She even had the lilting speech. She was a lady, in every sense of the word. I adored her."

"And what does that make you—the ugly duckling?" he chided. He tilted her chin up, searching her suddenly flushed face. "Nice eyes. Big and soft. Pretty little mouth. High cheekbones. Soft skin. You'll do, sugarplum, even without long hair. But let it grow anyway. I like long hair."

He turned her loose then and started out the door, still limping a little.

"Your knee...is it better?" she asked hesitantly.

He half turned toward her, his dark eyes alive and quiet. "It's no worse, at least. Why? Were you thinking of offering me a massage?"

"I don't go around playing with men's legs."

"Oh, you're one of those kind of women, are you?" he taunted. "Marriage or nothing?"

"I don't want to marry you. I'm sorry if that breaks your heart."

He smiled slowly, the sight of it almost knocking the breath out of her. Heavens, he was handsome! Bigger than the whole outdoors, sexy, sensuous…

"Tease," he accused.

"You're the one making references to playing with men's legs. Which I don't do."

He grinned at her high color. "I know a lot of things you didn't do until I came along," he mused, and his eyes went straight to her yellow sweater.

"Aren't your guests going to miss the plane?" she asked in a high-pitched parody of her normal voice.

"That's their problem, not mine."

"You're driving them, aren't you?"

The roar of the Jeep interrupted her.

"No," he answered as it sped away. "Mike's driving them. Gerald wants you in the office, by the way. He's got a hundred letters to get out yesterday."

"Thanks a lot," she muttered darkly.

"Better toe the line, honey, or you could get fired. Since you're throwing away money hand over fist lately, you do need the work now, don't you?" he asked, playfully looking down his arrogant nose at her.

It had only just occurred to her that he was teasing. It was new, like that look on his dark face, that twinkle in his eyes. Her heart skipped a few beats and she turned her head, a little unsure of this new Winthrop.

"Yes, I guess I do," she admitted. But the words didn't match what her soft, searching eyes were telling him. Not at all.

He tilted her chin up with a lean, strong hand and looked down at her. "I'm going out to check on my purebred herd," he murmured. "I'd take you with me, but you're a distraction, Kentucky girl."

Her pulse jumped again. "I thought...you said... you didn't want me around," she managed breathlessly.

"Did I say that?" he asked, lifting his eyebrows. "My goodness, it must have been the painkillers."

"Listen here, Winthrop—"

"Say it like that again," he whispered at her lips, taunting them from a fraction of an inch away, so close that she could almost taste him.

"What?"

"Whisper my name like that again," he repeated, and his nose brushed lazily against the tip of hers.

"Win...Winthrop," she obliged.

"Mmm," he murmured. His lips nuzzled hers, tempting them, urging her closer to him in the dim light of the hall. "Come up here...."

He actually lifted her off the floor with two steely hands at her waist. "That's better," he whispered. "Now open that pretty mouth and kiss me properly."

He had the most incredible way of getting to her. She was lost and witless, drugged on his nearness. She gave him her mouth, parted her lips, and moaned when he deepened the kiss hungrily and his arms swallowed her up against him.

Time got lost somewhere in the middle of that long, sweet kiss. A dog barked, and pans banged in the kitchen. A door opened and closed. Winthrop finally lifted his head, his breath coming hard and quick on her faintly bruised lips.

"Do you like it that way?" he whispered roughly. "Or do you want me to be gentle with you?"

She buried her face under his chin, trembling with reaction. "I like it…any way at all, with you," she whispered, clinging to him.

"Same here." He let her slide down his powerful body to the floor, savoring the feel of her against him. Her eyes were wide and soft and drowsy, and he couldn't help bending to brush her mouth once more with his. "Don't overdo it. You're not quite fit yet."

"Look who's talking."

"And no sass." He tapped her on the cheek. "See you."

He was gone, then, and she watched him until he was out of sight.

In between long talks with Sadie, Gerald managed to give a little dictation. Mrs. Todd had decided at long last to go and visit her sister in Florida, and it didn't really come as a surprise when Gerald announced a little hesitantly that he'd asked Sadie to marry him.

"It's about time," Nicky said, beaming. "Congratulations!"

"I can hardly believe it after all this time," Sadie sighed, leaning her head against Gerald's shoulder. "But I've never been happier."

"Neither have I. And I'm sure your mother's going to love Florida. The climate will be good for her. We can visit her every other week if you like."

"Well, maybe once a month anyway," Sadie compromised, her eyes bright with love and happiness.

Nicky had to look away. There wouldn't be any such happiness for her. She'd go back to Chicago and take up her job, and try to forget Winthrop. That wasn't much of a future. She wondered how she was going to manage without him. He might enjoy teasing her and kissing her, but he'd said too often that marriage wasn't for him.

"You look glum, Nicky. What's wrong?" Gerald asked.

She forced herself to smile. "Nothing at all. I'll get my pad and take down some of that correspondence you're so anxious to get rid of."

"Good girl." He smiled down at Sadie. "I think life is going to be a lot easier to cope with from now on."

For him, at least, Nicky agreed. Not for her.

She couldn't quite handle sitting at the supper table without the buffer of guests to protect her from Winthrop's dark, searching gaze. So she offered to have hers upstairs with Mrs. Todd. Mary gave her a hard look, but she fixed two trays and helped Nicky carry them upstairs.

"It is not like you to run away," Mary said stoically at the door to the guest room Sadie and Mrs. Todd were sharing.

"I'm very good at it, actually," Nicky replied. "Especially when I'm outgunned."

"The biggest fish are the hardest to land."

Nicky shrugged. "Sometimes they're the boniest, too."

Mary grinned. "Good bones, though." She opened the door. "Nicky is having supper with you," she told Mrs. Todd. "Thought you might enjoy some company."

"Why, Nicky, how thoughtful," Mrs. Todd said with a smile. "I'll enjoy that."

"Mary even fixed you a pudding," Nicky said, nodding toward the creamy vanilla treat.

"My favorite. How kind, Mary."

"No trouble," the older woman said. "I like them, too. Hearty appetite."

Mary left them, and Nicky arranged Mrs. Todd's tray and silverware before she sat down to eat her own food. It tasted like cardboard, but she forced herself not to pick at it. She'd have to get used to not seeing Winthrop across the table from her. Now was a good time to start.

"My sister is looking forward to having me stay with her," Mrs. Todd said. "She's been alone for five years now, since her husband died. She lives in one of those retirement communities, and she says there are lots of things to see and do. Best of all—" she sighed "—the weather is warm and sunny. This chill goes right through me. I haven't been comfortable with the cold weather, but I didn't have the heart to tell Sadie. She was so happy, especially when Gerald came here on his holiday."

"He really came to see Sadie, I think," Nicky laughed. "And I'm glad it all worked out so nicely."

"So am I. Sadie will take care of him, and he of her." Mrs. Todd's gaze searched Nicky's face curiously. "Why are you hiding up here?"

Nicky jumped. "Hiding?"

"Hiding. You can't tell me it's my company you want. Are you and Winthrop trading blows again?"

Nicky shifted restlessly, crossing her jean-clad legs. "We just agree to disagree, that's all."

"He's a stubborn man. You'll have to be patient if you want him."

"I don't want him!"

"Don't be silly, of course you do," Mrs. Todd said nonchalantly. She finished the last of her pudding. "When it comes time, he won't let you leave. Mark my words, he knows a good thing when he sees it."

"Think so?" Nicky wanted to believe the old woman's words, but she knew Winthrop too well. He didn't want a long-term relationship. In fact, he'd probably be happy to wave her goodbye. The thought depressed her even more.

The last thing she expected was to find Winthrop at the door when it opened suddenly. She'd thought it was Mary and hadn't looked up until she heard his voice.

"There you are," he said pleasantly. "I wondered where you'd gotten to. How're you doing, Mrs. Todd?"

"Very well, Winthrop, thanks to you." The older woman beamed. "It's been like old times visiting here."

"I'm glad you're enjoying it. I thought I'd walk Nicky down to the barn and let her look at my colt. She helped deliver him, you know."

"I didn't! Nicky, that's quite a feat for a city girl."

"But she isn't," Winthrop said proudly, watching her. "She's a country girl. Kentucky-born and reared. Her people were horse fanciers."

"How interesting."

"How is the colt?" Nicky asked, keeping her voice steady when her heart was racing wildly in her chest.

"Growing like a weed. Come on and I'll show you. Good night, Mrs. Todd. Mary will be up soon to check on you."

"Thank you, Winthrop. Good night, Nicky, and thanks for keeping me company."

"It was my pleasure," Nicky assured her, bending to kiss the wrinkled cheek. "Night."

She followed Winthrop out the door with faint hesitation. He seemed friendly enough, but she sensed something beneath the outward calm. Something disturbing. Exciting.

"Isn't it late to be looking at horses?" she asked as they walked down the staircase.

He glanced down at her. "Why? Are you afraid to be alone with me after dark?" he asked.

She hated that arrogant look. "Of course not!"

"Then why ask the question?"

"I thought you might have better things to do."

"I could do some bookwork, I guess." He glanced at her. "Or watch the VCR—"

"I'd just *love* to see the colt!" she interrupted.

He chuckled softly. "I thought you would."

He led her down the side hall and helped her into her coat and stocking cap. "It's still cold, although the snow has stopped."

She couldn't imagine why he wanted her company, but she was touched beyond reason that he did. It felt so good to be with him, alone with him under the wide sky, crunching through the snow toward the barn.

"Did Dad look at the colt while he was here?" she asked.

"He sure did. He thinks I've got a young champion on my hands. He said that if I wanted him to, he'd train him for me."

"That's not a rash offer," she said. "He's good with horses, and he's never backed a loser yet."

"So I hear." He took her arm and turned her at the barn door. "Turning down three million dollars is crazy. You could accept the trust and still give a million to research."

"I don't want to be rich," she said simply. "I tried it, and I didn't like it. My values got fouled up. I like them the way they are."

He sighed. "I can understand that. It just seems a waste. You could do a lot with that kind of money."

"You can only wear so many diamonds at a time, and fur makes me sneeze," she said with a straight face.

"You'll be working for the rest of your life, damn it. What if Gerald ever fires you? What will happen to you?"

The prospect really seemed to bother him. She searched his dark eyes, shadowed by the wide brim of his hat. "I might get married someday," she said. "I like children. I'd like to have a family."

He touched her arm lightly, smoothing her coat sleeve. "Yes. I'd like that, too, one day. Kids are nice."

"How many do you plan to adopt?" she asked.

His eyebrows arched. "Adopt?"

"You said marriage wasn't in your vocabulary," she reminded him. "So if you want children, you'll have to adopt them."

He moved restlessly. "A wife would be an encumbrance."

"So would children."

"It's not the same thing."

"It is."

He glared at her. "I won't marry you, honey, if that's what you're hinting at."

She glared back. "Who asked you? I don't want a walking icicle."

"I'm anything but an icicle in bed," he told her.

"Talk is cheap!"

"Not half as cheap as that statement," he returned. He scowled down at her. "How in God's name did we get on this subject?"

"You said you wanted children—"

"Well, I don't. Not anymore." He started walking again. He glared at the barn door as he opened it. "Women! They twist everything around to suit themselves."

"So do men."

He stood aside to let her enter the barn. "Marriage was invented by women to legalize sex."

"Don't look at me," she said airily. "I don't want to marry anyone. I'm just twenty-two. I have years and years of living to do before I tie myself to a man's housework."

"Time passes quick. Before you know it you'll be my age."

"God forbid." She glared up at him. "I'm not ready for the Home."

"Stop that," he grumbled. "I'm not old."

"Neither is the Statue of Liberty," she said with a sweet smile. "Where's the colt?"

"Over there."

She followed his irritated gesture and leaned over the gate, watching the little chestnut colt nuzzle at his mother's belly.

"Aw," she cooed. "Isn't he cute?"

"I'm not old," he repeated, still nettled by her offhand remark.

She looked up at him carelessly. "All right. You're not old. Isn't he cute?"

"Thirty-four is a man's prime."

"If you say so."

"It is, damn it!"

"Was I arguing?" she asked innocently.

He pushed back his hat with an irritable sigh. "Gerald says you and he are going back Monday to get the office shipshape so he and Sadie can get married Friday and have an extended honeymoon."

"That's nice," she said absently. She hadn't known, but it was good to have it out in the open. Two more days to be with Winthrop. It would be heaven and hell.

"You won't lose your pay. He's going to let you handle his office while he's gone."

"That's nice, too."

"Don't you know any other words?" He glowered down at her. "Look here, Nicole, we won't see each other again."

"Yes, I know." She looked up at him quietly. "That should please you. It must be hell, having a lovesick woman making calves' eyes at you all the time."

He shifted restlessly. "I've gotten used to having you around," he said reluctantly, but he wouldn't look at her.

Like an old shoe, she thought miserably. She watched the colt in silence for a few moments, then said, "I imagine you'll get used to not having me around just as easily."

"I guess so."

She peeked up at him. His face was hard and cold, but his eyes were glittering faintly as he looked down at her.

"I'll always limp," he said unexpectedly. "Gerald says I can work the kinks out, but the doctors don't agree. There's always going to be a degree of impairment."

"That's too bad," she said.

"Is that all you can say?" he growled.

Her eyebrows arched. "What would you like? Shall I sit down on the ground and start crying?"

"I'm a cripple!"

"Sure." She stared back at the colt. "You and the Marine Corps."

"Nicky..."

"If you want to limp, go ahead. I don't care."

"You aren't listening."

"Of course I'm listening. You're telling me what a bad risk you are, and I'm agreeing with you. You've been right all along, Winthrop. I need a younger man who doesn't limp, who wants marriage and children. You're absolutely right, so now I'm going to go back to Chicago to find one." She looked at the growing anger in his hard face. "That should satisfy you."

"Would you like to know what would satisfy me right now?" he asked under his breath.

"Not really. I'm tired and I'd like to go to bed."

"At last, we agree on something." He moved toward her.

"Oh, no, you don't. I'm saving myself for my future husband."

"Thank you."

"It won't be you," she told him doggedly. "I'm not crazy enough to think that. You aren't a marrying man, remember? You don't want commitment."

"I don't know what I want anymore," he muttered.

"Well, I do," she said. "I want to go home."

"To a lonely apartment in Chicago?"

"It won't be lonely long," she assured him. "I'm going to start my very own lonely hearts chapter."

"Over my dead body."

"Nobody would want to meet over your old dead body."

"Nicky…"

She got as far as the barn door and opened it to freedom. "You only want my body," she burst out. "And that's not enough!"

"Will you listen to me?!"

"No!"

She turned and ran for the house, easily out-distancing him. She passed Gerald and Sadie on the steps, shot up the staircase into her room and locked the door. So much for trying to reason with Winthrop. All he wanted to do was back her into a corner and seduce her. Well, he wasn't getting another chance to do that! She'd just avoid him until she could leave. Better to walk away with a broken heart than a broken spirit as well. She loved him, but she couldn't settle for a one-night stand. Not even with the only man she'd ever wanted.

She tossed and turned all night, thinking about the ironies of her life. Even if nothing else had come out of this trip, at least she'd made peace with her father. But she wished that Winthrop could have returned just a little of the feeling she had for him. Her heart was going to break in two when she walked out that door Monday morning. And Winthrop wouldn't even miss her. On that thought, she cried herself to sleep.

Ten

It was as if Nicky's impulsive action had brought a wall down between herself and Winthrop. He wasn't around the next morning when Gerald and Sadie and Nicky got into the Lincoln to go to church in Butte. He wasn't around when they got back, either, and Gerald remarked on it, because Winthrop almost always went to church.

The day wore on, and Nicky got her things packed since they were leaving early the next morning. The corporation jet was scheduled to pick them up about eight.

Gerald spent all his free time with Sadie, finalizing their wedding plans. A special plane was taking Mrs. Todd to Florida that afternoon, so that she could make the flight in luxurious comfort. Gerald had arranged everything, and Mrs. Todd was enthusing about her future son-in-law to anyone who had time to listen.

Since there was a chance that Winthrop might show up, Nicky stayed behind when Gerald and Sadie drove Mrs. Todd to the airport. But Winthrop was still missing.

"Gone hunting, he said," Mary told her with a curious glance. "Funny thing, to see him hunt on Sunday when he curses if others do same."

"He's avoiding me," Nicky murmured.

"Thought as much. What did you do?"

"He was telling me all the reasons I ought not to get involved with him and I agreed, that's all," Nicky sighed.

Mary grinned from ear to ear. "Just like man, to state truth and then get mad when others agree."

"I suppose he'll never speak to me again." Nicky was remembering their talk. Perhaps he'd been trying to say something and she hadn't given him the chance. Either way, she'd never know now. She was going home and he wouldn't follow. Most likely, he'd be glad to be rid of her.

"Winthrop is deep," Mary said unexpectedly. "Hard man to predict." She glanced at Nicky. "But be sure that he thinks before he acts. Weighs the odds. He is surefooted."

"I used to think I was, too," Nicky said. "But I'm not anymore."

"Give it time."

"Now that," she replied, "I have plenty of. What's for supper?"

"Something different," Mary told her secretively. "Old family recipe. You'll like it."

"But what is it?"

Mary leaned forward. "Moussaka."

"You're putting me on," Nicky laughed.

"Had Greek uncle. Taught me to make it, eggplant and all. Nice change of pace."

"I'll bet!"

"Here." She handed over the utensils. "Set the table. No doubt Gerald and Sadie will be late. They have much to discuss."

"They'll make a happy couple."

"Yes."

Since there was no more reply than that, Nicky went about her business and began to set the table in the dining room. And all the while she wondered where Winthrop had gone and why he hadn't come home. She had so little time left here. It was going to be agonizing to go off and leave him, and here he was wasting precious minutes they might have spent together. But why should he care? she reminded herself. He didn't trust her. He might want her, but he didn't love her. He'd said himself that love was an illusion. Besides that, he didn't ever want to marry. So why bother about him?

She finished the place settings and put napkins all around. At least her nice boss was going to come out ahead, she thought. Gerald would marry Sadie and

have a perfectly wonderful life while Nicky grew
old taking dictation. It didn't bear thinking about.

Maybe she could do what she'd threatened Winthrop with—get married and have children. Sure.
Nothing easier. First, she had to find a man. And
who could measure up to old stone face?

Even as she was asking herself the question, the
kitchen door opened suddenly and Winthrop came
in with something furry by the tail.

Mary stared, but Nicky went forward. "Oh,"
she exclaimed. "A wounded squirrel! Wait, I'll rush
and get a bandage!"

"Oh, for God's sake," Winthrop ground out. He
slid the squirrel onto the sink for Mary to deal with
and glared at Nicky as he eased out of his sheepskin
jacket and hat, dumping them untidily on the floor.

"There ought to be a law against shooting unarmed squirrels," Nicky muttered for something
to say.

Winthrop went to the sink to wash his hands,
ignoring her.

"Nice squirrel," Mary defended him. "Plump.
Make good stew."

"I'll bet he was somebody's daddy," Nicky murmured.

"You're breaking my heart," Winthrop said nonchalantly. He dried his hands on a towel and looked
straight at her. "Where's Gerald?"

Her heart was beating double time, but she
wasn't about to let him know it. "He and Sadie

drove Mrs. Todd to the airport. She left for Florida today."

"I know. I said goodbye before I went out. What's for dinner?" he asked Mary.

"Moussaka."

"That stuff with eggplant?" He made a face. "Whatever happened to beef and potatoes?"

"Need change of pace."

"No, I don't," he argued. "I like having the same thing every day. It gives me a sense of security."

"Then why go out and kill an innocent squirrel when you really wanted a steak?" Nicky asked.

"He wasn't innocent," he replied. "I have it on good authority that he was a rounder with unspeakable taste in women squirrels."

"Well, in that case, let's all eat him," Nicky agreed.

Winthrop actually grinned at her. She had to spoil it all by blushing.

"Sit down. I will bring the dishes," Mary told them.

Winthrop motioned for Nicky to go ahead, and even pulled out her chair for her.

"I'm impressing you with my manners," he informed her.

"Are you really?" She smiled vacantly. "When do you begin?"

"Watch it, Kentucky girl." He sat back in his chair and studied her intently while Mary brought in the main course, followed by rolls, vegetables and fruit.

"We leave tomorrow," she said when they all three were seated and enjoying Mary's exotic dish.

"Yes." He didn't seem disturbed. But when he finished his meal, he lit a cigarette. That was the first time Nicky remembered seeing him with one since her early days at the ranch.

"Bad smell." Mary scowled at him. "Why you do that? Thought you quit."

"I quit several times a month," he reminded her. "I'll start quitting again tomorrow."

Mary shrugged as she got up to fetch the coffee-pot for refills. "Your lungs, not mine."

"Thank you so much," he said with a mocking smile.

Mary hit him on her way to the kitchen.

"You sure are cheerful tonight," Nicky remarked. "It wouldn't be because I'm getting out of your hair tomorrow?"

"The thought did cross my mind."

"I'll bet it did."

She sipped her coffee and he stared at her for so long that her heart began to run wild and her breathing became quick and labored. She gripped the cup tighter so that he wouldn't see how badly her hands were trembling.

"You aren't limping," she said suddenly, shocking herself with the flat statement. But he hadn't been. He'd been walking straight and steady.

"I've been practicing," he replied easily. He

tapped the ashes into an ashtray. "Nice of you to notice."

"Are you going to cut Mary off by auditioning for the Rockettes yourself?" she asked demurely.

"I'd never pass muster," he replied. "My legs are too hairy."

"Ah, well, another career shot to hell by lack of a straight razor."

"Cute." He chuckled softly.

"Thank you, my mother always said I was."

"How did she die?" he asked unexpectedly, and stared at her until she was forced to answer.

"She fell into the swimming pool and drowned during a party," Nicky told him, and the dark memory was reflected in her eyes. "Nobody even noticed, can you imagine? She fell in front of two dozen people and drowned right there. And nobody noticed."

Something in her expression caught his eye. "And where were you when it happened?"

Her face drew in. "Haven't you guessed?" she asked in a faint whisper and forced a smile. "I was one of the two dozen people who didn't notice...."

He got up without haste, crushing out the cigarette in the ashtray and pulled her up into his arms. "Stupid," he accused, drawing her close to him. "Holding it in like that, never telling anyone."

"I didn't see her," she wept. "Winthrop, I didn't see her. I was dancing with Chase and I never even looked. Not until someone screamed...."

"Your father?"

"He wasn't around. I guess we both had our share of guilt over it, wondering if we could have saved her if we hadn't been so caught up in the glitter." Her hand came up to wipe away a tear. "She was so unhappy. And so alone."

"We're all alone," he replied quietly. "Some more than others."

She looked up at him, searching his dark eyes. "Do you remember your mother?"

He smiled. "Very well. She and my father were deeply in love. It never faded, all the long years." He touched her face lightly. "I was looking for something similar. I found Deanne instead."

"All women are not like Deanne," she said doggedly.

His thumb rubbed lazily across her lips. "Maybe. Maybe not."

"Cynic," she burst out, exasperated. "You're scared to death to find out."

His eyebrows arched. "I like not having my heart used for target practice. Which reminds me—your father said you were something of a markswoman."

"I used to be," she corrected. His thumb caressing her mouth was disturbing. "I used to ride, too. But I'm out of practice."

"You might come back with Gerald for the wedding," he said abruptly. "I could give you a refresher course."

Her heartbeat increased. But even as she heard

him say the words, she knew that the minute she left the ranch, he'd forget her. She'd be out of his thoughts. His offer was just a sugar pill—something to keep her happy until she left. He didn't mean it.

"That would be nice," she said, without any real conviction.

"Nicky…"

Whatever he was about to say was lost, because Mary came back in with the coffeepot and didn't lift an eyebrow at the two of them practically standing in each other's arms.

"More coffee?" she offered, and the spell was broken.

Winthrop watched Nicole for the rest of the meal, and then Gerald and Sadie came back, and the conversation centered on the wedding. Bedtime came and there wasn't a single opportunity for any more discussion. Nicky went to bed halfheartedly, more disappointed than she could ever remember being. She loved Winthrop, but he was making it patently obvious that he didn't return that feeling. But, then, what had she expected?

The next morning, before she had time to plan what she was going to say, she and Gerald were in the Jeep with Mike and being driven to the airport. Winthrop was long gone, apparently out hunting again. Nicky didn't even get to say goodbye to him before she flew back toward Chicago.

Eleven

Back at work, Nicky found herself haunted by a particularly vivid ghost. Winthrop drifted around in her thoughts constantly so that she couldn't eat or sleep or rest. She didn't understand why he couldn't have managed the time to say goodbye to her. Of course, there was always the possibility that he was simply indifferent.

She was a nervous wreck by the time Thursday rolled around. Gerald was equally anxious, all thumbs as he waited for the driver to take him to the airport. And tomorrow was the wedding at the ranch.

"Why aren't you packed and ready?" Gerald asked suddenly, as if it had only occurred to him that Nicky wasn't coming.

"I'm not going," she said quietly.

"But why not?" he asked, and smiled. "Winthrop invited you, didn't he?"

"I suppose he felt obliged to," Nicky confessed. She sighed heavily. "You see, I...well, I kind of...I told him I loved him," she concluded, and went scarlet. She buried her face in her hands while Gerald gaped at her. "Of all the stupid things I ever did, that was by far the stupidest. He told me right up front that he didn't want commitment. I should have listened."

"Oh, Nicky," he murmured. He patted her shoulder awkwardly. "Nicky, I'm so sorry. With all due respect, you could have found a more approachable man. Winthrop has too many scars and he's lived completely alone for so long.... I'm just really sorry. If I'd thought anything like this would happen, I'd never have forced you into going to Montana with me."

"It's not your fault," she reminded him. "I didn't have to go." She forced a smile. "But I can't quite manage the wedding. I hope you understand. Having to be around him, and having him know how I feel... I just couldn't bear the embarrassment."

"I'll make some kind of excuse for you. Don't worry." He studied her worriedly. "You'll be all right?"

"Sure I will. I thought I might go and spend the weekend with my father. Christmas is coming up in three weeks."

"So it is." He patted her shoulder again. "Can you cope while I'm on honeymoon?"

"You bet, boss," she said brightly.

"Okay. Well..." The driver appeared in the door and announced that he was ready when Gerald was.

"Kiss Sadie for me," Nicky said.

"I'll do that with pleasure. You'll have to come over for supper one night when we get back in town."

"That would be nice."

"I'll see you soon, Nicky."

"Yes, sir." She smiled, and waved goodbye to him.

She wanted to go to the wedding. It would have been heaven to stand and look at Winthrop just once more. But she'd do better to get him out of her mind, and going back to the ranch would only open old wounds. She'd had enough torment. And he'd never led her on. He'd told her exactly how he felt, so if her heart was broken she could only blame herself.

She settled back into the office routine the next day, fielding questions and phone calls and correspondence with a flair that would have pleased her absent boss.

She wasn't prepared for the phone to ring and an angry, irritated Winthrop to be on the other end of the line.

"Where in hell are you?" he demanded coldly.

She stared at the phone as if it had grown teeth.
"I'm…here. Working." She faltered.

"You were invited to the wedding," he reminded
her.

"Yes, I know."

"Then why aren't you here?"

She stared at her feet. "I didn't want to come,"
she said in a ghostly tone.

"I don't bite," he grumbled. "And I hadn't in-
tended to drag you off into the underbrush."

"I know that," she moaned. She bit her lower lip.
"I made a fool of myself," she said after a minute, almost choking on the words. "I…couldn't face you."

There was a pregnant pause. "Made a fool of
yourself? How?"

She twisted the cord around her fingers. "I threw
myself at you like a lovesick teenager."

"Was I complaining?" he asked unexpectedly.

"I know how you feel about women."

"Do you?" he asked in bemusement. "I'd
planned to take you hunting with me."

Her heart leaped. "Had you?"

"Your father tells me you can handle a .30-.30
with the best of them," he added. "I thought we'd
hunt deer."

"I would have liked that."

"It's not too late," he reminded her. "Gerald
could send the plane for you."

She closed her eyes and prayed for strength. "I
don't think it's a good idea, Winthrop."

"Why not, for God's sake?"

"Because I can't live on dreams," she burst out. "And the sooner I face it, the better off I'll be. I know you mean well, but it…it tears the heart out of me, that's all. I won't come."

She hung up quickly, before he could talk her into going to Montana. He was offering her comfort, but he didn't realize the torment it would cause her. Loving him, being near him, and knowing he didn't care for her would have been the last straw.

All the rest of the day she expected him to call back. But he didn't. And she went to Kentucky and spent the weekend with a surprised and very different father. They talked, she and Carol went shopping, and when the time came to go back to Chicago, she was frankly reluctant to go.

"This has been fun," her father remarked, grinning. "We'll have to have a big Christmas this year. I'll get a tree and everything."

"And we'll have a party," Carol added, clinging to his arm with real affection. "Nicky needs to meet some men her own age. I know at least one with a good character I could invite." She glanced at Nicky ruefully. "Notice I didn't say with money— just with character."

"Yes, and I appreciate that." Nicky grinned back. She liked Carol. The more she saw of the redhead, the more depth she found in the other woman.

"Come home for Christmas," her father coaxed. "We'll have a big time."

It would at least keep her mind off Winthrop. "All right," she agreed, smiling. "I'll plan on it. See you in a couple of weeks, then."

"I'll send a plane up to get you." He grinned.

She went back to her apartment feeling vaguely happy. But the bubble burst at work the next morning. Becky was waiting in her office with a cold message from Winthrop.

"The iceman calleth," Becky said, whistling through her teeth. "And was he in a snit! He said to tell you that you can—" She cleared her throat. "Well, that you can sit up here in the city and freeze for all he cares, and that if he never sees you again, it will be too soon." She cocked her head at Nicky. "Does he drink? Because he sounded as if he had a *snootful!*"

That didn't sound like Winthrop. "Are you sure it was Winthrop?" she asked.

"Boy, am I sure." Becky shook her head. "He even spelled it for me." She smiled with mischief in her eyes. "He got it right on the third try, anyway."

"Oh, my."

"Oh, my, isn't what the switchboard operator had to say. She's thinking of filing charges against him for his use of language." She turned to go back to her own office, still shaking her head. "Poor old guy. What did you do to him, Nicky?"

Nicky wasn't sure. But if he was that angry, she must have gotten under his skin a little. She sat back and waited for new developments.

But when a week went by with no more word from him, she fell into a black depression. Gerald came back to work a new man. The honeymoon in the Bahamas had been ecstatic, and he could hardly keep his feet on the floor while Nicky brought him up to date on what was happening in the office.

"Yes, I can handle all that." He sighed. He watched her closely. "I hear Winthrop called you."

She flushed. "Sort of."

"I hear he was drunk at the time," he added.

"How did you hear that?"

"Mary," he said. "She was snickering so hard that I could barely understand her. She said he went off into the mountains and dared anybody to bother him."

"Will he be all right?" she asked with concern she couldn't help.

"Winthrop?" he asked as if she'd taken leave of her senses.

"Well, he isn't Superman."

"Don't tell him that. He's just taken out another lease on the cape," he murmured.

"If he wants to go off in the mountains in a snit just because I wouldn't come to the wedding, that's his problem," she said shortly. "Anyway, he didn't really want me there."

"That isn't what Mary said."

"What do you want to do about this letter?" she asked, attempting to change the subject.

He started to speak, then changed his mind and

settled for work. They fell back into a pleasant routine, and Winthrop wasn't mentioned again. Nicky was sure that he was only angry because she hadn't fallen all over herself getting back to Montana. She didn't dare hope it was because he'd started to care for her.

He didn't call. He didn't write. Christmas Eve came and Nicky gave up hoping that she'd hear from him. She wished her boss a merry Christmas, sent her love to Sadie and went to Lexington for the holidays.

Her father met her at the airport in his Lincoln, with Carol beside him, and took time to have the driver run them through town so that she could see the beautiful Christmas decorations.

"It's just like old times," Nicky sighed. "I always did love the way they decorate the city."

"Me, too. You ought to see the decorations we have at the house," her father said with a twinkle in his eyes.

"And your present," Carol added, also twinkling. "It was really hard to wrap, so I gave up trying and just stuck a bow on it."

Nicole had presents for both of them in her luggage: a pipe for her father and for Carol a bottle of her favorite perfume. But she frowned, wondering what they could have gotten her that made them both look so smug.

She didn't have long to wait. They piled out at the steps and she walked toward the enormous brick house with feverish curiosity. It was decorated with boughs of holly and red velvet ribbon, and she took a minute to tell Carol how pretty it looked.

"Thanks," Carol laughed. "I did it all myself. With a little help from your dad," she acknowledged with a wink in his direction.

"Your present's in the living room," her father added as he helped Carol out of her mink coat. "We'll go see about some hot cider while you open it."

"Aren't you coming?" she asked.

Her father helped her out of her tweed coat, nodding at the pretty green silk dress that matched her eyes. "You look very nice. No, we're not coming. Not just yet. Go on, now. And merry Christmas, sweetheart."

He kissed her cheek and then went away, whispering to Carol, who glanced over her shoulder at Nicky and giggled.

Boy, it sure was some strange Christmas, she told herself as she opened the living room door. And then she stopped dead. Because her present wasn't under the huge lighted Christmas tree. It was sitting on the sofa, looking toward her furiously, with a glass of whiskey in one lean hand.

"Merry Christmas," Winthrop said curtly.

Her mouth flew open. He had a bow stuck on the pocket of his gray vested suit, and he looked hungover and pale and a little disheveled. But he was so handsome that her heart skipped wildly, and she looked into his dark eyes with soft dreams in her own.

"You've got a bow on your pocket," she said in a voice that sounded too high-pitched to be her own.

"Of course I've got a bow on my pocket. I'm your damned Christmas present. Didn't you listen to your father?" He got up, setting the glass down with enough force to shake the table, and started toward her, limping just a little. He didn't look like a present, he looked murderous. "I can't eat," he said accusingly. "I can't sleep, I can't work. I spent a week up in the mountains trying to get you out of my head, and all I got was drunk. I'm hungover, bleary-eyed and half mad with wanting you."

"Oh, I'm so glad, Winthrop," she whispered. Her heart went wild. "Because I'm half mad with wanting you, too… Oh!"

The tiny cry was lost under his devouring mouth. He had her up in his arms, barely pausing to kick the door shut before he carried her back to the sofa and stretched her out on its velvety length under the formidable weight of his body.

She protested the intimacy of his hold, but he shook his head and took her mouth under his again, glorying in its breathless response.

"No more fighting," he breathed into her parting lips. "There's no need. You're mine, now. That gives me the right to take any liberties I please with you, and this is only the beginning. You're going to marry me, lady. I've got all the necessary papers.

All we need is a blood test, and that's scheduled an hour from now. We're going to have a Christmas wedding."

Tears stung her eyes. She looked up at him through a drowsy haze, her body intimately pressed to his, her eyes wide and soft and loving. "You don't want to get married," she whispered.

"Yes, I do," he corrected her. He looked stern and solemn and very adult. But the look in his eyes was so tender that it knocked the breath out of her. "I just didn't know it until I let you walk out the door. And then I couldn't get you to come back. I thought I didn't care." He bent, brushing her mouth with exquisite gentleness. "But I can't quite make it without you, Nicky," he added huskily. "I've never been so alone. Come home where you belong. I'm too old, and too cynical, and not quite the man I used to be, but I…" He took a slow breath. "I love you, little one."

Tears ran down her face. She didn't imagine he'd ever said that in his life, and she felt the faint shudder that ran through his body when she arched hers to search blindly for his mouth.

"I love you, too," she breathed. "Deathlessly. Hopelessly. With all my heart!"

"Yes, I know, you say it quite often," he murmured, nuzzling her nose with his. "After a while, I began to enjoy hearing it. You got under my skin from the very first time I saw you, so busy at your desk. I convinced Gerald that he needed to bring you out with him," he confessed lazily, shocking her. "I didn't realize why, of course, until I had you in my arms. Then it all fell into place, and I did my best to run. But I was caught, even then. God, I've been miserable without you!"

He kissed her hungrily and she felt his hands at her hips, lifting her up into an embrace that made her shudder and gasp and go scarlet.

"This is part of loving," he whispered into her mouth. "Part of marriage. It's beautiful. Don't be afraid of it."

"I'm...not." She looked straight into his dark eyes and imagined how beautiful it would be joining with him in loving union, softness to hardness, tender rhythm on cool sheets in the darkness. And she gasped again. "Oh, my," she whispered shakily.

"Oh, my, indeed," he whispered. "Yes, sweet, just that way. Intimate and ardent...your body and mine. For all the long, achingly sweet nights of our lives. I'll be your fulfillment, and you'll be mine. And there'll never be another secret between us."

She cradled his head in her hands and pulled it gently toward her. "I'll give you children."

He smiled softly. "Yes." His head bent. "Merry Christmas, sugarplum."

She smiled back as she gave him her mouth. "You delicious Christmas present, you..."

Outside the door, two people with a bottle of champagne and four glasses were congratulating themselves on their little surprise.

"Should we knock?" Carol asked.

Dominic White pursed his lips. "Sounds a little premature." He grinned at the muffled laughter behind the door. He lifted an eyebrow. "Suppose we sample the champagne? Just to make sure it's not corked?"

"A brilliant idea," Carol agreed, linking her hand through his arm.

"I have another. How do you feel about a double wedding?"

Carol reached up and kissed his cheek. "Ecstatic," she sighed. "Can we get a blood test and a license in time?"

"Honey, I ain't a millionaire for nothin'," he drawled.

"As long as you know I'm only marrying you for your money," she reminded him with a mischievous smile.

"Mercenary hussy," he accused. And he grinned. They went into the office and closed the door. And after a minute, laughter was coming from that room, as well. Outside, the first flakes of snow began to fall. A white Christmas was well under way.

* * * * *

THE HUMBUG MAN
DIANA PALMER

One

Tate Hollister lived alone, which wasn't surprising to his nearest neighbor. He had a temper like black lightning and seemed to hate people in general, and boys in particular. Maggie Jeffries had gotten an earful about the taciturn rancher from her late father-in-law, and her son Blake was an ongoing verbal documentary on his life. If she hadn't loved the boy so much, she might have had some terrible fights with him over the incredible case of hero worship he had for Hollister. Maggie had seen their black-eyed neighbor from time to time over the years, but he avoided her the same way he tried to avoid Blake. But he didn't have a lot of success with the boy; Blake was almost ten and Hollister was his hero.

It was hard to overlook Blake's constant chatter

about the man, but Maggie loved her son, so she tried not to be annoyed. She also kept in mind that Blake had never known his father. Bob Jeffries had been a war correspondent. He'd died in Central America covering a story, leaving Maggie destitute and three months pregnant. She'd supported herself by working as a secretary to a printing corporation executive. When the company had moved its headquarters from Tennessee to Tucson, Arizona, Maggie had decided to go along with little Blake. Her parents were dead and her three brothers were scattered all over the country, but Grandpa Jeffries had still been alive. She wanted to be close enough that Blake could spend some time with him on his rural Montana ranch.

Over the years, Maggie had rapidly climbed to executive secretary and held a responsible job. Then Grandfather Jeffries had died unexpectedly in the fall and had left this small ranch to Maggie.

Blake, who'd been in military school for the past year, had jumped at the chance to go to Montana. Couldn't they, he pleaded, just for the Christmas holidays? Then Maggie could decide if she wanted to sell the place, couldn't she? After all—he played his trump card with a dejected expression that was only partially faked—they hardly saw each other anymore.

That had done it. Maggie missed her son, despite the fact that she wanted him to be independent and not tied to her apron strings. She'd asked for two weeks leave from her job, just through the Christmas and New Year's holidays. Then she'd found them a temporary secretary to take her place, and she and young Blake had left for the wilds of Montana.

And here they were. In two feet of drifting snow, on a rickety, run-down ranch facing the Bitterroot mountains, with no close neighbors except for the elusive and unfriendly Mr. Hollister, whom Blake seemed to worship from afar for God alone knew what reason.

The ranch house was more of a large cabin than a house, but it wasn't uncomfortable. It had just four rooms, two of which were bedrooms. The living room and dining room were combined, with a small kitchen in one corner and a bathroom that was definitely an afterthought. The furnishings were wood, and all of it had a definite Indian influence, from the blankets and rugs to the paintings that decorated the rough wood walls. The only difference now was the few Christmas decorations that Maggie and Blake had added, like the pine boughs around the fireplace with their red velvet bows and the cheerful red and green candles and the artificial holly on the coffee table.

Maggie found the idle pace of life in Montana familiar. It brought back memories of her childhood spent in the mountains of southern Tennessee, so close to the Georgia line that it had once been disputed border territory. She'd lived in the backwoods with her parents and her brothers, and it had been a satisfying life until Bob had passed through covering a story and had wooed Maggie out of her mountains and into Memphis and a small apartment.

Sometimes that part of her life seemed like a long-ago dream. If it hadn't been for the photos, she would hardly remember what Bob looked like, although she'd loved him desperately at the age of eighteen. Now she was twenty-eight, and there were faint threads of silver in her wavy, dark brown hair. She was tall and slender as a willow, but her eyes had a haunted look these days. She was restless lately, and sometimes she felt like she was searching—but she didn't know for what.

"It's fun here." Blake was grinning as he stared out the window at the snow. "I don't miss prickly pear cactus and creosote and roadrunners and dry washes, you bet."

"At least in southern Arizona we didn't have all that snow, or haven't you glanced out the window lately?" she asked, smiling, and her eyes crinkled at the corners. She had an elfin face, very mischievous, and an elegant carriage, which had come from her mother's insistence on proper posture. Those contradictions, added to the faint traces of her southern mountain drawl, made her something of an enigma. She did attract men occasionally, but her rigid Scotch-Irish upbringing didn't allow for a casual outlook on life, and most of the city men she ran across were as easygoing about sex as they were about letting a woman buy them a meal. It was a kind of life that suited many, but Maggie had too many hang-ups. So she was still single.

She wondered sometimes if Blake was being deprived of male companionship solely because of her attitudes. It bothered her, but she didn't want to change.

"Snow is awesome," he sighed, using a word that he used to denote only the best things in his life. Cherry pie was awesome. So was baseball, if the Atlanta Braves were playing, and football if the Dallas Cowboys were.

She smiled at his dark head, so like her own. He had her slender build, too, but he had his father's green eyes. Bob had been a handsome man. Handsome and far too brave for his own good. Dead at twenty-seven, she sighed, and for what?

She folded her arms across her chest, cozy in the oversize red flannel shirt that she wore over well-broken-in jeans. "It's freezing, that's what it is," she informed her offspring. "And it isn't awesome; it's irritating. Apparently, the electric generator goes out every other day, and the only man who can fix it stays drunk."

"That cowboy seems to know how," Blake said hesitantly.

Maggie agreed reluctantly. "I know. Things were running great until our foreman asked for time off to spend Christmas with his wife's family in Pennsylvania. That leaves me in charge, and what do I know about running a ranch?" she moaned. "I grew up on a small farm, but I don't know beans about how to manage this kind of place, and the men realize it. I suppose they don't have any confidence in working for a secretary, even just temporarily."

"Well, there's always Mr. Hollister," Blake said with pursed lips and a wicked grin.

She glared at him. "Mr. Hollister hates me. He hates you, too, in fact, but you don't seem to let that stand in the way of your admiration for the man." She threw up her hands, off on her favorite subject again. "For heaven's sake, he's a cross between a bear and a moose! He never comes off his mountain except when he wants to cuss somebody out or raise hell!"

"He's lonely," Blake pointed out. "He lives all by himself. It's hard going, I'll bet, and he has to eat his own cooking." He sat up enthusiastically, his thick hair over his brow. "Grandpa said he once knew a man who quit working for Mr. Hollister just because the cook got sick and Mr. Hollister had to feed the men."

Maggie glanced at her son with a wicked gleam in her eyes. "He probably fed them some of his razor blades," she murmured.

"Oh, shame on you," Blake said with a chuckle. "How did I wind up with a mother like this?" he asked the ceiling.

"Well, they ran out of ugly, mean ones, and here I was," Maggie sighed, striking a pose.

Blake laughed harder. He would have agreed with her if he could have stopped laughing. He thought she was the best mom in the whole world, even if she did have this annoying hang-up about his beloved Mr. Hollister. "But really, Mom, you're going to have to do something about the cattle and the men pretty quick," he finally said, sounding grown-up and almost knowledgeable. "The cattle are straying real bad. I saw some down on Mr. Hollister's place just this morning."

She drew in a breath. "Why didn't you say so? For God's sake, don't just sit there. Get some barbed wire, and I'll send for a few land mines…." She shuddered.

"He's a nice man. You just don't understand him," Blake said.

She lifted her eyebrows. "Are we talking about the same Mr. Hollister? The one who looks like a hat and mustache sitting on a rock?" she asked, turning away from Blake's amused grin. "I'll bet if he ever smiled, his face would break."

"Grandpa liked him," he reminded her. "I do, too. You just don't know him, that's all. He's a real jake guy."

"I don't want to know him. That's why I spent every minute I came up here hiding out from him. And I will never learn to understand the language you speak," she informed him. "It goes from mum-

ble to street jive to unintelligible—" A loud knock
at the door stopped her in midsentence. "Maybe it's
the man who can fix the generator," she said hopefully and went to open the heavy oak door.

A rush of cold air hit her in the face, temporarily blinding her. Montana in winter was uncomfortable, even for natives. The windchill factor was
nearly unbearable, and the snow never seemed to
stop. This small ranch that she'd inherited from
her father-in-law was located between the Bitterroot mountain range on the west and the Pryor
mountains on the east, with the Wyoming border
to the south. Tate Hollister's much larger ranch
and enormous house were on her north border and
only about a quarter of a mile from the small frame
house she shared with Blake.

She wasn't really surprised to find Tate Hollister on her doorstep when she got her eyes cleared
of snowflakes. He was tall already, but he seemed
to have grown two feet since Maggie last saw him.
He glared down at her from black eyes in a thin-
lipped, deeply tanned face, which was all hard lines
and sharp angles. He looked to be in his late thir-
ties, and he was as wild a man as Maggie had ever
seen. In his battered black ranch hat and sheepskin
jacket, worn jeans and black boots, he looked like
an outlaw. He needed a shave and his mustache
needed trimming. His thick, shaggy hair was disheveled. Just the sight of him was enough to in-
timidate most men, much less Maggie.

"Yes?" she asked with forced pleasantness, her head cocked warily as he removed his gloves and slapped them into his palm.

"Ten head of your cattle are grazing on my winter feed supply," he said without preamble. "What are you going to do about it?"

"Award them the Croix de Guerre for bravery above and beyond the call of duty," she answered without hesitation.

He stared at her as if he wasn't quite certain that he'd heard her. His head tilted slightly and his dark eyes narrowed, while Blake struggled with suppressed laughter. "I don't think you understand the situation," he tried again. "If you don't get them off my land and out of my hay, I'm going to throw down on them."

"That is an old Western expression," Maggie explained to Blake. "It means he's going to shoot them." She looked back at Tate Hollister. "I hope you plan to give them a sporting chance. They are, after all, unarmed." She smiled vacantly.

Hollister's dark eyes were shadowed with surprise, and his mustache actually twitched, but there was no smile on his lips. "Mrs. Jeffries, this isn't a laughing matter."

"Yes, sir." She curtsied. "What would you like me to do about the cattle?"

He looked as confused as a man could. He glanced at Blake, glowering at the boy's grin, which was quickly erased.

"Oh, for God's sake, where's Jack Randall?" he demanded, his deep voice like a bass fiddle with the wind howling outside the door.

She stared at him. "Jack who?"

"Your foreman, lady!"

She sighed. "Oh, him. He left two days before we got here."

"Left!"

She put a hand to her ear. "Please. I have sensitive ears. Yes, he left. He took his wife back east to visit her people for Christmas."

"Christmas!" he muttered, and Maggie stared at him wide-eyed, waiting for him to come out with a hearty "Bah, Humbug." The sentiment was in his expression, even if he didn't say the words, and she had to stifle a giggle. That made him scowl even more. "Are you really this boy's mother?"

Her eyebrows arched. Just because they'd never spoken to each other before was no reason for him to pretend he didn't know who she was. He'd at least seen her a time or two. "Of course," she said.

"I found her under a cabbage leaf," Blake volunteered with twinkling green eyes.

Hollister wasn't amused and after a moment, returned to the subject. "What about the other men?" he asked.

"They're out doing God knows what." She sighed. "We've only been here three days and I can't get one of them to stand still long enough to listen to anything I say. And the man who fixes the electrical generator is—" she hesitated, eyeing Hollister "—indisposed."

"He's out in the bunkhouse drunk," Blake countered, grinning when she glared at him. "Well, he is. I looked in the window."

"Honest to God, you'll die up here in a week," Hollister muttered, glaring at both of them. "City greenhorns! Why in hell didn't you stay in New Mexico where you belong?"

"Arizona," Maggie corrected. "And we don't really belong there. Blake and I moved there from Tennessee."

"Southerners," Hollister grumbled. "Easterners."

She hated that cold, arrogant black stare. She drew herself up to her full height and still had to tilt her head back to look at him. He made her home state sound like the worst kind of insult. Maggie lifted her chin, and her gray eyes sparkled like flint chips. "Well, let me tell you, Mr. Hollister, if I was back home, I'd have plenty of willing help," she replied. "These men seem to think they're being paid by the tooth fairy, and the only mechanic I've got can't walk unless he's carrying a bottle of beer!"

He didn't even flick an eyelash. "No cowboy in his right mind is going to take orders from a city woman with no savvy about ranching. As for the generator, I can fix that."

He antagonized her as no man in her life ever had. She wanted to tell him what he could do with his offer. Damned bossy so-and-so...!

"Well?" he asked, glaring. "I can't work and shine a light all at once. Get me a flashlight, boy."

Blake didn't hesitate. "Yes, sir!" he said smartly and rushed off to look for one.

"Don't order my son around," Maggie said quietly. "I don't like other people telling him what to do."

"If you didn't, you wouldn't have jailed him in a military school," he returned coldly, shocking her because she hadn't realized he knew so much about Blake.

She caught her breath, but before she could say anything, Blake was back with the flashlight. "I'll come and hold it for you," he offered.

"Your mother can do that," he replied with an arrogant smile. "Or don't you know how?"

Her gray eyes flashed, and it was a good thing she didn't see the expression of unholy glee on Blake's face as all his secret plans for bringing these two together seemed to be coming true.

"I'm an executive secretary for a printing corporation," she informed him with blatant hostility. "I can do a lot more than hold a light."

"Oh, I can see how valuable you'd be in an emergency, with all that specialized knowledge," he agreed and turned to open the door. "Get a coat on."

She absolutely gasped. In all her life, she'd never run into anybody like him. He threw out orders like a drill sergeant. And it didn't help that Blake was sitting there with a book on his lap, looking the picture of a studious, polite boy. She stuck out her tongue at him as she put on her leather jacket, and he grinned like a Cheshire cat.

"I'll get you for this," she mouthed at him and left him giggling on the sofa.

She followed the big man around the house, because he hadn't even bothered to wait for her to trudge through the snow with him. He had the flashlight in one enormous gloved hand. He paused by the housing that protected the generator, then thrust the flashlight at her while he uncovered the apparatus and then studied it silently.

"Hold the light on the damned thing, if you please," he shot at Maggie. "I can't see in the dark."

"My God." She whistled. "And you're actually admitting it?"

He muttered something she was glad she couldn't understand.

She grinned as she leveled the flashlight. Odd how refreshing it was to have a man actively dislike her. Most men seemed to feel obliged to chase her. This one wouldn't chase anybody, she mused. He wasn't a marrying man or a particularly romantic one, and it was really fun to antagonize him. She'd never tried to deliberately upset a man before, but it was wildly exhilarating. She felt alive in a way she hadn't for over ten years. Strange, really, since Hollister was the last man in the world she could feel an attraction for.

Hollister paused and scowled down at the generator. "This damned thing came over with the Ark," he muttered. "I don't understand why your father-in-law didn't replace it."

"He probably liked eating," she remarked, pulling her stocking cap over her ears. Snow was falling again. "He wasn't a wealthy man."

"Could have been," he murmured as he stripped off his gloves to reveal huge but elegant hands, which were long-fingered and darkly tanned—capable hands, with callused ridges on the finger pads. "But he kept putting off things."

"Maybe he thought money would corrupt him," she suggested.

His big shoulders shrugged. "It can." He caught her hand that was holding the light and positioned it where he wanted the beam with no regard for her posture. His hand was warm over her own, and curious little tingles went down her spine until he released his brief hold. "Keep it there," he said absently, scowling under the brim of his hat. "Damn. I hope I can splice that wire...."

He pulled out a pocketknife while Maggie watched with fascination. He was a fixer. Most men were, but this one did it with such style. She studied his profile in the faint radiance of the flashlight, fascinated with its hardness, the uncompromising nature it revealed.

He seemed to feel her intent scrutiny because his head turned. His black eyes caught hers and

THE HUMBUG MAN 259

held them, penetrating, questioning. "Well?" he asked curtly.

"You have an interesting hairline," she improvised. Her voice sounded odd. Probably because lightning was running down her spine from that intent black stare.

He lifted a shaggy eyebrow as if he thought she might need immediate mental counseling. "That's a new one."

"Thanks," she said with a grin. "I thought it up all by myself, too."

He tilted his hat back as he worked with the generator. "What the hell are you and the boy doing up here by yourselves?" he asked suddenly.

It was none of his business, and she almost said so. But she stopped herself in time—it wouldn't do to antagonize a man when he was that close to fixing her generator.

"It's almost Christmas. Blake wanted to spend some time with me," she said finally. "He doesn't really like military school, and I think he's out to convince me that I can run a ranch in the wilds of Montana while he sits on a fence and hero-worships you."

He looked at her with wide, disbelieving eyes. "I beg your pardon?"

"Sorry. It slipped out." She leaned against the wall, holding the light steady.

But he wasn't moving. His dark eyes were fixed on her face. "I said: I beg your pardon, lady."

How in the world could a man make an insult of the word *lady?* she wondered absently. She shifted. "Blake likes you."

"Well, I'm not much on boys," he returned shortly. "Or city women. Or even neighbors. I live alone and I like my privacy. I don't intend having it invaded by your son."

"That's plain enough," she returned, feeling her temper start to rise. "Now let me tell you something. I don't like men in general and you in particular, and what I think of your type of man would fill a book! As for my son, he's only nine years old and he never knew his father. His grandfather is the only male besides you that he's ever spent any time around. And Papa Jeffries was kind and gentle and loving—the exact opposite of you. Blake doesn't know what a man is, so you'll have to forgive his attachment to you!"

His left eye had narrowed and his jaw was clenched. "You are playing one dangerous game, lady," he said shortly.

"I'm so sorry if I've offended you, Mr. Hollister," she replied coolly. "And I promise you Blake won't be allowed within a mile of you for the entire two weeks we're in residence."

"You won't last two weeks if you don't get this outfit into shape," he said shortly as he looped a wire and stayed it with a screw. "There. Let's try it now."

He replaced the cover and started the generator. Maggie had to concede that Hollister was good with his hands. He was lucky, she thought venomously, that he had something to make up for his lack of looks.

Hollister slid his gloves back on and didn't glance at her. She brought back painful memories, she and her son. It had been six years, but he still grieved for his own family. He didn't want or need complications, but this woman could get under his skin. And that irritated him. She opened his wounds and made them bleed. The boy rubbed salt in them.

Blake opened the door and let them back in. "The heater's running!" He grinned up at the big, unsmiling man. "Thanks, Mr. Hollister. We'd have frozen to death but for you."

Hollister's black eyes went over that boyish face with something less than affection. The boy looked like a boy—all uncombed hair and eyes that sparkled with mischief. Just like his mother. The pair of them were going to give him problems. He could feel it in his bones. He missed the old man, because Jeffries had never bothered him. But Blake had, at every opportunity. When he'd come to visit Jeffries for the summer, Tate couldn't walk for bumping into him. It had been irritating at first, and then frankly painful. He'd been glad when the boy left at the end of summer and went back to school. Now here he was back again, and Hollister was feeling the same old stabs of memory, only they were worse. Because now she was here, too, and he'd been a hell of a long time without a woman. She aroused sensations that he'd forgotten he could feel, and he hated them. Damn it, he hated the world…!

Maggie glanced at him, surprised by his cold reaction to Blake's gratitude. He was a cold man, though, she thought as she got out of her cap and jacket and boots. Thank God he wasn't going to be around very much.

"Yes, thank you for fixing the generator," Maggie agreed. "I suppose you need to get home, so I won't offer to make coffee…."

She didn't want to, she meant. Oddly enough, that irritated Hollister. He didn't like the way she reacted to him. He knew he wasn't pretty, for God's sake, but did she have to make it so obvious that she found him ugly?

"Those cattle have got to be moved. I'll find your men and set them to it."

"Thank you," she said, deciding against arguing because it would only keep him here longer, and she didn't want that.

"Wouldn't you like a cup of coffee?" Blake invited, while Maggie felt herself choking. *No, Blake,* she moaned inwardly.

Hollister saw that look in her eyes and just for the hell of it, he said yes.

Maggie forced a smile to her lips. *Be generous,* she told herself. *He fixed the generator. You won't freeze. The least you can do is give the poor cold man a cup of hot coffee*. If only she could have managed to get him in the pot with it….

"What do you take in your coffee, Mr. Hollister?" she asked with forced sweetness.

He took off his hat, revealing his thick black hair. Snow flaked from the hat as he placed it on the hat rack and shed his thick coat. Under it he was wearing a red flannel plaid shirt and as near as she could tell, no undershirt. The flannel was unbuttoned halfway down his brawny dark chest, and it had the thickest covering of hair she'd ever seen on a man.

She stared at him. She couldn't help it. Despite her very brief marriage, she knew almost nothing about men. Bob had been as inexperienced as she, and as shy, so she'd learned little during those few fumbling encounters in the dark. But Hollister had a savage masculinity, an untamed look that made her blood run crazy and her pulse do unexpected things. She didn't even like him, but he had a dangerously sensual appeal. She forced her eyes back to the white mugs she was pouring coffee into.

"I take my coffee black, Mrs. Jeffries," Hollister said quietly.

She'd known that somehow before she'd posed the question. He looked that kind of man. No frills, no embellishments. She'd have bet that he drank his whiskey straight and never put catsup on his meat. She looked up as he came close to take the cup, smelling of wind and fir trees and leather.

"I'll bet you never put catsup on a steak," she said without thinking.

He searched her eyes curiously. "As a matter of fact, I don't," he agreed. His heavy brows moved together faintly. "What brought that on?"

She dropped her eyes to her coffee. "I don't know." She lifted it, even though it was hot. Involuntarily her gaze went to Hollister's hands. They fascinated her, now that she knew how capable they were. They were huge. Lean. Darkly tanned, with thick hair on the wrists and hard muscle in the long fingers. Flat nails, very clean. She could imagine those hands doing anything that was necessary on a ranch, from fixing generators to helping a calf be born.

"Do you still have that big Aberdeen Angus bull, Mr. Hollister?" Blake asked. He'd joined them at the table and was sipping a cola from a can he'd gotten out of the refrigerator.

Hollister hated having the boy ask him questions. But the youngster had a natural feel for ranching, and he remembered vividly the ease with which Blake had helped old man Jeffries deliver a calf and doctor one of the bulls. "I've still got him," he replied tersely. He glanced at Blake, his eyes suddenly curious, losing their sharp edge as he realized that the boy was really interested and not just asking inane questions. "And I've bought a new Hereford crossbreed bull as well. I'm doing a three-one cross this next year. Angus to Beefmaster, Beefmaster to Hereford, and back to Angus again."

"Angus are easy calvers," Blake said knowledgeably. "And Herefords are hardy. And Beefmasters are good choice grade beef."

"With good weight gains ratios," Hollister agreed. The boy had been putting in some study to learn all that. He was impressed despite himself. "I had to sell my Brangus bulls. After two years of inbreeding, you can create some problems for yourself if you don't introduce some new blood into your herd."

"That's a fact," Blake said, sipping his cola.

Maggie, lost, glared at both of them. Hollister happened to glance her way and lifted an eyebrow. He came as close to smiling then as he had in six long years. "Something bothering you, Mrs. Jeffries?" he asked in his deep, slow tone.

"She doesn't know a lot about cattle," Blake said. "But she's a whiz at math and accounts payable and organizing things. She's the top secretary at Skyline Printing Services and a computer expert."

Maggie shifted restlessly. "Don't brag about me that way," she told her son. "I only learned accounting to get out of typesetting. And I learned computer programming to get out of accounting."

"Most women aren't good at math." Hollister's dark eyes narrowed in his hard face. "My mother could barely count hens."

"It was always my best subject in school," Maggie replied. "My dad was a farmer. He kept a tally book, and I was his payroll clerk. He taught me to add columns of figures in my head."

"Her parents are dead now," Blake volunteered. "I have three uncles, but they're spread all over the country and I never see them."

"A farmer?" Hollister persisted. "What kind of livestock did he have?"

"Cattle and hogs," she answered. "He had some high pastures, too. Right on the side of the hills, but he did very well. We had Jersey cows and a few Holsteins."

The tall man finished his coffee. "But you don't know how to breed cattle?"

"A handful of cows, mostly milk cows, doesn't qualify anyone to handle several hundred head of beef cattle," she reminded him. "It's a totally different proposition. And I was only eighteen when I married Blake's father and left the country for the city. I've forgotten most of what little I knew about the management of it."

Hollister's big hands toyed with the empty cup. "I went to school with Bob Jeffries," he said. "He was a grade behind me."

She sat very still. "He died in Central America before Blake was born. We'd been married less than six months." She sighed. "It seems like a dream sometimes. Except for the talking proof sitting there trying to look invisible while he drinks his soda," she added with a dry grin at Blake.

Blake just grinned back, but he was listening.

"Bob loved danger," Maggie reminisced, aware of Hollister's narrow gaze on her face. "He fed on adrenaline. Just after we were married he tried to give it up." She smiled sadly. "It didn't work out. For him it was like trying not to breathe."

"I never knew him," Blake sighed. He looked up at Hollister. "You aren't married, are you, Mr. Hollister?"

Hollister stared into the empty coffee cup. "I was." He put the cup down on the table and turned. "Thanks for the coffee. I'll round up your hands and point them in the right direction." He put on his coat and cocked his hat over one eye, glancing back at Blake and his mother without smiling. "If I were you, I'd stay inside until this snow lets up. And I'll have that fence fixed before I let your men come home."

"Thanks for fixing the generator," she said, alternately relieved and irritated by his shouldering of her own problems.

He opened the door. "No problem. Good night."

He was gone in a whirl of wind and snowflakes, and Maggie stared after him feeling oddly empty and alone. How strange to feel that way about a man she disliked.

"He must be divorced," Maggie said absently.

Blake joined her in the kitchen, draining his can of soft drink. "No, he's a widower," he told her. "Grandpa said his whole family was killed in an accident in the Rockies. Mr. Hollister was driving. His wife and son died, and he didn't." He shrugged, oblivious to the shock and horror on his mother's soft face. "Grandpa said that was why he lived like he does, alone and away from everybody. That he was punishing himself because he didn't die, too. Too bad. He sure is a nice man."

He glanced at his mother and did a double take at the look on her face. She actually looked interested. And that made him smile, but he was careful not to let her see him doing it.

Two

❄❄❄❄❄

With the electrical generator fixed and the snow diminishing, thank God, Maggie spent a day going over the ranch's financial statement. Blake busied himself with a new computer game while listening to Christmas music on a local country and western radio station. She wondered how Grandfather Jeffries had ever made a go of ranching in the first place, having spent so much on adding new land to his ranch when interest rates were sky-high and spending so little on herd improvement.

What little she'd gleaned from Hollister about crossbreeding had piqued her curiosity. She wondered if her father-in-law had been trying that angle, or if he'd just raised beef without worrying about bloodlines or grades at auction.

The really big problem, though, wasn't what

the ranch's past had been. It was what its future was going to be. She hated to sell it. There was something majestic and real about rural Montana. About mountains that touched heaven and trees almost that tall. There was space here, not unlike the Arizona she'd come to love, and there were basic values. Blake would love staying on the ranch, having cattle to raise, and he'd have a heritage to inherit. But how was she going to keep it solvent all by herself? As she'd admitted, she knew nothing about the daily routine of ranching, even about how to breed cattle. The worst thing in the world would be to tackle it without expertise. She'd fall flat on her face and lose everything, and where would she be then?

Blake, noting the lines of worry on her oval face, saved the game he'd been playing and, carefully removing the disks first, cut off the computer. He lowered the volume on the radio and turned to face her.

"Something's wrong, isn't it?" he asked.

She smiled. "I'm no rancher," she sighed. "That about sizes it up. This place needs a cattleman, not a vacationing secretary."

"There's always—"

"Mr. Hollister," she bit off with a glittering stare in his direction. "Don't you know any other words?"

Blake grinned, not at all chastened. "His first name is Tate."

She rolled her eyes toward the ceiling and went back to the figures. "I'll never be able to make it work."

"We have a great foreman," Blake said sensibly. "And that's mainly all we need."

"You make it sound so easy," she replied and smiled wearily at him. Probably at his age everything was easy. It was only when people grew up that life got so complicated. "Well, I'll think about it," she promised.

But Blake went to bed that night frowning because she'd had that look on her face. The one that said: I'm quitting while I'm ahead. And at all costs, he couldn't possibly let her out of these mountains before he got a good chance to bring her and Mr. Hollister together. They were both alone, about the right age, and he doted on them. Why wouldn't it work? He turned off his light so his mother would think he was sleeping, and before he dropped off to sleep he had the answer.

Maggie made pancakes the next morning, and Blake ate two helpings before he got up from the table, put on his boots and thick parka and announced that he was going to hike down the ridge to the river and see if it was frozen.

"You be careful," she cautioned as he went out, reminding herself that young boys had to have some independence and that she couldn't keep him indoors for the rest of his life.

"Sure I will," he promised. He chuckled. "See

you in a couple of hours. I've got my watch on, so I'll know when I'm due back, okay?"

She smiled gently. "Okay."

But two hours passed, joined by two more, and still he didn't return. Maggie was frantic. She tried searching, but she didn't have any idea how to find which way he'd gone. She didn't trust the men, either. Not with Blake's life. She grimaced and gritted her teeth and tried to stay calm. There was only one person in the world she did trust to find Blake. In a fever of impatience, she got into the four-wheel-drive Bronco that Blake had talked her into buying in the summer and went quickly down the road to the Hollister place.

The Hollister house was a big rugged retreat, with a varnished wood exterior, all angles and glass. Every possible view had its own window, and judging by the number and size of the chimneys, it must have as many fireplaces. Maggie had never set foot inside it, but she'd seen it often enough from the road.

She jumped out of the Bronco, tugging her leather jacket closer against the biting wind. The windchill in these parts was formidable, even in December.

The front porch was long and rambling, with plenty of chairs, but she didn't stop to admire the view. She knocked frantically at the front door and only then wondered what she was going to do if he wasn't home. What if he was gone for the day, or out on business, or...

The door opened. Tate Hollister eyed her over a cup of steaming coffee, his blue-checked flannel shirt the only bright and welcoming thing about him as he stared down at her.

"I don't recall inviting you to lunch," he said.

She glared at him. "Blake's missing," she said hesitantly. Now that she was here, it was even harder than she'd imagined. He did look like stone, mustache and all.

"Don't look at me," he said imperturbably. "I don't have him."

"He said he'd be gone two hours." She gnawed her lower lip. "He went down to the ridge to see if the river was frozen. That was four hours ago, and it's snowing again." Her soft gray eyes looked up at him helplessly. "I can't even find tracks."

"He's playing a prank," he told her easily. "When he's had enough, he'll come home."

"He's not," she argued. "Blake is like me. If he says he'll do something, he'll do it. He doesn't play pranks."

"You don't know much about boys, do you?" he mused.

She was freezing, and his attitude wasn't warming her at all. "No, I guess I don't," she admitted flatly. "I've been too concerned with trying to support us to have much free time to learn, either, and Blake is a handful sometimes."

His dark eyes went slowly over her face, as if he hadn't really looked at it before. Around them, the wind blew and snow peppered the porch, but he didn't seem to notice.

"He might be hurt," she said with involuntary softness. "I'm afraid."

He pursed his lips, the mustache twitching. "It's a prank," he repeated. "But I'll come. You can wait inside if you like, while I get my coat."

She didn't understand why, but she didn't want to go in that house. She thought suddenly of the wife and child he'd lost, and her feet froze to the porch. It would be like trespassing.

"No," she hesitated. "I'll...I'll just wait out here, thanks."

He frowned slightly, puzzled, but he shrugged and went off after his coat.

She was standing by the Bronco when he came out, his torso and lean hips covered by the thick shepherd's coat, his thick black hair under the wide brim of his black Stetson and what looked like a rifle in one hand. At closer inspection, it was, and she frowned.

"You can drive if you like..." she began, but he was going the other way. "Where are you going?" she called, running to keep up with him as he went toward the stables down the road from the house.

"You're crazy if you think I'm taking a vehicle, even with four-wheel drive, down that ravine," he said easily. "I'm going out on horseback."

"With a rifle? What are you going to do with it?"

He spared her an impatient glance. "Oh, for God's sake, woman, I'm not going to shoot the boy."

"I didn't say so." She faltered.

He made a sound that refuted that and kept walking while she ran along behind him.

"You can wait in the house or go home," he said. He opened the stable door, and she saw a wide alley filled with wood chips with bright, clean stalls on either side, some of which housed horses.

"He's my son. I want to come, too."

He turned, staring at her. "Can you ride?"

"Of course I can ride," she said irritably.

"Well, well. You aren't quite the lily I thought you were," he mused as he went to the tack room.

And what did that mean? she wondered, but anxiety kept her quiet. He saddled a quiet little chestnut mare for her and a huge buckskin gelding for himself. Snow was falling steadily as they stood outside the stable.

"Molly won't toss you, but she has a tendency to scrape people off against tree trunks, so keep your eyes open," he said as he held the mare for her to mount.

She swung easily into the saddle, sitting tall, the reins held lightly in her hands.

He looked up. His dark eyes approved her excellent posture and he smiled. It was the first time she recalled ever seeing him smile, and his face didn't even break.

"No hat," he said then and went back to the tack room again, returning with a beat-up old Stetson, which came down to her ears but did keep the snow off. "Let's go." He swung into his own saddle and took the lead. "Keep in my tracks," he said over his shoulder. "And don't stray off."

"Yes, sir, Mr. Hollister," she muttered under her breath.

"What was that?"

She averted her eyes from that black stare. "Not a thing."

There might have only been the two of them in the world as they rode out through the tall lodge-pole pines and aspens, where the snow was less thick, and Maggie thought irrelevantly that this was the best way to see Montana. Not in a car, or on foot. But on the back of a horse, with leather creaking as they rode, and the smell of the fresh mountain air and the bite of the wind and snow on her face. If she hadn't been so worried about Blake, she might have even been able to appreciate it.

She was still tense, but somehow she knew that whatever was wrong, Hollister would be able to handle it. She glanced at him curiously, wondering at the sense of security she felt with him, even in an emergency like this one. Which brought her mind back to Blake and to the hundred things that might have happened to him, the least of which was enough to make her nauseous. He was all she had…!

"I said," Hollister repeated curtly, "which way did he go when he left the house?"

She looked up, to see her own cabin just before them. She had to blink twice to get her mind back on track. "Sorry." She bit her lower lip. "He went there." She nodded toward the back of the cabin, down the long hill behind.

He spared her an irritated glance before he urged his mount forward, so much at home in the saddle that he seemed part of the big buckskin. Halfway down the ridge, he held up his hand and swung down, kneeling in the snow to look. He went on foot from there, stopping to examine limbs, his eyes keen and quick as they darted around the mountainous terrain of the forest.

"He went through there," he murmured, his eyes narrowed as he studied the downward slope. His head went up, and he listened. Maggie heard it, too—a voice.

"Blake!" Hollister's deep tones cut through the wind, carrying, bellowing.

"Hellllp!"

The cry was definitely Blake's, and there was an odd note of fear in it. Maggie almost cried out herself, feeling that piercing cry to her soul.

Hollister didn't spare Maggie a glance. He whipped his rifle out of the sheath on his saddle and swung back up onto the horse, wheeling the animal in the direction of the shout.

Maggie urged her mount after him, terrified. Hollister wasn't a hysterical man. If he reacted that way, there was a reason. But even as she was thinking it, she heard the sound, and it chilled her to the bone. A sob caught in her throat. She knew the howl of coyotes, but this sound was deeper, richer, more threatening. It was the howl of a wolf...

Hollister urged his mount down the ridge at a clip Maggie did her best to follow, frustrated that the snow made it such an ordeal to get to Blake.

With her heart hammering in her throat, blind fear choking her, she held on to the reins and felt her heartbeat shaking her as she heard Blake's shrill voice.

Ahead of her, Hollister made his way quickly through another thick stand of aspens, through the thick underbrush, and Maggie, right on the heels of his mount, caught a horrifying glimpse of a small dark head far below, near the ribbon of stream that cut through the snow. Blake! And only a few yards away, stalking, a big silver wolf.

Maggie felt her heart stop. Her son. Her boy! She saw Hollister swing out of the saddle, heard his voice.

"Don't move!" he yelled at Blake and sighted down the rifle barrel with an economy of motion that was as menacing as the wolf itself.

There was a sudden report, and then another

and another, the crack of rifle fire echoing with horrible violence down the ridge and up the next slope, at odds with the pastoral beauty and peace it disturbed.

"Blake!" Maggie screamed, tears sliding down her cheeks as she swung out of the saddle. There was smoke from the rifle in Hollister's hands, but even before it cleared, he was down that slope, his big frame absorbing the shock of his steps with grace and ease. Maggie was right behind him.

"Mr. Hollister! Mom!" Blake cried, his voice excited and high-pitched with pain.

Through her tears, Maggie could see the unnatural angle that Blake's left leg was lying at. Broken for sure, she thought sickly, and thanked God for Tate Hollister.

The man knelt quickly beside the boy, the rifle cast aside as he felt the lower leg, and Blake winced. Maggie got on Blake's other side, hugging him, shaking with reaction.

"Broken," Hollister murmured. "A simple fracture, thank God, not a compound one. What happened?"

"Lost my footing." Blake tried to grin. "I came out…to check the river. Gosh, Mr. Hollister, that wolf sure was a beaut. I guess that's why you didn't kill him, huh?"

"Timber wolves are damned near extinct," Hollister said as he got up and broke two limbs off a tree. "If he hadn't turned tail, I wouldn't have had a choice, but I flushed him. I hate killing when I don't have to. Maggie, I need some cloth to make a splint," he said as he pulled a folded blanket from its position just behind the saddle on his horse. He wrapped the limbs to make a cradle and then very carefully drew the cradle under Blake's leg.

It was the first time he'd ever called her by name, and Maggie couldn't understand why her heart ran wild. She let go of Blake long enough to hand him the wool scarf around her neck.

"Will this do?" she asked in a quivering tone, handing the scarf to him while Blake gripped her hand tightly and tried to reassure her that he was all right.

"Hi, guy," she said and spoiled her stiff upper lip by bursting into tears.

"Aw, cut it out, Mom," Blake muttered. "It's just a broken leg."

"Excuse me," she said, trying to laugh. "You know how mothers are."

Hollister glanced at her, but he didn't say anything. He whipped out his pocketknife and made a neat slit right down Blake's boot so that the whole thing was laid bare and easily removed. Then he positioned the sticks he'd broken on either side of Blake's leg and put his wool bandanna next to Maggie's. "Okay," he told Blake quietly. "This is going to be rough. I have to straighten that leg and splint it, and it's going to hurt like hell. Want something to bite on?"

"Oh, but you can't—" Maggie was already pro-testing.

"Shut up," he told her, his eyes black and steady and challenging.

She did, instantly, without an argument, because that hard glare was like a dash of cold water.

"I'll be okay," Blake said through his teeth, nod-ding. He clenched his hands at his sides and propped himself on them. "Go ahead."

Maggie felt tears spurt from her eyes as Hollister worked, his hands deft and sure. Blake cried out just once and almost blacked out when Hollister pulled the leg straight, but the boy never let out another sound, even while the makeshift splint was put on and tied in place. But his face was as white as plas-ter when Hollister finished.

"Okay?" Hollister asked, and his voice was dif-ferent. Gentle. Deeper. He smiled at the boy.

Blake beamed. He managed a grin because it was like a turning point in his relationship with the taciturn rancher. "Okay," he agreed.

"Here." Hollister handed his rifle to Maggie. "Wait a minute. Let me put the safety on." He did that and handed it back. "Don't shoot yourself in the foot," he cautioned.

She glared at him. "I know which end to point, thanks."

Tate didn't smile, but his dark eyes twinkled. He lifted Blake very carefully, but Blake's breath sucked in at the pain the movement caused. "This is doing it the hard way, I know," he told Blake as he carried him to the buckskin, "but it can't be helped. Back in the old days, the Plains Indians made a travois and pulled injured warriors back to camp on it."

"A...travois?"

"That's right." Hollister propped Blake on the saddle while he swung into it behind him and turned him over his knees, wonderfully gentle even though Maggie could see the pain in Blake's young face. "I'll tell you about it on the way back," he said, nodding to Maggie who'd managed to get the rifle back into Hollister's saddle horn before she'd mounted the mare.

She let Hollister take the lead, wondering at his skill as a woodsman as he led them right back up to the cabin with no fuss or side trips, talking softly to Blake the whole time, his deep voice steady and comforting. It dawned on her then that he wasn't just making conversation. He was keeping Blake calm so that he didn't go into shock.

She wondered what she would have done if Tate hadn't been around. She'd have done her best, but would it have been good enough? Just the thought of that wolf made her blood run cold. But the man she'd imagined Hollister to be would have killed the wolf without a second thought. Instead, he'd managed to run it away because he didn't like to kill things unless he had to. Her gray eyes watched his tall form quietly, curiously, and new feelings began to bud inside her.

"Keep him warm," he told Maggie after they'd gotten back to the cabin and he'd put Blake carefully on the sofa. "A couple of aspirin wouldn't come amiss until we can get him into Deer Lodge to the doctor. Keep him talking. It will help him fight off shock. I'll take the horses home and bring the Bronco back as quick as I can. You left the keys in it, right?"

She nodded and started to speak, but he was gone before she could get her mouth open.

"Isn't he something?" Blake sighed through his pain.

"He is that," Maggie agreed. She brushed back his dark hair. "Are you going to make it?"

"Sure," he said, grinning. "I'm tough."

"I guess you are, at that. I'll get those aspirin."

By the time Hollister got back, Blake was in a little less pain, although he was still groaning a little.

"I'll put him on the backseat," Hollister said, lifting Blake gently. "You'd better sit back there with him. The way the snow's coming down, we may slide a bit getting down into the valley."

"I wish I could thank you enough—" she began.

"Get the door," he said tersely, ignoring her efforts to tell him how she felt.

She sighed softly and did what she was told.

All the way to Deer Lodge, holding Blake's head in her lap, she wondered at her new acceptance of Hollister's rough demeanor. He made her feel feminine. Watching the easy, confident way he handled the Bronco, she recalled the same ease with which he'd repaired the generator, handled the emergency of Blake's broken leg, routed the wolf and got them down the mountain in deep snow. He was simply amazing. And she was suddenly hurt that he had a past that wouldn't allow him to lose his heart because it was dawning on her that she wanted it. She wanted to learn everything there was to know about him. She wanted to smooth away the hard lines from that dark face and make him laugh. She wondered if he even knew how to laugh, with all the tragedy he'd known.

Dr. Peters examined Blake's leg at the small clinic and set it, commending Hollister's knowledgeable first aid treatment as he put on a thick plaster cast. He wrote Maggie a prescription for pain pills to give the boy, praised him on his bravery and told him when to come back to have the cast removed.

Maggie didn't even think about it until they'd stopped by the pharmacy to get the prescription and were on the way back up the mountain. They'd be back in Tucson when that cast had to come off. She'd have to be back at work, but how could she possibly send Blake back to military school? She frowned, gnawing her lower lip as the thought of leaving the ranch began to make her feel sick.

"Reaction," Hollister mused, watching her. She was sitting in the passenger seat now, because Blake had a dose of sedative in him and was almost asleep on the backseat. "Don't worry. I wish I had a nickel for every broken bone I've set over the years. He'll be fine."

"What?" she asked quietly.

"Now that it's all over you're going green, Mrs. Jeffries," he murmured dryly. He was smoking a cigarette, the acrid smell of it filling the cab as he easily handled the sliding motion of the Bronco on a patch of hard ice and whipped it around the next horrible curve as they wound back up to the cabin.

"I think I'm entitled," she said gently and smiled at him.

His dark eyes studied that smile, intent on her soft mouth, and his thick eyebrows drew together. "Yes," he said after a minute, dragging his eyes back to the road. "I guess you are."

"Don't you ever smile?" she asked suddenly, the words popping out before she could stop them.

He didn't look at her. "Not often. Not any-more."

She wanted to say more. She wanted to ask him about the accident. She wanted to tell him that he shouldn't live in the past. But she didn't have that right, and she was shocked at her own forward-ness. She loved her own privacy. It was odd that she should feel free to infringe on his.

She blushed as she looked out the window at the distant majesty of the mountains all around, blue and white against the gray sky.

"Now what is it?" he asked.

She shifted restlessly. "Nothing."

"You colored."

He saw too much. "I wanted to thank you for what you've done," she said. "You...make it difficult."

"I don't want thanks," he said simply. He lifted the cigarette to his chiseled lips. "Up here, we look out for each other. It's how we survive."

"I can't imagine you letting anybody look out for you," she sighed.

He glanced at her with both eyebrows arched.

She shivered, pulling her jacket closer. "Well, I can't," she said doggedly, and her silvery eyes glinted at him.

The mustache twitched, and his dark gaze had a twinkle in it as he turned his attention back to the road. "I'm glad the boy was all right."

"Yes, so am I." She shivered again. "Just thinking about that wolf..."

They were at the cabin now. He stopped the Bronco and cut off the engine, turning to look at her. It was almost dark, and in the going light he could see the strain in her face, the worry darkening her eyes. A woman alone with a boy was hard going, especially when she was their only support. He wondered if she'd ever let herself lean on a man since the death of her husband and figured that she probably hadn't.

"He's all right," he reminded her.

"No thanks to me," she laughed huskily and heard her own voice break.

His chin lifted while he studied her. "Come here," he said, catching her arm with his free hand. "Come on," he said when she hesitated. "I guess you need a good cry."

It seemed strange, letting him hold her when they'd been strangers. But he didn't feel like a stranger anymore. He'd saved Blake and taken care of everything, and she felt safer with him than she'd ever felt with anyone. She sighed, giving way to the tears while he held her, one lean hand smoothing her hair, his deep voice quiet and comforting at her temple.

"I'm sorry," she said after a little, embarrassed at her lack of composure. "It frightened me."

"It should have. Don't let the boy wander off like that again," he said, his tone firm and commanding. "This isn't downtown Tucson. There are wolves around here and even a few bears."

"He isn't likely to go far with a broken leg," she reminded him, her gray eyes meeting his.

"No, I guess not." He was looking into those silvery pools and forgot what he was going to say. He couldn't seem to look away. His body tautened and his breathing seemed to go haywire. God, she was pretty! His face hardened. He didn't want or need this…!

Maggie was having problems of her own. Her heart was going wild from that look. She felt like a young girl with her first beau. Involuntarily, her eyes dropped to his mouth under the thick black mustache, to the beautifully cut lines of his hard lips, and she wanted to kiss him.

"Oh, no," he said suddenly, and his lean hand contracted in her hair, tugging her face up to his. "No, you don't, lady. I'm not going that route again in one lifetime." He let go of her all at once and opened the door.

Maggie felt nerveless. She didn't understand what he'd said, unless he was insinuating that he'd loved his wife and didn't want to risk his heart twice. She even understood. But she hadn't been trying to tempt him...or had she?

She watched him get Blake out of the Bronco and thanked him tersely as he laid the boy on the bed in his room and went back out again.

"I'll bring the Bronco back later, when I get one of my men to ride with me," he said coldly. "Is there anything you need?"

He was as icy as the wind. She wouldn't have asked him for a crumb if she'd been starving. "No, thank you, Mr. Hollister," she said with remarkable calm, considering how churned up she felt. She even managed to smile faintly. "Thank you for all you've done."

He searched her face with eyes that didn't want to see the pain he'd just caused with his remoteness. He turned to the door. "No problem," he said curtly and left without a backward glance.

Three

Blake rested fairly well that night, thanks to the medicine the doctor had prescribed for him. But Maggie was wakeful and restless. Her mind kept going back to Hollister, to a day that was going to live forever in her memory, like the man who was such a part of it.

She hadn't wanted this complication in her life. For years she'd kept men at a safe distance. She'd dated, but with the careful stipulation that she was searching only for friendship. Once or twice she'd had to ask to be taken home because some of her dates had been quite sophisticated and certain that they had the perfect cure for her reserved attitude about sex. But Maggie wasn't interested in cures or even in men. Her brief marriage had left her unsatisfied and a little embarrassed at her own sexuality.

She didn't understand the restlessness she'd been feeling lately or her rather frightening attraction to Tate Hollister. She knew so little about men and intimacy. Far too little to handle a violent emotional upheaval in her life. All she wanted now, she told herself, was her job and her son. Or she had. The trouble was that Tate Hollister was suddenly coloring her world.

It was the longest night in recent memory. She didn't sleep until the wee hours of the morning and woke to freezing cold. Dragging herself out of bed in her blue flannel pajamas, she went to the thermostat and tried to turn on the furnace, only to discover that there was no electricity. Again.

She moaned. Well, wasn't this just the berries, she thought gnashing her teeth. Infuriated, she went to the fireplace, where she'd laid a fire the night before, and searched for matches. Then she remembered that she'd used up the last one and hadn't thought to ask Hollister for the loan of a pack. Not that they'd have done much good. She didn't have any wood except what was in the fireplace. Nobody had cut any more.

She sat down on the sofa and burst into tears. Her whole life seemed to be falling apart.

The knock on the door came as a shock. She stared at it, frowning because it was barely dawn. Could it be one of the men? She went to it, hesitating because she was in her pajamas and didn't have a robe handy. She opened the door just a crack and found a familiar hard, mustached face.

Her heart jumped, and the light that came into her face seemed to paralyze the man on the porch for a split second. He studied what he could see of her with a faint twinkle in his own eyes.

"Your generator's down again," he said.

"Yes, I noticed. How did you know?"

"I wanted to see if my jury-rigging was going to hold since the temperature dropped so much last night," he said with a curious inflection that made her suspicious.

"Did you?"

"I can't fix it without the proper supplies, anyway," he said impatiently. "So I guess that being the case, you and Blake had better come home with me until this weather lets up."

Her heart ran away. She had doubts about it, and she wanted to ask more questions about that generator because he did look suspicious. But his dark eyes had found hers, and she couldn't quite look away from them.

"Come…home with you?" She faltered.

"Mmm-hmm," he murmured, as oblivious to what they were saying as she was. She was pretty even without makeup, and her gray eyes were oddly welcoming.

"Would you…like some coffee?" she asked, without realizing that if she didn't have any power, she certainly couldn't make any.

"Sure," he replied.

She opened the door, moving back, and she flushed scarlet when he came in the door and got a good look at her pajama-clad, barefoot figure.

"Oh," she exclaimed, pausing while she tried to decide what to do.

His dark eyes raked over hers, and there was a faint flush high on his cheekbones.

"I...I'd better get something on," she began.

"You better had," he agreed.

But she couldn't seem to convince her legs because they wouldn't move. She stood helplessly, feeling her breasts swell, feeling her heartbeat shaking the low V of the pajama top so that he had to be able to see it. In fact, his eyes had dropped there and narrowed as he looked, and that flush on his cheekbones that was so puzzling got even darker.

Her lips parted. No, it wouldn't work. She was afraid to go with him, afraid of what was happening. "Blake and I...had better stay here," she said huskily. "But thanks anyway."

Her breath stopped as he suddenly bent and lifted her in his hard arms, carrying her straight back to her bedroom. His booted heel caught the door and slammed it. He put her down then, slowly, with her back to the door.

"What are you afraid of?" he asked quietly.

She felt the cold door at her back and the even colder floor under her feet, but her body was blazing with sensation as he paused just a foot away. "You," she confessed.

His dark eyes went over her like hands, fascinated, intent. "I guess that should flatter me?"

She moved restlessly under the pressure of his black stare. "You've been married," she said hesitantly. "So have I, but only for a few months, and I haven't dated very much since Blake was born."

That surprised him, although with what he was learning about her, it shouldn't have. He tilted his hat back, watching her face. "No sex?" he asked quietly, not dressing it up.

She blushed scarlet and her eyes dropped. She shook her head.

His lean hand went to her chin, tilting it up, and for all its cool deftness, it didn't insist. "Yes, I was married," he said gently. "To a woman who avoided the very touch of me."

She stopped being afraid and just stared, astonished. "But...you had a child."

He sighed heavily. "Most people think that. I've let them think it to prevent gossip for the sake of her people." He touched her hair lightly, as if its dark silkiness fascinated him, while her rapt gaze remained fixed on his hard face. "She was my brother's girl. He was killed in a skiing accident several years back, just weeks before they were to be married, and he left her pregnant with his child. She was from good stock, churchgoing people with hard ideas about anticipating marriage vows. It was my nephew she was carrying. So we married, for the child's sake."

"She didn't love you?" she asked gently.

His chin lifted pugnaciously. "I'm not a lovable man," he said with a cold smile. "No, she didn't love me. She loved my brother and grieved for him the whole time we were married. Even after the baby came, she could hardly bear to let me touch her." He studied her mouth as he spoke, as if the words were coming harder by the second. "We'd taken Kip on a camping trip, up into the Rockies, and for the first time, Joyce was showing some interest in life. I'd let them ride in the trailer we were towing, against my better judgment." His eyes closed, his whole body going rigid. "The coupling came loose. They went over…."

She didn't even stop to think. She slid her arms under the shepherd's coat, around him, and pressed close, holding him as hard as she could, rocking him. "I'm sorry," she whispered, her eyes closed as she gave him what little comfort she could. "I'm so sorry."

He was astonished at the gesture. His hands touched her shoulders lightly as he tried to decide what to do. The feel of her lightly clad body under his coat was disturbing him. He could feel her soft breasts pressing into him. She was clinging too hard, making his mind whirl with sensation, with soft woman smells coming up into his nostrils and making him hungry in a way he hadn't been since Joyce's death.

"It was a long time ago," he said finally. His lean hands smoothed over her hair, holding her cheek to his chest as he stopped fighting it and gave in to the feel of her against him.

"You loved her."

He hesitated. "I thought I did, yes," he agreed and wondered why he qualified it that way when he'd always assumed that it was love. Now it seemed more likely that he'd pitied Joyce, that he'd wanted to make up to her the loss of his younger brother. But now, with Maggie holding him, he wasn't sure anymore.

"And the boy."

He drew in a steadying breath. "Especially the boy," he confessed. "I missed him like hell. I still do, Maggie."

The sound of her name on his lips made her go warm and soft all over. That startled her into stiffening.

"Sorry," she said, starting to draw back.

But he held her. "No," he said quietly at her temple. "I haven't had a woman this close in years. It feels good."

His admission was shocking. She lifted her gaze to search his black, intent eyes. "Years?" she asked hesitantly, and with that one word, she was asking how experienced he really was.

He didn't want to tell her. But the way she

was looking at him wasn't mocking or amused. He touched her cheek with the back of his hand. "Years," he confirmed, and that strange flush was back on his cheekbones.

Her lips parted because she wanted to know, needed to know, had to know. "Were there... many?" she whispered.

He swallowed. His eyes went over her face gently. "No," he whispered back. His jaw clenched. "Only one, if you can't live without having the whole truth," he added harshly, because he hated admitting it. In fact, he didn't know why he was even telling her.

She had to catch her breath. He looked so sophisticated, so worldly. And he was telling her blatantly that he was as inexperienced as she was. She felt a thrill go through her body that was beyond anything she'd ever felt.

He was rigid, waiting for the laughter. It didn't come. And the way she was looking at him made fires in his blood. His head lifted, and he looked down at her quietly, curiously. "No smart remarks?" he asked, challenge in the very set of his dark head.

"Oh, no," she whispered, her expression soft, adoring. "There was only my husband, you see," she replied. "And I was innocent and very young. He wasn't terribly experienced, either. We did a lot of fumbling, and I don't know if either of us was ever...satisfied." She buried her red face in his hard chest, feeling his heart pounding under her forehead. "I could never say that to anyone before. I could never talk to a man like this."

He felt like throwing his head back and laughing with the sheer delight of what he was learning about her. He smiled to himself, secretly, triumphantly. "And here I thought you wrote the book on city sophistication," he murmured with a soft sound that was almost a chuckle.

"Fooled you, didn't I?" she asked dreamily.

In more ways than one, but he wasn't letting his guard down that far. His hands smoothed her hair, savoring its softness. "Then come home with me, you and Blake. Until the snow's gone, at least. You'll need help bathing him, if nothing else," he persisted. "I remember how I was at his age. I'd have raised hell before I'd have let my mother give me a bath."

She laughed delightedly and lifted her head, her gray eyes sparkling, beautiful in her soft face as she looked at him. "I guess he would, too," she agreed.

"I won't hurt you," he murmured. "I don't have enough experience to seduce women. Even green little girls like you."

She smiled even wider. "Thank you, Tate," she said gently.

The sound of his name in that soft, husky tone made his heart stop beating. He searched her eyes, watching the smile falter at the intensity of the look they were exchanging. "Say my name again," he whispered.

"Tate," she obliged, her voice breathless now.

His lean hands framed her face, and holding her eyes, he bent toward her. His hard lips touched her mouth hesitantly, the mustache tickling. He was a little awkward, and his nose got in the way before he finally pressed his mouth to hers.

"God, I'm rusty," he whispered on a husky laugh. "I think I've forgotten how!"

She laughed, too, because it was delicious being with a man who was as inexperienced as she was herself. It was the sweetest kind of pleasure. She reached her arms around him and tilted her head back. "I don't mind," she whispered. "Could we try again? I'm kind of rusty, too."

He smiled, a real smile this time, and bent again. This time he wasn't awkward. His hard lips brushed hers, once, twice, and then settled, moving gently until the contact suddenly became electrically charged.

She felt the very moment when his big body stiffened, when his breath caught. She started to speak. The opening of her lips coincided with the downward movement of his, and he tasted her.

"Maggie," he groaned. He eased her back against the door, and his big body moved down, pinning her there with exquisite strength but so gently that it didn't frighten her. She felt his mouth, tasted its hard, moist crush, and her lips parted for him with a soft little cry.

She couldn't remember the last time a kiss had

aroused her. Even during her brief marriage she hadn't felt this oddly weak and trembling vulnerability. Tate might be inexperienced, but there was a powerful chemistry between them if this shuddering need was any indication. She loved the hard crush of his lips, even the abrasive tickle of his mustache. And the feel of his muscular body so close was making her tingle from head to toe.

He lifted his head, and his dark eyes were black as they searched her face.

She felt drowsy, hardly capable of standing alone. "Tate," she whispered, lifting her mouth toward his blindly.

"No, honey." He moved away from her then, the endearment coming without any effort at all, although he'd never used them in his life. He held her until she got her balance back, his hands gentle but firm on her soft upper arms. "We have to stop."

She looked up at him with blank eyes that slowly darkened as she became aware of reality again. She flushed and dropped her eyes to the heavy rise and fall of his chest. "Oh, my," she said inadequately.

"You'd better get dressed," he said, fighting for reason. The bed was just behind him, and he could already feel her soft bareness against him. He shook his head to clear it. "I'll go roust Blake and help him dress."

"Thank you."

He moved her gently to one side, his hands still

warm and comforting on her arms. "Maggie, are you all right?"

She forced a smile. "Just a little shaky, that's all," she said and laughed at her own weakness.

He laughed, too, because it was new to be vulnerable. And because he didn't mind if she saw that he was. She was just sweet hell to make love to. That could cause some problems, but he wasn't wasting time thinking about consequences right now.

"Me, too," he murmured, lazily studying the way her pajama top was shaking with her heartbeats. Her breasts were hard tipped. He could see their outline, and he wished for a moment that he had more experience, but since she wasn't put off by it, why should he worry?

"Stop that," she whispered, embarrassed, and crossed her arms over her chest.

He chuckled. He liked her reactions. He liked her. "Get some clothes on."

He opened the door and went out, and it was almost a minute before Maggie could even move. She tasted him on her lips, she smelled the clean scent of him on her pajama top. She and Blake were going to his house, to live with him until the snow stopped.

Until the snow stopped. She blinked. Christmas was next week, and soon she and Blake had to leave Montana. She winced. It was going to be harder than she'd expected. She didn't want to leave Montana. She didn't want to leave Tate. She turned back to her chest of drawers to get out a blouse, wondering how this sudden attachment to him had come about and how she was going to cope with it.

Tate had his own four-wheel-drive Jeep outside, and he carefully loaded Blake into it, then Maggie, along with the clothes she'd packed quickly, and they headed for his place.

Fortunately, it was a big house, and there were four bedrooms. Tate had renovated one of them and made it into an office where he did his book work, but there were three rooms with beds left. Tate had the biggest, filled with antique furniture in dark oak shades and a bed that was king-size and boasted a quilted coverlet with a Western motif.

The others were alike, pine-paneled rooms with modern furniture and trimmings in shades of brown and beige and green. Earth colors that suited him. Maggie took one room and Blake had the other.

"Who cleans the house for you?" Maggie asked as she joined him in the huge living room with its cathedral ceiling and large stone fireplace. The furniture was heavy and dark, made for comfort. There were stone ashtrays and several potted cactus plants, and even a rubber tree in one corner.

"One of my men has a compassionate wife," he murmured, smiling at her curiosity as she went around the room looking at the Indian pottery on the mantel, at the huge Hereford bull whose masculine beauty was captured in a painting above the mantel.

"Who is he...was he?" she corrected, indicating the bull.

"King's Honor," he said proudly. "He was a champion sire. Lived to be twenty years old and kept the ranch going when nothing else could. His progeny are still well-known in cattle circles."

"I wish I knew more about ranching."

"Plenty of time to learn," he said, his eyes twinkling as they met hers.

She loved to look at him. It became a habit as the day wore on. Maggie cooked supper, grilling steaks on the big expensive range in the kitchen. She made creamed potatoes and cooked some frozen beans and even made bread to go with it.

Tate was fascinated with the bread. "I didn't know women still made it," he confessed as he finished his third buttered slice.

"Mom loves to cook." Blake grinned.

"Mostly out of laziness," she confessed. "I hate eating out."

He laughed gently. "So do I." He glanced at Blake's sudden grimace. "How about something else for that leg?" he asked the boy.

"I don't really need it," Blake said.

Tate turned his chair around, staring at the boy. "I broke my leg once. Got backed up on by one of my bulls. I learned that pain hurts, and that if you don't overdo pain medication, it gets you over the bad spots. You don't have to prove anything to me," he added with a quizzical smile. "You kept your head eye to eye with a wolf. That told me all I needed to know about you."

Blake actually flushed with pleasure. "It wasn't so bad," he mumbled.

"Now how about that capsule?" Tate persisted.

Blake sighed. "Okay."

Tate waved Maggie back down when she got up to get it. Instead, he rose and brought back the bottle. "Have one, then I'll teach you how to play chess. Or do you already know?"

"I can play checkers, but nobody ever taught me chess."

"No time like the present to learn," Tate said and smiled at the boy.

Maggie did the dishes and then curled up on the sofa to watch the game. Tate was patient in a way she'd never expected him to be, going over and over the moves with Blake until he understood. Her first impression of him had been that he never stopped or slowed down for anybody. But all those first impressions were undergoing change. She found that he had a dry sense of humor, that he wasn't really a bear at all and that he was rather a lonely kind of man. There was nothing in this elegant house to indicate that he was wealthy, except for the sheer size of the ranch around it. He didn't put on airs, but she imagined that he could have if it pleased him.

"It must get lonely," Maggie said absently, smoothing one of the Indian blankets that lay over the back of the sofa.

Tate looked up from the chessboard while Blake frowned in concentration over his next move. "It does," he answered her. "Especially for a woman."

She blinked, averting her eyes.

"I guess loneliness is pretty portable, though," he added, watching her. "Because I've known people who could be alone in a crowd."

"That's true enough," she conceded, trailing her finger over the design in the blanket while the fire roared like a fiery lullaby in the hearth. She was oddly sleepy. That was new, because she'd been a little jumpy at the cabin, even with Blake nearby. But here, in Tate's house, she felt safe. She smiled secretively and closed her eyes.

Tate's dark eyes wandered slowly over her face, aware of that dreamy expression on it as he tried to reconcile his misgivings with a new and staggering hunger.

Blake caught the look on the man's face before he could erase it, and he had to bite his tongue to keep from smiling. So far, so good, he thought.

Four

Blake went to sleep during a chess move, and Tate lifted him carefully, cast and all, and carried him into his room.

"Get me his pajamas," he called over his shoulder, "and I'll get him into them."

"It will take a miracle to get them over that cast," she sighed.

He smiled at her gently. "Good point. Well, get his jacket anyway, and I'll loan him a pair of my bottoms."

"I can see him now with the legs tied around his neck to hold them up," she mused.

He actually laughed. He put the boy down on the bed, hesitating as he stood watching him sleep. His dark eyes narrowed. "Nine going on ten," he said softly. "He's a hell of a boy."

Maggie caught her breath at the quiet affection in that statement and wondered if he realized how much emotion he was betraying. But after a minute he moved, frowning, and went toward his own room as if he was preoccupied.

She got Blake out of his flannel shirt and into the pajama top just as Tate came back with a pair of cotton trousers that looked new in one lean hand.

"Oh, you shouldn't let him have your newest ones...." she protested.

He gave her a faintly mocking smile. "Honey, I don't wear anything in bed. I keep a couple of pairs in case of fire."

She flushed beet-red without understanding why. After marriage and a child and despite his admitted lack of experience, he could so easily reduce her to shyness.

"Sorry," she said, then added as she backed toward the door, "Well, I'll leave you to it."

He turned toward Blake, still smiling.

Minutes later, he was back. He eased down onto the sofa beside her and lit a cigarette while the fire crackled and wind occasionally whistled down the chimney.

"Does he miss not having a father?" he asked with studied carelessness.

"Sometimes I think so," she confessed. She tucked her feet under her, bare below the hem of her jeans, and folded her arms over her cotton top. It was the same shade of blue as the one Tate was wearing, and she wondered if he'd noticed that their taste in color seemed to match. "It's especially hard on him at school, although a number of the boys have divorced parents. Most of their mothers seem to have remarried or at least have boyfriends who come to the events at school."

He leaned a long arm over the back of the sofa and studied her face openly. "And there aren't any men in your life."

She smiled, not embarrassed. "I'm hopelessly old-fashioned," she explained. "I guess Blake thinks I'm a dinosaur."

"I'd bet you that he doesn't," he replied, surprising her. "He told his grandfather that he thinks you're the best mother a boy could possibly have."

Her breath caught, and she smiled. "He said that, really?"

"That's what Jeffries told me," he agreed. He took a draw of the cigarette. "I used to spend a lot of time at his place, when you and the boy were in Tucson. I heard about you until I felt as if I knew you. But I didn't, of course. Not at all. I had a totally different picture of you. I thought you probably went out a lot, but were very discreet," he added with a faint smile.

"I wouldn't know how," she sighed. "If I were involved with someone, Blake would know it instantly. I can't hide how I feel."

"Thank God," he said and meant it.

Her eyes came up, curious.

"I hate lies," he said unexpectedly. "I hate social convention and subterfuge and polite verbal warfare. I say exactly what I think, and I appreciate it when other people do. You and I got off to a rough start, but after what we said to each other back at your house, I think we're on the way to something good."

"What kind of...something good?" she asked, still a little wary of an intensity in him that she didn't quite understand.

"You tell me, Maggie," he replied quietly. He bent then and brushed his mouth very softly over hers. "Sleep tight."

He got up in one smooth motion, leaving her staring after his broad back.

"It's only eight o'clock," she said to the room at large.

"I get up before dawn. Cattle don't keep city hours," he added with a slow smile. "Turn out the lights when you're sleepy."

"Okay."

She sat a little longer by the fire, spinning dreams, thinking about how it would be if they were a family, she and Tate Hollister and Blake. But they were only dreams, she reminded herself, and soon enough she'd be back at her desk at work, with only memories.

The next morning, something woke her before daylight. A sound. A movement. She got up, feeling bright eyed because she was accustomed to rising early when she had to work. She dressed in jeans and a pullover gray jersey, pausing to run a brush through her hair before she tiptoed down the hall to Blake's room and peeked in.

He was still sound asleep. She smiled, closing the door, and went into the kitchen in search of coffee. Only to find somebody else bent on the same course.

Tate was there, in his stocking feet wearing nothing but his blue jeans. She stopped dead in the doorway, her eyes helplessly drawn to a body that would have made a male centerfold look anemic. Muscles rippled under darkly tanned skin as he rose from peeking into the oven, and when he turned toward her, she wondered if it was permissible for a modern woman to swoon.

His chest was completely obscured by thick black curling hair. Muscles rippled in his big arms, down his flat stomach, and she knew there wasn't an ounce of fat anywhere on him. She'd never liked hairy men, but this one was a work of art. He didn't have tufts of hair on his arms and shoulders as some men did. No, it was all on that broad chest, thick and gleaming with faint moisture, as if he'd just come from a shower. Probably he had, because his shaggy head was a bit damp as well, his straight hair falling roguishly over his forehead.

"Good morning," he murmured, his eyes running over her face with blatant interest. "No makeup?"

"I hate the stuff," she blurted out.

He laughed. "So do I. Get some cream out of the refrigerator and I'll pour you some coffee."

"I didn't think you were so handy in the kitchen," she remarked as he took up the toast he'd been watching under the broiler and added it to a platter of thick bacon and scrambled eggs.

"Oh, Jeffries used to tell a story about one of my hands quitting because I fed him, but I'm handy enough, I guess. I was a marine, honey," he added with a quick glance as he filled two thick white mugs with coffee. "Cooking is one of the easy things you get taught."

She opened her mouth to make a comment but thought better of it. He put the coffee on the table and sat down.

"I didn't expect you to be up and about this early," he said as he filled his plate.

"I like to watch the sun come up," she confessed. "It's magic in Tucson, when dawn hits the Santa Catalina mountains. They change color. Sometimes they're red, sometimes black, then they turn pink and rust...they haunt me."

"I've seen my own mountains change, but from blue to purple," he told her. "And dead white in winter. Have some eggs. You need feeding up."

"I never gain weight," she confessed as she reached for a piece of toast to go with her slice of bacon. She watched as he dumped eggs on her plate. "That's too much," she told him.

"If you're going to live on a ranch, you have to keep up your strength. Blake will tell you that." He was through his eggs already and working on homemade jam and toast.

"I won't be out pitching hay and fixing fences and checking on cattle," she reminded him.

"What did you plan to do?" he asked curiously.

"I thought I'd clean the house, if you don't mind—not that it needs it, but the beds will have to be made." She dropped her gaze. The sight of his bare chest at close range was making her weak in the knees. "I wouldn't want to interfere with your cleaning lady, of course."

"You won't interfere. Do whatever you like. Within reason, of course. I get funny about lace on my undershirts."

"Do you wear one?" she blurted out, and blushed as she realized how intimate the question sounded.

He was watching the way her eyes glanced off his chest, and she couldn't know how much a man her shy appreciation made him feel. His dark eyes narrowed on her face. "No, I don't," he answered the question. He finished his toast and swallowed the rest of his coffee. "Want a second cup?"

"Yes. I'll get it." She got up, but as she went past him, his lean hand shot out and caught her wrist.

"No, you won't," he murmured dryly, and jerked.

She fell across his lap, gasping, one slender hand coming into sudden, shocking contact with all that bare chest. She couldn't even protest. Her gaze fell to where her hand was half-buried. She didn't want him to see how vulnerable she was, but it took too much work to try and hide her blatant interest.

He pressed her hand flat against him, looking at the small ovals of her nails without polish. She had nice hands, very slender and graceful. "Stop hiding from me." He tilted her face to his so that he could see all the doubts and nervousness. His black eyes were kind for all the darkness growing in them. "This is as new for me as it is for you, so don't think I'm going to make fun of the way you're looking at me. I'd be staring just as hard at you if your shirt was off."

Her lips parted. "Really?"

"Really." He moved her hand against the thick hair and hard, warm muscle beneath it, watching the movement, feeling its instant effect on him. He laughed, the sound deep and low and pleasant in the early morning stillness. He looked up to see an arrested fascination in her eyes. "I thought I was immune. Feel." He put her hand over his heart and let her feel its hard, heavy beat.

"I guess none of us are…immune, that is," she whispered.

"Is yours beating that hard?" he asked softly and, still holding her gaze, his lean hand pressed just under the soft breast. But his other arm came up at the same time, arching her, and he eased her down into the crook of it while his long fingers spread. The tips of them just touched the soft underswell of her breast, bare under the jersey, and she couldn't breathe. She began to tremble and her eyes darkened to old silver, staring up into his black ones.

"Tate," she whispered huskily, her breath catching.

"I suppose there are rules about this sort of thing," he said tautly, holding her eyes as his fingertips traced the swell of her breast. "Back in the Dark Ages when I was a boy, nice girls would slap a man for what I'm trying to do to you."

"I'm a widow, not a girl," she breathed shakily. "And I...like...what you're doing to me."

"You aren't supposed to tell me that, Maggie," he whispered as his head bent toward her. He brushed his lips over hers once, twice, and then they settled on her mouth. His hand searched for the hem of the jersey, found it and went up until it found a warm, soft mound with a hard tip that arched into his palm even as she shuddered with rapt sensation.

She moaned under his mouth. He tasted her, felt her hunger, drowned in her yielding softness.

When she tensed again, without taking his mouth from hers, he pushed the jersey out of the way and pulled her against his bare chest. She tensed, gasping as her breasts melted into the thick hair and warm muscle of him. His head lifted, because he wanted to see her face.

His dark eyes narrowed. She looked…wild.
Abandoned. Her lips were swollen, her eyes half-
closed, misty and faintly savage all at once. She was
flushed and her body arched toward his.

His eyes went down to her breasts, and he looked
at the contrasts between what he could see of her
pink and mauve flesh and his hair-matted darkly
tanned chest. His arm tightened, but he lifted a little away, because it had been years since he'd seen
a woman without clothes, and he wanted to look
at Maggie's soft breasts.

She saw him visibly start at his first real sight of
her that way. His face hardened, his eyes began to
glitter. He frowned slightly, looking intently at her
body. As if fascinated, one lean, dark-fingered hand
came up to touch the round contour with its blatant
hardness, and she gasped at that tender tracing because the excitement she was feeling was so intense.

His black eyes moved back up to hers. "You fas-
cinate me," he whispered tautly. "All of you. Your
body, your heart, your mind. I've always thought
of women in physical terms until now. But I touch
you and I wonder…"

"Wonder what?" she asked in a soft whisper, because it was almost reverent with him.

"I wonder how it would be if I gave you a child,"
he whispered, his tone full of awe.

She stopped breathing. His words held that kind
of impact. Her eyes searched his face, and she lifted
her hand to touch his mouth, to trace the thick

mustache, the hard cheek, the thick brows. His eyes closed and he sat quietly and a little tensely while her soft hand went over him, learning the contours of his face.

She arched then and touched her mouth with aching tenderness to his. Her fingers found his, pressing them down over the softly mounded flesh, holding his palm there while her mouth made slow, sweet love to his.

"You're killing me," he whispered on a tortured laugh.

"You aren't doing my metabolism much good, either," she whispered at his lips. She was sitting up on his lap, with both hands on his chest, and her eyes were full of emotion. Their color was soft, like gray doves.

He took a deep breath and forced himself to pull her jersey down, smoothing it around her waist. "I've got to go to work," he groaned. "My God, I hope I can pitch hay bent over double."

He was laughing, though, and her eyes blazed with triumph, with delighted knowledge on her part in his downfall. She smiled at him, and her hands smoothed back his thick dark hair, lingering at his temples.

"What would you like for lunch?" she asked.

"Anything," he replied. "As long as I get to look at you while I eat it."

"Oh, Tate." She put her mouth over his and

clung to him, feeling him move, feeling his lean hand gather her hips suddenly against his.

He felt her tauten. His head lifted and he looked into her wide, frightened gray eyes. "I won't hurt you, Maggie," he whispered. "I just want you to know how much a man I am with you. It isn't a threat. It's..." He paused. "I don't know. Pride, I think," he decided finally, and it was in his eyes, in his whole look.

She met his level gaze and the fear was gone, all at once. She relaxed into him, forcing her taut muscles to give, forcing her body to trust him. "It's difficult," she said softly. "I've spent years holding back."

"I understand." He kissed her closed eyelids and then he let her go, helping her back onto her feet as he rose and towered over her. "I didn't bring you here to seduce you," he added, framing her face in his warm, strong hands. "There's nothing to be afraid of."

"But I am afraid," she whispered, frowning as she looked up at him. "Tate, I... We mustn't..."

He put a long finger against her soft lips. "I have to go." He brushed his hard mouth over her forehead, and the mustache tickled. "Let's live one day at a time. Okay?"

She forced herself not to panic. "Okay," she agreed.

He smiled. He seemed to do a lot of that lately,

she thought, watching him go down the hall to his bedroom. But, then, so did she.

The days that followed were magic. Tate didn't touch her again, although she could see the banked-down fire in his eyes when he looked at her; she could read the hunger there. He spent time with Blake at night when he wasn't working, talking cattle and marketing, things that went right over Maggie's head, but that Blake seemed to understand and really enjoy. And when Tate loaned him his *Stockman's Handbook* to study, the boy was over the moon.

"It's got a whole section on feedlot management," Blake said enthusiastically.

"We could use a feedlot around here. I just never seem to get time to look into the possibilities," Tate said, leaning back on the sofa with a cup of black coffee and smoking a cigarette. "But it's interesting all the same to see how they're operated. There's more to it than just grouping numbers of cattle together and feeding them twice a day."

"This is interesting, about the danger of explosive gases," Blake murmured.

Maggie looked up from her *Ranch* magazine, where she was going over a recipe for a beef casserole. "Gases?"

Blake went into a long and nauseating explanation of how the unvented waste from livestock could create explosive and toxic gases, while Tate watched, faintly amused at her wide-eyed disgust.

"Son, I don't think your mother's in raptures over the gory details," he murmured. "She might find some tips on range management a little easier to take."

"Right," Blake agreed readily, flushed because his idol had actually called him "son." He looked at Tate with more emotion than he realized, so hungry for a father of his own that he was as open as a book.

Tate, watching that expression unfold, felt a wild stirring inside himself. A protective stirring, just as he had the morning he'd shot at the wolf when it threatened Blake. The boy and the woman were getting to him, growing on him, taking him over. Once, he'd have drawn back in anger from that kind of affection. But now...

He looked at Maggie, his eyes quiet and tender on her down-bent dark head as she read her magazine. She and Blake were already part of his life; it was as natural as breathing. He looked forward to coming home at lunch, at night. He looked forward to every new day. That was when it dawned on him that Christmas was five days away and they'd be going back to Arizona soon afterwards. He felt sick all over.

To ward off thought of the future without them, he got to his feet. "What are we going to do about a tree?" he asked suddenly.

They both stared at him.

"Well, we have to have a tree," he explained. "It's going to be Christmas in five days."

Maggie felt the same sickness he'd just experienced at the thought of what came after the holiday, but she forced herself to smile. "What are we going to put on it?" she asked. "Do you have any decorations?"

"We could put one of my hats on top, I guess," he mused, "and whip a rope around it for a garland."

"We could put it in one of your boots," Blake chuckled and got a black glare for his pains.

"Suppose we make decorations?" Maggie pondered. "I can bake cookies in different shapes to go around it, and do you have some popcorn and thread?" Tate nodded and she grinned. "We can make garlands of popcorn. But what about Christmas dinner? Tate, can you get a ham and a turkey?"

"There are three hams in the deep freeze," Tate replied. "But a turkey..." He frowned. "I guess I could get one from Jane Clyde, over the mountain."

"Is it far?" Maggie asked.

"Just an hour's drive or so."

She thought of him on that winding road, of how dangerous it was in snow and ice. "We don't need a turkey," she said. "Really, I hate turkey. And so does Blake," she added, daring her son to argue.

But he was quick, was Blake. He'd already followed her reasoning and was agreeing with enthusiasm that turkeys were the curse of civilization.

Tate didn't say anything else about going over the mountain to get a bird. But he smiled to himself when he left the room. They weren't fooling anybody—he saw right through them.

For the next few days, Maggie and Blake worked on decorations and made presents. Since the nearest store was down the mountain, they decided to make do with what they'd brought with them from Tucson. Maggie had Tate run her back to the cabin to check on everything, and she dug out the shopping bags full of things she'd brought with her from the city for Christmas.

"More decorations," she murmured, tossing out tinsel and gently laying a box of colored balls on the sofa. "And this is what Blake especially wanted for Christmas." She showed him a computer game, one of the very expensive ones with graphics and three diskettes.

He pursed his lips. "Very nice. I have a PC compatible, but I hadn't realized that Blake had an interest in computers."

"You have a computer?" she asked with vivid curiosity because she was thinking up a present for Tate, since he was the one person she hadn't foreseen a need to buy one for.

"Sure. Over 600 kilobytes of storage space, double disk drive, with a modem and a daisy wheel printer." He smiled at her fascination. "I keep my herd records on computer these days. It beats the hell out of having to handwrite every entry."

"Do you have a spreadsheet program?" she fished.

"I do, indeed," he said and named it. It was one of the more expensive ones, so that program was out.

"What I don't have—" he sighed, studying Blake's disk "—is a good word processing program. I could use one of those to write letters with." He glanced at her, noticing her rapt expression, and he grinned again. He had two word processors, but he wasn't about to tell her. He'd rush home and hide those disks, fast!

"My, my, they do come in handy, don't they?" she mused and quickly hid the one she'd bought for Blake. Blake could wait another Christmas for a word processing program; he wasn't getting this one.

They loaded her packages in the car after she'd taken time to wrap them. "Tate, I never thought," she said as they got into the Jeep, "is there anyone you spend Christmas with? Your family?"

"My parents are long dead, Maggie," he said quietly. "I have no one."

"I'm sorry, I didn't mean to pry."

He took her slender hand in his and pressed his mouth to the palm. "You and I aren't going to have any secrets from each other," he said tenderly. "I don't mind telling you anything you want to know."

He let go of her hand and started the Jeep, and she thought about what he'd said all the way home.

Home. It felt like home. She finished the last of the icing on the Japanese fruitcake she'd made, with its one mince layer and two white layers and exotic candied fruit icing with coconut all over it. It was like the cake her mother had always made back home. She wondered if she could ask Tate later about phoning her youngest brother Michael on Christmas Eve and charging the bill to her phone in Tucson. Oddly enough, she hadn't missed having a telephone at the cabin, but she knew Tate had one because she'd heard him talking on it occasionally. Michael still lived in Tennessee, and he kept in touch with the rest of the family. Maggie wanted to know how Jack and Sam and their families were, and Michael was always good about passing messages along. Dear Michael, with his hair as dark as her own and eyes almost as gray as hers.

"What are you dreaming about?" Tate asked, reaching past her to refill his coffee cup while he and Blake took a short break from one of the old computer games Maggie had brought over.

"About Michael," she said without thinking and looked up to see a flash of lightning in Tate's black eyes.

"Who's Michael?" he asked tersely.

"Oh, I like that," she said softly and smiled up at him. "I like the way you sound when you think there's another man in my life. But there isn't, you know. Michael is my younger brother. He's just twenty-two, and he looks like me, except in places."

He mellowed. His lean fingers brushed back her thick hair. "Does he?" He bent, nuzzling her cheek with his. "I'm getting possessive. Does it bother you?"

"Look at another woman and you'll see how much it bothers me."

He lifted his head, searching her eyes quietly. "I see what you mean," he mused.

"What?"

He rubbed his nose against hers. "I like it, too."

His breath was on her mouth. "Like what?"

"Having you get possessive. Open your mouth."

She did and his brushed against it, open, too. He bit at her lip, his mustache abrasive, his mouth hard. He grasped the back of her neck and pulled her closer, crushing her mouth under the warm pressure of his.

"Would you bring me a cola, Mr. Hollister?" Blake called suddenly from the office, shocking them apart.

Maggie could hardly breathe. Tate seemed to be having a bit of a problem in that direction himself. He stood up, blinking. "A what?" he called.

"A soda."

"Sure." He shook his head, whistling through his teeth as he got one out of the refrigerator. "Heady stuff."

"What is, cola?" she murmured dryly, although her heart was still pounding.

"You," he whispered and kissed her again, softly, as he went past her to the study.

She leaned against the counter, watching his broad back disappear into the room with the computer, and she thought dreamily how sweet it would be if they were married and she never had to go back to Tucson.

But despite their closeness and the way Tate was with them, she had to remember that she was only a guest and in less than five days she and Blake would be in Tucson and this would only be a memory.

Tears stung her eyes as she finished icing the cake. Only a memory, perhaps, but one that would haunt her the rest of her life. The thought of being away from Tate now was worse than the threat of death. And whatever he felt, he was keeping his own counsel. He wanted her, that she knew. But there was a chasm between wanting and loving, and one was nothing without the other.

Five

Getting Blake to go to bed on Christmas Eve was like trying to put a pair of pants on an eel, Maggie thought as she watched him make his fourth reappearance.

"Mr. Hollister, is there or isn't there a Santa Claus?" he asked Tate.

Maggie stared blankly at Tate, who was struggling valiantly not to give the show away.

"Santa Claus is like a spirit, Blake," he finally told the boy as he sipped his coffee on the sofa. "So in a sense, yes, he exists."

"But he doesn't come down fireplaces?"

"I didn't say that," Tate replied.

Blake bit his lower lip, leaning heavily on the crutch Tate had loaned him. "But there's a fire in it," he groaned.

"Fire," Tate improvised, "can't possibly hurt a Christmas spirit like old Santa. He can get right through it to the stockings."

"Are you sure?" Blake asked worriedly.

Tate put his hand over his heart. "Blake, would I lie to you?" he asked.

Maggie had to bite her tongue almost through to keep from laughing at the expression on Tate's face. But Blake let out a pent-up sigh and grinned.

"Okay," he said. "I just wanted to be sure. Good night. See you early in the morning!"

"You, too, darling." Maggie smiled, kissing his forehead gently. "Sleep well."

"Ha, ha," he muttered, glancing ruefully at the huge pine with its homemade decorations in the corner by the window. All lit with colorful lights and smelling of the whole outdoors, it had turned out to be a better tree than anyone had expected. But the crowning touch was some soap flakes that Maggie had found in the kitchen cabinet. She'd mixed them with water and made "snow" to go on the branches. The finished product was a dream of a Christmas tree, right down to the paper snowflakes that Blake had cut out—something he'd learned to do in art class in school.

Maggie sighed as she looked at the tree. "Isn't it lovely?" she asked absently.

"Not half as lovely as you are," Tate remarked quietly, his dark eyes possessive on her body in its sleek silver dress, a long camisole of sequins and spangles that had impressed her with its holiday spirit. With her dark hair short and curled forward, she looked like one of the twenties flappers.

"I'm glad you like it." She curtsied for him with her coffee cup held tightly in one hand. Like him, she didn't drink—rarely even a glass of wine. They were celebrating Christmas with black coffee, despite her dress and his suit slacks, white shirt and navy blazer.

He turned off the top light, leaving the winking, blinking colorful lights of the tree to brighten the room. His arms slid around her waist as they looked at the paper angel Blake had made for the tip-top. "I'm sorry we couldn't get you up there," he mused. "You'd make a pretty angel."

"I'd rather be just a woman," she said, turning. Her eyes ran over his face quietly although her heart was beating her to death. It had been forever since that morning when he'd made such sweet love to her in the kitchen. And she wanted that, and more, tonight. Her whole body ached for him.

He touched her throat with the very tip of his forefinger, watching the pulse throb there, watching her lips part. She was his. She didn't even have to tell him. He could see it in her eyes, in her face, in the body that leaned toward his in the semi-bright darkness.

He took a step forward, so that he was against her, and his head bent to hers. His mouth brushed her open one, feeling with shock the sudden darting movement of her tongue against his upper lip.

He caught his breath and her eyes opened lazily, looking at him.

"It...it's something I learned when I was in my teens." She faltered.

"It's damned arousing, do you know that?" he asked quietly. "Having Blake in the house wouldn't even slow me down, Maggie, so don't look for miracles if you start something tonight."

He made it sound as if she was making him a proposition. Well, she was, but he didn't have to make her feel cheap for it. She'd taken certain things about their relationship for granted, but perhaps she'd presumed too far. She'd wanted a memory of him, something warm and private, just for the two of them. A Christmas memory that she could take back to the desert with her to last all the long, lonely years that she was going to spend grieving for him.

Her head bent. Her hands clenched around her coffee cup. "I'm sorry," she whispered.

His breath caught. He hadn't expected her reaction. He hadn't meant to shame her, for heaven's sake. He'd just been hesitant to let things get out of hand before he could get up his nerve to ask her if she might consider staying at the ranch—she and Blake. He started to speak when a thunderous knocking at the front door broke the spell.

He jerked it open and a man was standing there,

a very old one in a ragged hat. "Sorry to bother you, boss, but Katie Bess is due." He grinned. "I knew you'd want to be there."

"Yes. I do. Thanks, Baldy."

He closed the door and turned. "Katie Bess is one of my Shetland sheepdogs," he explained. "We use them to help us herd cattle. Katie Bess is our newest, and she and her pups are purebred."

"Christmas babies," Maggie said with a smile, trying to live down her humiliation. "Can I come, too?"

"Sure. But not in that," he said with a faint grin.

"I'll hurry and change."

"What's going on?" Blake called as they went past his door.

"Never mind." Maggie peeked in his door and told him, "Go back to sleep. Santa may come while we're outside, but only if he thinks you're snoring."

"I am, I am!" he promised, snoring loudly.

Maggie laughed as she closed the door. She got into her red flannel shirt and a pair of jeans, thick socks and boots, grabbed her parka and rushed out into the hall. Tate was already ahead of her, his boots making loud thuds as he went toward the hall closet and jerked out his shepherd's coat and hat.

She followed him to the stable where the mother sheepdog, who resembled a small collie with her fluffy tan and white fur, was lying in a clean stall. There were already three tiny furry bodies nuzzling close as the puppies nursed. And even as they watched, a fourth and fifth were born. Tate and Baldy spoke encouragingly to the dog, of which they were both obviously fond, and commented glowingly on the pups. They were like patchwork in color, beige and brown and white and brown and tan and white, and Maggie would have loved to pick them up and cuddle them. But they were too tiny just yet, and she satisfied herself with watching, adoring the tiny things with her eyes.

When she was a child, her parents had always kept her away from the animals when they were about to give birth. Far from thinking it would be an interesting experience for her, they were horrified at the thought that it might frighten her. But this wasn't a frightening experience; it was a humbling one.

The dog bent, licking the soft little coats. Her liquid brown eyes were as tender as a human mother's, her tired body shivering a little in reaction.

"I'll get some milk for her," Baldy said, moving away.

Tate's lean hand found Maggie's in the semidarkness under the central hanging light bulb. "She's been sick," he explained, "and we were afraid she might need help. But as you can see, she was up to it. That's a fine litter, Katie Bess," he said gently to the dog, who wagged her tail and looked up at him as if she loved him. "Good girl."

Baldy came back with milk and some fresh meat.

"I'll take care of her now, boss. Looks like more snow coming, but merry Christmas anyway."

"Merry Christmas, Baldy," Tate chuckled. "I guess we've both got our presents tonight."

"Guess we have, although yours looks a mite prettier than mine, but just a mite, mind," the old man said with a smothered chuckle.

Tate didn't seem to take offense. He wished the old man a good night, and he and Maggie went back toward the house.

The snow was coming down softly, but the wind was calm. They could see for miles in the white landscape, the snow lighting the way as surely as a lamp. Tate stopped to light a cigarette and slid his arm around Maggie's shoulders as they walked.

"Was it hard for you, when Blake was born?" he asked unexpectedly.

She looked up at him. "You mean, was it hard physically?" He nodded, and she let her eyes slide back to the house, silhouetted against the snow and the mountains and the dark sky. "I guess it was. But it's his face I remember, not the pain. Life is like that, isn't it? We may remember the cut, but it's the kiss that came afterward that stays in the memory."

"Profound thoughts on a Christmas Eve," he murmured.

"Yes. It's a profound night." She sighed, feeling his strength near her, dwarfing her, supporting her. "A night for miracles."

"I haven't celebrated Christmas since the accident," he said. "I haven't cared about much. But you and Blake have made the color come back into the world for me," he added, looking down at her. "You've brought me out of the past, out of the shadows. I think I'd forgotten how to smile until you came along."

She smiled up at him, but her heart felt heavy. Was that a way of saying goodbye and thanks for the hand? Or was it more? She was afraid to ask him for anything.

"I'm glad you've remembered how again," she said, forcing her eyes back to the path.

"About what I said in there," he murmured, nodding toward the house. He hesitated. His dark eyes cut down to hers. "I didn't mean to embarrass you. Maggie, if you want me, all you have to do is say so."

The blatant shock of the words stunned her. She couldn't even answer him for a few seconds. Yes, she did want him all right. But he made it sound matter-of-fact, like offering a thirsty traveler a drink of water. She flushed violently.

"I...I'm sleepy." She faltered. "I'd better get some rest so that I can cope with dinner tomorrow. Thanks for letting me see the pups!"

She practically ran up onto the porch and through the quiet house to her room, tears glistening in her eyes. She couldn't look at Tate, and that was a shame, because the look on his face would have told her everything she needed to know.

After she'd put on her pajamas, the same blue ones she'd worn at the cabin, she paced the floor with the lights off. She paused at the window, looking out into the snowy darkness with eyes that didn't see. Christmas was tomorrow. Then, in two days, they'd be gone.

She closed her eyes on a groan and got into bed. She had to forget. No, she had to make plans. She'd been coasting, loving Tate, getting to know him. But there was no future in it, and she'd been making dreams, not plans. Now she had to decide. Did she keep the ranch? Did she send Blake back to school? Did she go back to Tucson?

She worried the question for hours. Finally, in desperation, she got out of bed. Surely Tate would be asleep by now, and she needed a cup of coffee and an aspirin for the headache she'd given herself. Hopefully she wouldn't run headlong into Santa Claus out there, she mused.

But when she went into the dark kitchen and collided with a warm shape, she let out a faint gasp until she saw Tate's face silhouetted in the light from the Christmas tree.

"What are you doing up?" She faltered.

He let his dark eyes run slowly over her body in the pajamas, and he smiled because she was so obviously embarrassed at not having on a robe.

"I'm about to make coffee," he mused. "But now that you're up, you can do it while I put some clothes on."

That was when she realized that he didn't have anything on. She kept her eyes on his face with wide-eyed apprehension that tore a deep laugh from his throat.

"My God, is it that much of a shock?" he whispered wickedly.

"I've never even seen a naked man!" she screeched, and it was true because she'd never looked at her husband, not once.

His eyebrows arched in the faint light from the tree. "And you were married? Well, lady, you're overdue."

"No, I'm not." She closed her eyes tight, and he laughed as he turned back down the hall.

"All right, coward."

But she peeked. Just as he went into his room, the streaming light from it silhouetted him and she got an eyeful. He was the most magnificent man she'd ever seen, with or without clothes. She turned into the kitchen feeling poleaxed. He could have been a centerfold, all right, she thought dazedly.

He was back in less than five minutes, but only clad in his jeans. His feet were bare, like hers, and so was the rest of him.

"I thought you'd gone to sleep," she murmured. She plugged in the percolator, having already filled it with water and coffee and laid out cups and saucers and cream.

"I couldn't sleep," he said quietly. "I wanted you too badly."

Her eyes lifted. "But…"

He shrugged his broad shoulders. His lean hand touched her cheek. "I know. I frightened you off. Maybe I meant to." He sighed heavily. "I'm still in the learning stages about seduction."

"I thought you didn't want me."

"I finally realized that," he said on a soft laugh.

She managed a tight smile and let her eyes fall to his chest, but the bare expanse of it disturbed her, so she averted her gaze to the tree.

"I forgot to call Michael," she mentioned.

"Is it too late?"

"The time zones are a couple of hours apart," she recalled, "and it's later on the East Coast. I guess he's asleep. It's just as well, anyway. I haven't quite decided what I'm going to do."

He caught her waist and leaned back against the kitchen counter, bringing her lazily against him. "Decided to do about what?"

"About the ranch. And Blake." She stared at his chin. "And me."

"Well, I can't see any real problem, honey," he said carelessly. "I want to buy the ranch, so that gets it out of the way. And Blake doesn't want to go to military school; he wants to live here and learn the cattle business. That takes care of him. Which only leaves you and me."

She swallowed. Her heart was going wild. She looked up hesitantly, her eyes faintly pleading. "You and me?"

"Mmm-hmm." He bent, brushing her nose with his. He smiled softly. "And that means," he whispered at her lips, "that you're not going anywhere until I say so, pretty girl."

"But I can't…my job…responsibilities…" she protested weakly, the words muffled by his lips.

"Hush," he chuckled, and his mouth opened lazily, taking her lips with it. She made a faint sound, but he held her close until she gave in, and then he unbuttoned her pajama jacket.

"Tate!" she protested against his hungry mouth.

"God, you're soft," he whispered as his hands tenderly took the soft weight of her breasts. He eased the fabric away from them and pulled her against him, holding her there, drawing her lazily from side to side so that the thick hair on his chest made delicious patterns on her softness, so that the hunger got worse by the second and she began to make noises that he liked.

Her nails bit into his shoulders and she clung, her mouth as eager as his.

His lean hands slid down to her hips and pulled them gently against his thighs, pressing her to him so that she could feel how much he wanted her. "I go crazy when I get close to you," he said huskily. "Eventually I'll give in to it, and so will you. We have to do something about it."

Her hands slid over his broad chest, savoring the feel of it, adoring him. "Yes."

He bit at her mouth. "When?"

Her eyes opened. "What?"

"When do you want to get married?" he asked simply, his black eyes soft, tender.

She stared at him blankly. "You...you want to marry me?" she stumbled.

"Of course I want to marry you." His shoulders lifted and fell and his mustache twitched. "Can you see us living in sin with Blake around?" he chuckled.

"But marriage," she said quietly. Her pale eyes searched his dark ones. "You haven't wanted anyone around you."

"Yes, that's true," he said honestly. "But you know how it's been for the past week. You have opened doors for me." His hands slid up her bare back and down again, smoothing her breasts against him, shuddering a little with the sweet pleasure of it. "Maggie, I've learned that I can't live in the past. And I don't want to, not anymore. I want a family. I want you. And Blake. I don't want to spend the rest of my life alone, and I don't think you want to, either." His dark eyes narrowed. "Or have I read it wrong? Is it just a physical thing with you?"

"I want you like crazy," she admitted without embarrassment. "But it isn't just a physical thing. I love being with you. I feel safe and happy." She stared down at his chest, where her fingers were buried. "I..."

"Don't stop now, for God's sake," he whispered huskily. "Say it."

She looked up, flushing. "You didn't."

"I won't—not until you do," he said. "What's the matter, city girl, balking at the last fence?"

Her chin shot forward and she glared at his smug expression. "Well, you know already, don't you?" she challenged.

"Of course I know," he said with barely concealed impatience. "You were trying to seduce me before we went to see the pups, weren't you? That isn't the kind of thing a virtuous woman does unless she's pretty stuck on a man."

Her blush got worse. "Maybe I just got hot and bothered," she muttered.

"Fat chance. Say it." He nibbled at her mouth and his hands slid up her sides, smoothing blatantly over her breasts and making her moan. "Say it, woman, for God's sake!"

"I love you," she murmured. "I love you, you horrible, wonderful man—" His hard lips cut her off, and her mouth was taken, possessed, absorbed, the second the last word was dying on the air, his hands strong and warm and tender on her soft breasts as he made them burn with pleasure.

He bent, lifting her, his big body shuddering with unconcealed hunger. "It's been years," he whispered roughly, "and I want you like hell. But I'll be gentle with you."

Her arms tightened around his neck and she buried her face in his throat, trembling. "I don't care

if you aren't," she whispered. "I love you so much.
I want you just the way you are, Tate."

He groaned, laughing, as he carried her down
the long hall. "My God, this is going to be sweet,"
he whispered.

She flushed, laughing. "I go all giddy and wild
when you touch me."

"Just remember that Blake's a light sleeper," he
whispered.

She nibbled at his jaw as he carried her, savoring
the feel of his broad, warm chest, the clean scent
of his body. He was going to be her lover, and
she could hardly wait. This was like nothing she'd
ever experienced, not even in the excitement of
her first marriage. This was the promise of heaven
and only the beginning of a long, achingly sweet
relationship....

"Santa Claus!"

They'd just passed Blake's room and were at the
door of Tate's when the sleepy young voice froze
them in place. If Tate hadn't been quite so hungry, the look on his face would have been comi-
cal as he swung around with Maggie close in his
arms to see Blake ambling slowly toward the living room with his crutch under his arm and cast
bumping the floor.

"Santa Claus!" Blake called again.

"Damn," Tate whispered huskily. "He thinks he
heard Saint Nick."

"Thank God," Maggie whispered back, frantically buttoning buttons while her face blazed with embarrassment.

He put her down, smiling faintly at her panic. "Calm down," he said gently. "Nothing happened."

"By the skin of our teeth," she moaned. She looked up at him and her heart stopped. "Oh, I love you," she breathed huskily. "And if it had happened, I wouldn't be sorry."

"I wonder," he mused. He bent and brushed his mouth gently over hers. "I lost my head, but I think it might be a good idea if we do it by the book. For Blake's sake."

She smiled dreamily. "That sounds nice. Too bad your heart's giving the show away," she added, pressing her hand over its hard, heavy beat.

"My body and my mind don't always agree," he confessed, but he was smiling, too.

Lights went on in the living room. "Wow!" came a hearty exclamation from a young voice. "Mom! Mr. Hollister! Wake up! Santa's been here!"

"Make that Mom and Dad, Blake," Tate called down the hall.

There was a short, shocked pause, a gasp and then a yell that could have awakened the dead.

"I think he's pleased," Maggie murmured.

"Do tell," Tate said, grinning. "I am, too. Well, we might as well go and open our presents, since we aren't going to give each other our best one just yet."

"There'll be time for that," she replied.

His dark eyes searched her gray ones. "All the time in the world," he agreed. "But we get married first."

"Yes, Mr. Hollister," she whispered.

Blake was already through his first two packages when they joined him, his eyes bright with love as he showed Tate and Maggie his new copy of the *Stockman's Handbook* and the software for his computer.

"But my best present," he told them, "is my new dad."

Tate ruffled his hair affectionately. "I hope it was worth that broken leg," he murmured dryly.

Blake flushed. "You knew?"

"I used to be a boy myself," Tate chuckled. "Yes, I knew."

"But how?" Maggie asked gently.

He gave her a rueful glance. "Well, you see, honey, while he was trying to get himself lost, I was busy sabotaging your generator so you'd have to spend Christmas week with me."

"Tate!" she gasped.

He smiled at Blake, who was laughing openly. "A man gets lonely. Maybe old Scrooge had a humbug attitude toward Christmas, but I wanted a tree and someone to help me enjoy it." He shrugged. "Hard to find company up here in the mountains, unless you trap it."

Maggie hugged him on one side, and Blake did on the other. He held them both gently, fighting the sting of moisture in his dark eyes. Christmas had brought him gifts he'd never imagined, and he had them in his arms.

A week later, Blake was in school in Deer Lodge, crutches and all, and Maggie and Tate were just home from the justice of the peace's office. They'd just been married, with Blake as a witness, and had dropped him off at school on their way back to the ranch. Maggie and Tate were alone for the first time, and she was afraid.

It was harder than Maggie had realized, the newness of belonging to a man after so many years of being alone. She felt like a beet when she glanced at her husband and hated her own feelings of inadequacy and nervousness.

He took her gently by the waist and looked down into her soft, frightened eyes. "Listen," he said gently, "I'm just as nervous as you are. Probably more, because I've got to set the pace. So just relax, Mrs. Hollister, and we'll kiss each other stupid and see where it gets us. Okay?"

She lifted her face to his, smiling shyly, and closed her eyes as his mouth settled gently on hers.

As he'd thought, once she relaxed and stopped being shy with him, everything fell into place. Minutes later, they were on his king-size bed, fighting the clothes that separated them until nothing did, not even the faint chill of the air.

"Slowly," he whispered, stilling her movements,

holding her. "Slowly, honey. Yes. Yes, like that," he murmured against her mouth as she shifted, letting him guide her. His lean hands caught her hips and held them as he moved. His mouth became demanding then, his hands insistent. He paused, breathing roughly, and felt her trembling. Then he moved again and it was easy. So easy. So sweet.

She clung to him, feeling his movements, feeling him breathe, feeling the wildness of his heartbeat over her breasts as his body slowly merged with hers. She'd been afraid, but there was nothing to be afraid of. He was her husband and she loved him, and this was the most beautiful expression of love that she'd ever dreamed of.

Her eyes closed as he shifted again and she opened her mouth against his throat as she heard him whispering, heard the words, burned with the passion in them. She arched, trembling, clinging, and heard his breath catch even as her body began to echo the sweet rhythm of his. And all at once they were soul to soul, as close as flesh could get to flesh. One.

She could barely breathe at all, and she was still trembling in the aftermath when she felt his eyes on her face. She opened her eyes, looking up, fascinated, into the black tenderness of his gaze.

"I love you," he whispered huskily.

"I love you, too." She reached up, clinging to him, shuddering in completion. "Tate, it was...it was never..."

"Never like this," he finished for her. He nuzzled her cheek with his. "I know." He wrapped her close, savoring her soft warmth in his arms. "You know," he whispered, "if we do this enough, you might get pregnant."

She smiled into his throat. "I've heard it said that a ranch needs lots of sons."

"Well, we've got lots of time," he whispered, lifting his head. "And I'd like to give you children, Maggie," he said, bending. "I'll love you all my life. All the way to the grave. Good times, bad times, all the times we share. You're my world."

"Oh, Tate, you're my world, too," she whispered brokenly, burying her face against him.

"Come here," he whispered. "Show me."

She tried to answer him, but there was so much emotion in her throat she couldn't speak for it. Two lost, lonely people had found a miracle this Christmas. And as she pressed against him, she managed to smile through tears of exquisite joy, her heart brimming over as she thought of all the Christmases yet to come that she and Blake would share with him—Christmases bright with laughter and filled with love.

★ ★ ★ ★ ★

Snow, sleigh bells and a hint of seduction

Find your perfect Christmas reads at
millsandboon.co.uk/Christmas